About the Author

As a divorced mother of three, I've spent a lot of time in my fantasy world. Then it crossed my mind that I should share my fantasies with others. So, this is my first book. Most of the stories are pure fiction, but some are based on real life experiences.

I've always loved sex, I like being a tease, and I've always relished being admired for my looks. Despite all my exploits, I see myself as a lady.

I certainly don't regret any of my adventures, as 'I did it my way.' Life is for the living.

Love Sheila

Sheila's Little Black Book

Sheila Allen

Sheila's Little Black Book

Olympia Publishers
London

www.olympiapublishers.com
OLYMPIA PAPERBACK EDITION

A CIP catalogue record for this title is
available from the British Library.

ISBN: 978-1-78830-890-8

This is a work of fiction.
Names, characters, places and incidents originate from the writer's
imagination. Any resemblance to actual persons, living or dead, is
purely coincidental.

First Published in 2021

Olympia Publishers
Tallis House
2 Tallis Street
London
EC4Y 0AB

Printed in Great Britain

Dedication

To my favourite pussy cat, Napoleon

Introduction

I've given the introduction to my book a lot of thought. Should it describe in detail which stories are real and which are total fabrications? The reality is that I now have difficulty disentangling them as every story has some element of truth in it, but they have all been exaggerated in order to satisfy the demands of my fantasy life.

I have always enjoyed sex, and I have always enjoyed the company of men, there is no point denying it. I like being a tease, and I've always relished being admired for both my looks and my dress sense. Despite all my exploits, I see myself as a lady.

I certainly don't regret any of my adventures, as 'I did it my way.' Life is for the living.

I hope you enjoy my book.

Love,

Sheila

P.S. This is a book of fantasies; please remember to practise safe sex.

The Wedding

Sheila was not a virgin on her wedding day, but she was very close to it. Her fiancé had acquired the nickname 'Wormy' as a child because he liked eating worms. As far as Sheila knew, he had managed to kick the habit, but she wasn't 100% sure. Anyway, back to Sheila's virginity. There had been several fumbles in the back of Wormy's old banger during which his hand, toe or cock might have caused her to lose her maidenhead.

It certainly wasn't intercourse of the 'bang, bang, how's your father' variety or the slow, romantic type you see in the early black-and-white films. As she was on the pill, Wormy could have had as much as he wanted. Sheila was certainly up for it; she was a lusty little minx with a very healthy appetite. She had never seen Wormy's penis, but it did feel a bit on the small side—not that she had actually touched it without many layers of clothing protecting it.

Sheila had attempted to carry out a detailed survey on more than one occasion, but Wormy had got cramp and jumped out of the car. On another occasion, he hadn't put the brake on, and the car started moving. She had put these events down to inexperience, but Wormy wasn't exactly the best example of a hot-blooded, knicker-ripping male that Sheila secretly desired. But she had the wedding and the honeymoon to look forward to.

It wasn't long before the day of the wedding came around. Everything went well with the registry office, the photos and the wedding car, and then they were off to the Nags Head at Eastbourne for the reception. Speeches were spoken, dances were danced, and fun was had by all. People nearly always comment on how beautiful the bride looks. In Sheila's case, this was absolutely true. She looked stunning with her long, black, curly hair, fabulous, curvaceous figure and large, brown, sparkling eyes. She was a pretty little thing that had a smile that captivated everyone—a smile that said, 'Life is for the living.'

Sheila looked virginal in her long, flowing wedding dress, but her thoughts were anything but. She was looking forward to a night of bliss. She wanted to be taken. She wanted to be thrown on the bed and ravished. She wanted to feel like a real woman. She was getting a bit hot and bothered just thinking about it.

Wormy, on the other hand, had already drunk more than he should have. He had a strange habit of picking up other people's drinks and knocking them back. If he weren't the bridegroom, he would have got his nose bashed in. Wormy had the unique skill of making any clothes he wore look dishevelled. His hair was a mess, and his shirt had red wine stains down the front. He was struggling to control his indigestion, and he kept burping and farting nonstop.

Sheila was getting concerned that her night of bliss was looking more and more unlikely. She urged him to stop drinking. She asked Colin, the best man if he could get Wormy under control. Colin was a tall, good-looking man with bright blue eyes and a Roman nose. He knew how to handle himself in most situations. In reality, he didn't know Wormy that well, but he felt quite honoured when he was asked to be his best man.

Sheila whispered to Wormy that it was time to go to bed for their night of passion. Wormy replied that he was far too tired for anything like that. Colin tried to sober Wormy up, but all Wormy wanted to do was sleep.

Sheila and Colin managed to carry, or rather drag, Wormy upstairs to the honeymoon suite. They threw him onto the double bed. Sheila put her hands on her hips and said, 'It doesn't look like I'm going to get a good seeing to tonight, does it?' Colin said that he had always fantasised about fucking another man's bride on her wedding night.

Sheila bent over the bed with her bum in the air and pulled down her tiny, white panties, exposing her fanny to full view. It was a glorious sight: lots of white wedding dress material with a cute little bum in the middle. You could see the dark hairs of her bush and her vagina in the centre. Colin was suddenly overcome with desire. He pulled his cock out of his trousers and started rubbing the foreskin up and down.

He said to Sheila, 'I can't fuck you because I'm married.' Sheila wiggled her bum in a scandalous and suggestive way. Colin was finding it difficult to resist. Colin said, 'I can't fuck you because you just got married to one of my friends.' Sheila wiggled her bum in an even more erotic and sensual manner. In a very sexy voice, she asked him to fuck her.

Sheila said, 'Please, give me a hard, serious fuck; be as rough as you want.'

Colin dropped his trousers and pants and thought, 'If she wants it hard and serious, then she is going to get it hard and serious.' Colin was proud of his cock. It was a good eight-incher with enough girth to satisfy any woman. He also had real staying power.

Colin stood at the end of the bed and dragged Sheila's bum towards him. Her fanny was now at the perfect height to support a fast and vigorous todgering. He pulled Sheila backwards a second time, and at the same time pushed his cock forward so that its full length entered her cunt in one go. She gasped for air. He withdrew and forcibly thrust his cock back into her, again and again. A very steady rhythm was building, and Sheila had a strange sensation in her stomach—or was it in her loins? She wasn't sure what it was, but it felt good.

Colin thought to himself, 'Well, she asked for a good seeing to, and she is going to get one.' However, the sexiness of the situation—and the silkiness of her soft fanny—was getting to him. She was much more enthusiastic than his wife. Then he thought to himself, 'That will soon change after a few years of married life.' Colin managed to maintain a steady but increasing rhythm that made it difficult for Sheila to remain in position.

Sheila thought that next time she might have it a bit gentler, but it was great, nevertheless. She and her cunt were thoroughly enjoying the experience. She noticed that she was getting hotter; her hands were getting hotter, her fanny was dripping, and her nipples ached. She could feel a tension growing. Something was going to happen. Should she ask Colin to stop? It was too nice to stop. Then, everything burst. It was an experience opposite to pain. Joy, pleasure, relief. Did the world stop? Nice, very nice. What had happened to her?

Colin was also delirious—elated, happy, smiling and mumbling that it was brilliant. He put his hand on Sheila's bum and said, 'That was the best fuck of my life.'

He slowly removed his prick. His semen rolled down her

bum. He put a couple of fingers in Sheila's fanny and looked at the semen, thinking to himself that that was the largest ejaculation he had ever experienced.

Colin walked around the bed and gave Sheila a long, lingering kiss on the lips. He said that he would never forget that day, and he hoped that she had enjoyed her orgasm. He wished her a wonderful honeymoon.

Sheila now knew what an orgasm was. She wanted more of that. She hoped that Wormy would be ready for an early morning session.

When Wormy woke up, he found that he had wet himself overnight. Sheila's passion suddenly disappeared, but there was still the honeymoon to look forward to. She wondered if Colin fancied a trip to Great Yarmouth!

The Waiter

Sheila went to Benidorm with her best friend, Tessa, for a girlie weekend, and husbands were not allowed. Sheila was mostly looking forward to some autumn sunshine. She had only recently got married and was determined to be a good girl. Tessa wanted sun, sex and booze, but not necessarily in that order.

Sheila was a very pretty girl with long black hair, a slim body and curves in all the right places. There was no doubt that she was a real looker. In her bikini, she looked stunning and had to fight off the Spanish lads. Tessa had a good figure, a pretty face and a nice complexion. She was a real tease and very popular with the boys. Together, they were a good catch.

In the late seventies, it was difficult for two attractive girls to fight off the desirous local Spanish lads. The girls were seen as "easy prey". Sheila and Tessa were being followed by a gang of six lads in the Old Town of Benidorm. There was a lot of noise and much banter. On two occasions, one of the boys rushed up and pinched the girls' bottoms, which made them scream. They didn't feel threatened, but they wanted it to stop.

A waiter saw what was happening and beckoned them into his restaurant. He waved the irritating lads away and gave the girls each a glass of wine. Sheila wasn't really a drinker, so Tessa consumed both glasses and the next two that followed. She wasn't inebriated, but she was nicely merry. Tessa started flirting with the waiter, who responded by kissing her neck. Tessa offered no resistance, and she invited him back to their shared hotel room. Sheila made it fairly obvious to the waiter that she wasn't that interested.

Regardless, all three walked back to the girls' hotel room. The waiter held both of their hands, which made Sheila a bit nervous. They entered the bedroom and grabbed some drinks from the minibar. Tessa laid on the bed with her skirt slightly up, exposing her legs. The waiter joined her on the bed. Sheila was sitting on the edge of the bed, as there were no chairs in the room. She decided to put the TV on to act as a distraction.

She looked around to see what was going on. The waiter, who was called Pedro, had his hand up Tessa's skirt. It was possibly in her knickers, as Tessa was making a series of small grunting sounds. The waiter kicked his shoes off, and one just missed Sheila. She was pretending to watch TV, but she was keen to keep an eye on what was going on. Tessa's dress was lifted over her head, and Pedro pushed her bra to one side so he could suck her nipple.

Tessa responded very positively to the nipple sucking. She literally pushed it into his mouth so that he could suck it harder. Sheila wasn't too keen on that as her nipples were very sensitive. One of Pedro's hands was playing with Tessa's fanny. Sheila couldn't quite see what he was doing. She shifted her position slightly to get a better view. Pedro caught her looking and suggested that Sheila join them. It was clear that he wanted a threesome. Sheila wasn't having any of that, although she could feel herself getting aroused. She was starting to feel quite horny.

Tessa managed to get Pedro's flies undone, but Pedro wanted more action and was soon on his feet, removing his trousers and pants. His fully erect ten-incher was aching for satisfaction. Sheila didn't know where to look. Actually, she did, and that was a problem. The sight of his proud monster really got her juices flowing. It was two or three times longer than her husband Wormy's, and the girth was more than double. She hadn't realised that a prick could be that big. She found it hard to believe that it could fit into a fanny, especially hers. She started to understand what she had been missing.

Pedro returned to sucking Tessa's nipples and playing with her fanny. Whatever he was doing was definitely working. Tessa was arching her back and breathing heavily. He ripped both her bra and knickers off, along with his shirt. They were both now totally naked. Sheila was mesmerised. She had never seen Tessa's fanny before. It was really, quite beautiful. A long slit with a fluffy brown topping of hair. The pink interior was just about visible. Her little clit had swollen with Pedro's constant rubbing.

Tessa shook all over and said, 'Thank you, Pedro.' Sheila assumed that she had climaxed. Pedro's cock had got larger and much stiffer. Sheila had dropped all pretence of watching the TV. She wanted to see Pedro's cock enter Tessa's sweet little cunt. She thought that it wouldn't be long now, but Pedro was a professional, and he knew how to play a woman's body.

He sucked both of Tessa's nipples hard, causing her body to convulse. He then lowered his head down to Tessa's clitoris and sucked it fervently. Sheila wasn't sure if Tessa found it painful or not, as her contorted facial expressions were worrying. She then let out a long sigh of relief. Pedro repeated this over and over again. Tessa kept saying, 'Please, stop.' But he continued relentlessly. Tessa seemed to be having one orgasm after another.

Without any warning, he plunged his engorged ten-incher into Tessa's little love hole. She shouted out and wrapped her long legs around his body as if she were trying to suck him in. Tessa was panting and covered in sweat. Pedro slowly withdrew his cock and then plunged it in again. This was followed by another slow withdrawal and another hard thrust. Tessa's body convulsed again, and before she could recover, he was in and out once more. This continued until he suddenly stopped and withdrew. Tessa felt like part of her body had disappeared.

Pedro turned Tessa over so that she was on all fours. Sheila was almost sitting directly next to her fanny. Pedro seemed to enjoy having an audience. He gradually eased his todger back into Tessa's warm embrace. Sheila was so close to the action that she could count the folds of Tessa's labia and smell the muskiness of her cunt. She could see Pedro's pre-cum. In many ways, it was a threesome.

Pedro had given Tessa multiple orgasms. Now, it was his turn to have some fun. He liked to just about come and then stop. If he could do this a few times, then the final orgasm would be remarkably intense. It was tough on the woman, as the fucking could be quite brutal, but he was sure that Tessa could take a pounding.

Pedro started the process of deep, hard fucking. Tessa was enjoying every stroke as her poor little fanny was being punished. He was almost there, and then he stopped. This surprised Tessa because she was prepared to take his spunk. He started up again; this time, he was even more forceful. Tessa was struggling to keep on all fours. It was like a battering ram hammering against her fanny walls. He was nearly there, and he stopped again.

Tessa was sweating profusely. This was hard work. She felt a bit like a piece of gym equipment. Pedro started again, thrusting repeatedly. She was just about to tell him to stop when she had a mighty orgasm. It hit her hard, and she collapsed with the intensity of it. Pedro was still in her vagina. His thrusting continued until his lust was satisfied. He came big time. He was just so pleased that he had saved Tessa from those ruffians.

This was really a string of firsts for Sheila. It was the first time she had looked at another woman's fanny close up. It was the first time she had seen such a large penis. It was the first time she had watched a man fuck a woman. It was the first time she had witnessed a female orgasm.

Pedro asked whether she wanted a fuck as his cock was still hard. Sheila declined, although part of her was tempted. She wondered what a cock that size would feel like in her fanny. She guessed that she would never know.

Pedro got dressed and left, but not before promising to come back tomorrow. Sheila laid down on the bed and cuddled Tessa, who was nearly asleep. She stroked her naked breasts, and as she encountered no objection, she gently sucked them. It didn't do much for her, but it was interesting. She enjoyed the intimacy of the moment and the softness of the breast. The sucking of Tessa's nipples somehow took her back to her childhood and reminded her of her mother.

Sheila thought that she would be daring and lightly stroked Tessa's bush. She gently flicked Tessa's clit, which caused her body to twitch. Sheila very gently eased her middle finger into Tessa's private little cavity. She felt the soft, silky walls of her vagina. Sheila found the pubic bone. She could feel Tessa responding to her touch. 'The little minx has had more than enough for today,' she thought. She covered Tessa up with a sheet, and they both went to sleep.

Sheila phoned Wormy next day. He asked how the previous day had gone. Sheila told him that they had received excellent service from a local waiter. Wormy agreed that they did have better-quality waiters over there. Sheila decided that she could do with a better-quality man.

Lady Chatterley Falls in Love

I had always been keen on amateur dramatics. If I could say so myself, I had talent but not the looks. In my mid-forties with a bit of a paunch and a balding head, I was hardly an Adonis.

I went along for an audition at the local village hall and surprisingly won the role of the gardener in a production of Lady Chatterley's Lover. It wasn't too shocking as I was the only male candidate. Sally, the organiser, emphasised that the role contained nudity and simulated sex. She said that bare bums also brought the locals in. It had previously been their only sold-out show.

I asked if Lady Chatterley had been cast. She said that the role had been offered to a local girl that had just got married. She was waiting to see if her husband would give his approval. She wasn't sure if he would be up for it. Fortunately, he was.

There had been several rehearsals, and the cast got on really well. Sheila, who was playing Lady Chatterley, was a bubbly brunette with a fine bust and curves where you would want them. I had never really seen her legs, but I was looking forward to it.

In many ways, Sheila was a classic English rose. She had that unique ability to be both innocent and slightly tarty at the same time. Sparkling eyes and pouty lips painted bright red completed the package.

The rehearsal for the nude love scene was getting nearer.

The director called me over and explained that Sheila was very nervous and that we had to take things slowly. He suggested that we have three sessions: one with Sheila fully clothed, one with Sheila in her underwear and one with Sheila fully naked. He suggested that I should be naked throughout to help her get used to my nudity. That was all right with me, but it seemed a bit unfair considering the first live performance was tonight.

Sally stood on the stage, waiting for the rehearsal to start. It was evident that she liked the frisky parts. I explained to her that I was also a bit nervous, as I had never been naked on stage before. She said that I would be fine. I also expressed concern about achieving an erection on stage. She said, 'Don't worry about that; we are all looking forward to seeing a stiff cock. The ladies in the WI have been talking about it all week.' I wasn't sure if that helped or not. I was now worried that my performance would make me a laughing stock. What if the old man stayed limp throughout the play?

Anyway, at the first rehearsal, I stood there in my naked glory, waiting for Sheila to arrive. She looked me up and down, smirked and slowly got into bed. The director asked me to start the simulation. I climbed on top of Sheila and began rhythmically thrusting my hips. The director shouted at Sheila to respond, and she pushed back. 'Play with her breasts!' the director yelled, and I responded by pawing at her thick, ribbed cardigan. Sheila asked if that was necessary, and the director nodded. Hardly the most romantic series of events, but my penis slowly responded.

The director called for us to halt and congratulated us both on an excellent first attempt. He explained that more passion was needed. He looked at me and said that he could tell that I was getting into the role. I was immediately conscious of my erect penis. Sheila looked at it in horror. I tried to explain to her that it was just a natural by-product of the acting and that she was safe with me.

Sally said that it was a good start and that my penis was doing a fine job. She was going to report back to the WI that things were looking up and that they should expect an eight-incher. Sally leaned forward to give me a peck on the cheek and tugged my todger at the same time. She said that she couldn't resist as she wanted to see how hard it was. Apparently, I passed the test. I explained that what she was doing was sexual harassment, but she said that I was a big boy and should be able to handle it.

An hour later, we were ready for our second rehearsal. Sheila stood there in a surprisingly skimpy set of bra and knickers. You could see the outlines of her pubic hair through the flimsy material. She explained that she got the outfit, especially for the rehearsal. She had a fabulous body, and I certainly was not disappointed with her legs. I thought that the bra was a bit on the small side for her ample bosom.

Before I got on the bed, I could feel my erection starting. This time, I actually acted and simulated the love-making in a romantic and caring way. Sheila responded in a similar manner. Sheila being less covered up probably helped.

Sheila must have felt my rigid penis rubbing against her silky knickers as we dry humped, but what could I do? She lifted both her legs so that I had full access to her pubic mound. I was accidentally pounding her clitoris, which seemed to be becoming increasingly sensitive.

The director once again said to play with her breasts. I responded by placing my hands under Sheila's bra and gently caressing her boobs. Her nipples were as hard as bullets. She whispered that playing with her breasts made her very wet. I started rubbing them more vigorously, but to be honest, I really wanted to chew them.

Sheila was breathing hard and making those sorts of sexy sounds that get a man excited. She twisted and turned her body, rubbing my cock almost to the point of no return. If she hadn't been wearing knickers, her cunt would have been full of hard, pulsating cock. I was finding it impossible to control my pre-cum. We both simulated an orgasm, and the director called an end to the scene.

We were congratulated this time on being very convincing. The director asked if there were any concerns. Sheila said that she was worried that when we did it fully naked, my penis might accidentally enter her vagina. She was particularly worried because her husband would be in the audience.

The director said that it did happen occasionally, but then again, we were all professionals. Neither of us knew what that meant. Sally, who had returned, said that there were some flesh-coloured knickers in the storeroom that could be used to prevent that. She returned with a pair that put us all in hysterics, as someone had painted a large black triangle on the front.

Sheila agreed to continue with full nudity, but she looked me in the eyes and said, 'You must not enter my fanny. That is reserved for my husband. Do you understand?' I nodded. As she walked away, I could not help noticing how wet she was —very wet indeed. Maybe she wasn't the English rose I'd first suspected.

An hour later, Sheila felt ready to carry on. I removed my towel, and Sheila slowly took off her bra. I loved the way her soft, fleshy breasts announced themselves. They were magnificent. Her nipples were already hard. Her knickers slowly followed, taking their time to fall to the floor. She wasn't undressing; she was stripping. She made sure that my eyes lingered on every curve. I really wanted to fuck her. The audience was in for a treat. My penis became fully erect, and my balls started to ache like never before.

Sally walked over with a mug of coffee for each of us. She winked at me and said that the WI was not going to be disappointed. Sally told us to enjoy ourselves and said that there might be some dessert later if we were interested. She started spraying the stage with air freshener as it already reeked of sex.

We quickly jumped into bed, and the rhythmic thrusting soon got underway. There was now a real passion between us. I tried to position my penis so that it rested above her pubic bone, but her thrusting kept making me lose control. I tried angling my todger so that it rubbed against her bottom, but she wasn't having it. Sheila was driving the situation.

I stopped abruptly as I felt the tip of my penis poke the entrance to her fanny. The director shouted at me to carry on, and Sheila said, 'Don't stop,' so I plunged straight in. I fucked her hard and steadily until she screamed.

The director called an end to the scene as I came. Sheila got up and raced to the toilet. The director said that he had never seen such unbridled passion on stage before. Little did he know that it was genuine. I ran after Sheila and apologised. She said that it was more her fault and that in one day she had felt more turned on than she had in weeks with her husband. She hadn't known that she could come so hard.

She wasn't sure if she could continue with the play. I said

that the show must go on. She said that her husband would be in the front row of the audience. She wasn't sure if she could perform with him watching.

Being a trooper, she was on stage that night waiting for me to bed her. This time there was real emotion. I played with her breasts until she was soaking wet; I didn't need the director to instruct me. There was no holding back, and I fucked her until we both came. I'm not sure if the audience saw my spunk running down her leg or not. Standing at the edge of the stage, Sally certainly noticed it.

Sheila's husband was extremely impressed with the play. He thought that the love-making scene, in particular, was remarkably realistic. Fortunately, the dim stage lighting obscured the more intimate moments between us.

As the play continued its run, Sheila explained that watching us in bed together seemed to turn her husband on, and she was getting a second session each night. That explained why she sometimes looked a bit tired the day after.

I was feeling much the same way, with rehearsals in the afternoon and the play in the evening. She was reasonably restrained during the day, but at night, Sheila became a tiger. I could do anything I liked to her—anything. She teased me constantly, sucking my cock and making me take her from behind, much to the horror of the director.

I think she was using it to punish her husband somehow. During the last night's performance, I accidentally poked her anus. She said to go for it, and I plunged in. She screamed out loudly. I'm not sure if it was a scream of pain or pleasure. The continued plunging in and out of her bum gave me the most amazing orgasm. I think my cock just exploded. She whispered that next time she would need some warning. I thought that there wouldn't be a next time as the final curtain had closed on the play's run.

Sally cleaned up the stage afterwards. It definitely needed cleaning. She said to me with a wink, 'That was some acting. The WI were very impressed!'

The Gambler

Wormy came home from work in a quandary. His boss was flying over from America to review the situation in a week. Business was slow, and the recession was hitting them hard. He was confident that he could turn things around, but he would need a bit of time. He had to convince his boss to give him that time.

Sheila, his wife, who was an attractive brunette in her early thirties, knew that Wormy was worried. She comforted him, and he patted her bum. They had a fairly miserable, unadventurous sex life. She would have liked it if Wormy were a lot more manly. She would have liked him just to come home, throw her on the ground and take her. But then again, Wormy wasn't Poldark.

Wormy said that his boss was a keen gambler. Back in the USA, he was a preacher, but when in the UK, he was known as a dirty old man. He was bringing over a few of his friends for a poker match. He asked Wormy to organise the drinks and arrange for a couple of girls to act as waitresses.

His boss had made it clear that the girls needed to be a bit risqué to create the right atmosphere. The men wanted a night of fun and heavy card play. He had asked Wormy a couple of times if he knew what he meant. Wormy had nodded, but to be honest, he wasn't too sure. He discussed it with his wife. Sheila assumed that they just wanted a couple of pretty girls in skimpy waitress outfits to add a bit of glamour.

Wormy told her that his boss had given him a thousand pounds to organise it. 'A thousand pounds?' Sheila said. 'We could do with that.' She said, 'My friend Mandy and I could do it. We'll hire a couple of waitress outfits, spend the night dishing out drinks and we'll be a thousand pounds better off.' Wormy said that while the idea was utterly ridiculous, he agreed that they could do with the money.

Actually, the thought of seeing his wife and Mandy in waitress outfits was quite appealing. Mandy was a sexy little thing at the best of times. After a few drinks, she was up for anything. Wormy agreed with Sheila that for the night, they would not be husband and wife, so as not to spoil the atmosphere.

The night of the poker party arrived, and Sheila and Mandy got into their costumes. Wormy had never seen his wife look so attractive. Her 36C boobs were fighting to escape her top. Only two or three buttons were protecting her modesty. The skirt just about covered her bum, and her skimpy knickers were almost continuously on show. Wormy suggested that she should put on some more modest knickers, but Sheila said that it would spoil the effect.

Mandy just looked dirty—there was no denying that she was a good-time girl. She was a natural blonde with curves in all the right places. He could see the edge of her nipple poking out. Her tight knickers exposed her cameltoe. 'The dirty, little bitch,' Wormy thought.

They arrived at his boss's hotel room, made their introductions and got two small card tables ready for the action. Drinks were prepared, and the lights were lowered. Everything was ready for the guests to arrive.

Ben, Wormy's boss, complimented him on his choice of waitress. He particularly liked the brunette. He said that he was looking forward to getting his hands on her tits later, which made Wormy squirm uncomfortably.

The guests arrived, and the gambling got underway. Drinks were flowing, and both girls were being regularly groped. Wormy was helping as much as he could. He mentioned to Sheila that some of the men had put their hands up Mandy's skirt. 'Mine too,' she said. 'There's not a lot you can do when you have a tray of drinks in your hands.' Wormy said that he would have a word with them if necessary. But she just laughed and said, 'Don't worry about it.'

Wormy turned around to see that Mandy's breasts were on full display. A young man was giving them a serious sucking while another had his hand up her skirt. Ben announced that it was time to get Sheila's tits out. He gently undid the two buttons, and out popped her big, bouncing breasts, much to the delight of the men. There were cheers all around. Sheila seemed to be enjoying the attention. Ben got what he wanted and was giving her breasts a really good working over.

Sheila managed to get herself free so that she could organise some more drinks. Wormy followed her to the bar area. 'Are you not going to cover yourself up?' he said. She argued that there was little point as they would only get them out again.

'Besides,' she said, 'I've also lost my knickers.' She lifted her skirt to reveal her bare, shaven pussy.

'What made you shave down there?' he said.

'I didn't want any pussy hairs showing out the side of my knickers.'

'Well you have got to be careful,' he said. 'You don't

know what might happen next.'

As they returned to the group, they were confronted with Mandy on the table, stark naked. Her legs were in the air, and a large, bald man was giving her one. His large, pulsating cock was showing her no mercy. A young lad had his cock in Mandy's mouth. The other two were fondling her breasts and masturbating.

Ben shouted out to Sheila to put the drinks down and come over to him. She looked at Wormy, and he shook his head. Sheila slowly walked over to Ben, unbuttoning the rest of her dress on the way. She stood in front of three men naked, with her shaven pussy on full display.

All of them had already fingered her pussy. She had even experienced a finger up her bum. As she had said before, there was not a lot you could do when you have a tray of drinks in your hands. Ben gestured for her to bend over the table. Her breasts hung loosely over the other side. In no time at all, Ben entered her fanny. He was not interested in her. To him, she was just a fanny that he was going to use to pleasure himself, which he did. It was clear that he was experienced, as he didn't rush it. He even asked someone to get him a drink halfway through.

Before she could wipe off Ben's semen, another man entered her. This was a friskier, more demanding fuck that made her boobs bounce all over the place. Ben reappeared and put his cock in Sheila's mouth. Sheila could taste the mixture of her fanny juices and Ben's salty cum. The stranger in her fanny came with a powerful thrust and another outpouring.

A young lad of eighteen, who turned out to be Ben's son, then took advantage of her. Ben told his son to give her a good seeing to as he wouldn't find a better fanny back home. He came very quickly and noisily.

While this was going on, Mandy had entertained all four of her guests. Wormy looked at her spread legs and thought, 'What the hell.' He quickly released his stiff beast from his trousers and entered her. It was difficult to create any friction as she was so moist and dripping with a whole range of fluids. He gave up, but his prick was desperate for more action.

Then he heard Ben shouting his name. 'Come and fuck this one, she is a real beauty.' Wormy walked over to see his wife spread-eagle on the table. Her naked pussy was on view to the world. He took no time at all entering her. Sheila couldn't feel Wormy as he was so small, but she made out that he was fantastic. She called him an animal. Ben congratulated him on his performance.

Ben thanked Wormy for a great night. He asked if he could arrange to have the same two girls on his next visit. He said that he wanted to give that brunette a really good seeing to in privacy after the next party.

Wormy considered it a good evening in the end. He was pissed off that three men had fucked his wife, but then again, he had also fucked Mandy. They were a thousand pounds richer, and he still had his job. Sheila was looking forward to the next party.

The Life Class

Sheila owed Mary a favour as she had looked after her cat a few times. Despite being well into her sixties, Mary was a life drawing model. Sheila knew that she stripped off, but she wasn't too sure what exactly she had to do. Sheila felt a bit sorry for the class as Mary had definitely seen better days. Mary had spent far too much time in the sun; her skin was very wrinkly. She was a skinny, gaunt woman who blinked way too much.

Sheila, on the other hand, was a vibrant, happy sort of person who had undoubtedly kept her figure, particularly her bust and bottom. She had many admirers. Her slim, curvaceous figure turned many a head. She had been told that she had the best legs in Brighton.

Mary explained that she had been double-booked and wondered if Sheila could help her out by modelling for a class. She explained that there was nothing to it. She just needed to stand still in different poses for a mixed group of artists and photographers. Sheila said, 'Don't you have to stand there in the nude?' Mary replied that it was a life class, so obviously she'd need to be naked. She emphasised that it was all very professional, although it could get a bit fruity on the odd occasion.

Mary explained that she desperately needed Sheila's help as she had let them down in the past and could be struck off the Life Model Register. She also mentioned that Sheila would get a fee of £100. Sheila reluctantly agreed to do it, but only one night. She was even more reluctant when Mary left, but by then she'd felt trapped.

Sheila arrived at the old institute building where the evening classes took place. There was a tatty poster on the wall announcing the life class. It said that there had been a change and that Sheila and William would be the models for that evening's glamour session. It welcomed attendance from members of the general public.

Sheila met a young man in the corridor who was removing his shirt. She asked him if he knew where the changing room was. 'This is it,' he said. 'You must be Sheila. I'm William.'

William was a fit, young man in his early twenties. He had been a life class model for a few years. It helped to pay his university fees. A keen rugby player, his body was made for modelling. Sheila explained that this was her first time working as a life model. William said that she would be fine, especially as she was far more attractive than the models that they usually hired.

Sheila managed to strip off and put her dressing gown on without exposing herself, which was rather amusing as shortly she would be standing naked on stage. William had no such qualms. She looked away when he was naked before he put his dressing gown on.

A door opened, and a man who introduced himself as Dave said that they were ready for Sheila. She entered a well-lit room which contained thirty-plus people. When she looked around more carefully, they all appeared to be men. There was a mixture of easels and different types of camera set up everywhere, with a little stage in the middle of the room. She was surprised how close everyone would be to her. If they put their arms out straight, they could touch her.

Dave indicated that she should go to the centre of the room. She stood there and tried to muster enough courage to remove her large, pink dressing gown. This was her last refuge. She slowly eased off the gown and exposed her naked body to the audience. There was a round of applause that gave her some confidence.

Dave directed her through several positions. In her mind, they seemed to get ever so slightly more revealing. Photos were being taken at every opportunity. Some were close-ups, which she hadn't expected. Dave asked her to bend over, to open her legs wider and to hold her breasts up. She felt like a prize animal at a fair. Her nipples started to ache as they had been erect for so long.

A pretty young lady brought a tray of drinks into the room. Sheila looked for her dressing gown, but it was nowhere to be seen. The men crowded around her; one touched her bottom while another placed his arm around her shoulders. She felt a nipple being gently touched. Dave came over and told the men to give her some more space. It didn't help much. The men still crowded around her, and the groping continued.

Dave then announced that the second half was starting and that William would be joining Sheila for the glamour session. Sheila wasn't too sure what this meant. William walked in as naked as a jaybird. Sheila couldn't help noticing that his large penis was already slightly erect. Dave asked them to cuddle in several different positions. William wasn't shy about where he put his hands.

Dave asked William to fondle Sheila's breasts and then stroke her bum. He needed little encouragement. Her mind was confused; she was naked onstage being caressed by a handsome young man. William's hand flicked over her clitoris, giving her a bit of a surprise. She was sure that it had been deliberate. Photo flashes were constantly going off as the photographers took more and more close-ups.

Dave asked Sheila to bend over with her breasts hanging down in front of her. An elderly man from the audience approached with a wooden chair for her to hold on to. Strangely, he managed to touch her breasts in the process. William stood behind Sheila with a fully erect penis. She could smell his manly sweat, and there was even a slight odour of his pre-cum.

Dave asked Sheila to move back slightly, only for her to find William's penis resting against the entrance to her fanny. Dave said, 'Stop there so we can take some photos.' William was clearly keen and pushed slightly so that his cock moved her flaps to one side. He then slowly entered her fanny, giving everyone the chance to take even more photos. Then William pushed hard, entering her fully. Everyone clapped.

William carried on humping Sheila to much general applause and merriment. She could tell that he was about to come when he let out a huge roar. He withdrew and deposited his load all over her naked bum. Spunk started to run down her legs. She was just about to start cleaning it up when the men stopped her. They wanted photos of the final act.

She had hands all over her, grabbing her tits and fingering her pussy. She decided to run and made a break for it. She couldn't find her clothes, so she decided to push modesty aside and bolt for the car. At least one young man outside got an unexpected eyeful.

Driving home, Sheila thought that she would have to clean

the seats later. She decided that she was going to give Mary a piece of her mind. When she did get around to seeing her, Mary explained that she hadn't been double-booked after all and could have done it herself. She then asked what Sheila had thought of William.

The story doesn't end there. A photo of Sheila appeared in the local paper as an anonymous woman running naked through a car park. Apparently, she had become famous as the 'Brighton streaker.' Lastly, she received a folder of photos through the post. They didn't leave anything to the imagination.

The Photo Shoot

Wormy was not the greatest lover in the world. For a start, he was not that well-endowed. His and Sheila's love-making was an embarrassing disaster; it totally lacked passion. Sheila wanted to be thrilled. She wanted orgasms that blew her head off. Sheila wanted adventures where she was whisked off her feet; where she was taken roughly in the hay. She knew that she wanted to be used but was too shy to initiate anything. She also knew that she could never cheat on her husband.

Sometimes life was just too trying with the kids, work and the mortgage. Sometimes she just wanted to escape to a deserted island, perhaps, or a five-star hotel in Monaco. Instead, she settled for the odd cappuccino with her friends.

Sheila looked in the mirror and liked what she saw. She was a slim, pretty brunette with long legs and curves where you want them. Wormy had always complimented her on her bum and boobs. In her late thirties, she could still turn a head. She looked after herself and dressed well. Many of her friends had gone to seed; some looked twenty years older than her.

It was coming up to Wormy's 40th birthday, and she wanted to do something special. He had nagged her in the past for some nice photos of her. Well, more fruity than nice. She wasn't too sure what he meant, but semi-nude, perhaps. Just a little daring; it might get him going, especially as his libido was on the wane. To be honest, it had never really been there.

She found an advert in the paper for 'Glamour Photography: 'Don't be shy—Give your husband a surprise.' 'Perfect,' she thought. She had always been a bit naïve, but she built up enough courage to phone. 'Yes, we do glamour,' the man who answered said in a very blunt, matter-of-fact sort of way. He asked what she wanted. She said some discreet nude pictures for a friend; she wasn't sure why she didn't say, husband. Perhaps she was just too embarrassed.

He asked, 'Do you just want tits or the whole lot?'

'Whole lot,' she said without a second thought.

'OK,' he said. 'How about tomorrow afternoon?'

'That's fine,' she said without hesitation. 'Do I need to bring anything?' she asked.

'Just a towel,' he gruffly replied.

'What have I done?' she said to herself. She quickly organised a hair appointment for later that day and also got her nails done. If she was going to do it, then she needed to look her best. While her hair was being cut, she fantasised about being nude in front of another man. She could feel her pussy getting damp. That evening, she masturbated until she came three times. She tried to get Wormy interested, but he said it was a workday tomorrow and just turned over.

Angrily, she thought, 'I will show you; there are other men out there who want me.'

The next day, Sheila arrived at the photography studio— if it could even be called that. It was an old converted garage that had seen better days. The exterior urgently needed tender love and care. Just a good weeding session would make a difference. Even cleaning the windows would help.

She tentatively knocked on the door. 'Come in,' a voice shouted. A man in a dirty vest and beer-splattered shorts offered his hand. 'You must be Sheila,' he said.

'That's right,' she said, not wishing to hold his hand too tightly.

'You want some dirty pictures for a friend,' he said.

'Well, not too dirty,' she responded.

'I'm Tom, by the way,' he said, grinning. 'You said you wanted glamour shots?'

'That's right,' she nodded.

'Well, you have come to the right place. We do glamour really well, me and my mates.'

'Your mates?' she asked.

Tom said, 'Bill is doing the lighting and Darren, my son, will be assisting you.'

There was a knock on the door and a tall man, probably in his late sixties, and a young lad in his middle teens entered. 'Oh, here they are,' said Tom. 'We can get started now.'

Bill quickly set up the lighting, and Darren changed out of his college outfit into shorts and a figure-hugging vest. 'Not a bad figure,' she thought to herself. A space was cleared in the middle of the room. An old bar stool was strategically placed for her to sit on.

'Now,' said Tom, 'the plan is to take some fully dressed photos of you both standing and sitting. Then we will have you in your underwear. Then topless, followed by fully nude. Things could then get a bit more interesting if you're up for it.' She didn't really understand what he meant by the last point, but she nodded anyway. 'There are a few other points that I need to make.

As you know, cameras nowadays are digital. We don't have to worry about expensive film. Later, you can choose the photos you like best. Secondly, skin can get very sweaty and shiny, which spoils the photos. Consequently, Darren will be wiping you down regularly.' Again, she nodded her consent. In some ways, she liked the attention.

Sheila brushed her hair, straightened her clothes and sat on the stool. She was wearing a short blue skirt and a blouse but hadn't bothered with any tights. Darren came over and gently powdered her face and lower legs. The camera started flashing, the lighting was adjusted, and she smiled.

Tom asked her to show a bit more leg, which she did. He nodded to Darren, who returned to do a bit more powdering. She thought that he lingered a bit too long. Tom asked for more leg, and she obliged. She was enjoying this.

Tom asked if she could undo a couple of buttons on her blouse. It seemed wrong, but then again, she was doing this for Wormy. Her breasts were heaving and partly exposed. Tom constantly shouted, 'Well done!' His enthusiasm was infectious. Darren took off his top as it was getting hot under the lights. She couldn't help admiring his body. The same could not be said for the other two. Bill was clearly a dirty old man.

Tom asked if she would stand and slowly remove her blouse. 'Slowly,' he said. She felt a bit like a stripper—where was the music? The blouse came off, and she stood there in her skimpy bra. It was one that she had purchased to entice Wormy. Her ample cleavage was held up in two balconies. She knew she looked good.

Darren came over to give her a good powdering. He was very thorough in powdering her back, stomach, arms and chest. Especially her chest. Tom explained that because breasts protrude, they tended to pick up a lot of light. It was clear that Darren liked his job, as there was the first sign of an erection appearing in his shorts. She smiled to herself; proud that she could turn on a teenager. It was her Mrs Robinson moment.

Tom thought that the skirt should come off next so that they could get some underwear shots. She wondered if she should have been a bit more selective regarding the knickers, as they were somewhat small and semi-transparent. Tom spotted her hesitation and said, 'We can stop whenever you want. These are your photos, please don't feel that you are under any pressure.'

'That is very sweet of him,' she thought. They had all been accommodating. Anyway, she didn't want to disappoint Darren.

Tom shouted, 'If the skirt is coming down, then do it slowly.' She obeyed and shifted back into stripper mode. She was now just in her bra and panties. She could tell that they were all impressed. She knew that Darren would be over shortly.

Darren should have been at football training, but he thought that this job beat football hands down. He slowly powdered Sheila's legs and thighs. Darren 'accidentally' brushed her fanny through the knickers, which made her jump. He apologised and then turned her around to powder the parts of her bottom that were on show. She wondered how much powdering would be needed when her underwear was entirely off. Then she thought, 'Dirty cow,' as she was looking forward to getting the rest of her kit off.

Tom said that she was a natural, and if he hadn't known better, he would have assumed that she was a professional model. This helped her confidence to no end. He asked if she wanted to continue, and she nodded. 'Before we do that, let's get some different poses,' he said, which also relaxed her.

Tom asked, 'Top or bottom? It's up to you.' She slowly unclipped her bra. She knew now that things needed to be done gradually. Bras are never the easiest things to undo, especially when you have an audience, but slowly, it came off. Like most women, she instinctively covered her bare breasts as the bra fell to the floor.

Darren, as expected, rushed over with his powder. He caressed each one of her breasts, one at a time. Daren didn't hurry. He made her feel beautiful. Darren couldn't hide his erection now; it was trying to pop out of the top of his shorts. Tom got nearer to get some close-ups of her cleavage, and his hand reached over to tweak her left nipple. He looked at Darren and said, 'That's how it's done.' Darren tweaked her right nipple. As far as she was concerned, they could carry on tweaking all day.

Tom quickly apologised to Sheila. He explained that Darren was still learning his trade. He explained that all models had their nipples tweaked so that the nipples were erect. How many pictures of naked women do you see without erect nipples? He asked if Darren could do a bit more to get some practice. She nodded; she found it hard to say no.

Tom knew that this was getting her excited. There was a pleasant aroma in the room. Things might get a lot more interesting later. He thought that Darren could be a bit of a winner. He'd only met him yesterday for the first time. Sometimes there are too many lies in this world.

Sheila knew that she should have said no. She didn't think that Wormy would like the fact that a student was sucking her tits. Why didn't Wormy want to suck her tits anymore? She didn't believe her nipples could get any harder than they were, but they did.

44

Tom shouted at Darren to stop as they didn't have all day. Both Darren and Sheila wanted to carry on. Tom asked her to bend over the chair so that her boobs dropped before her. Darren desperately wanted to suck them again, but then he changed position to admire her bum. The almost transparent fabric of her knickers was stretched over her tight buttocks. Little was left to the imagination; you could clearly see the outline of her fanny, particularly as her dampness made her knickers even more transparent.

Tom said that Sheila's friend was a fortunate man. Then he thought to himself that it could be a woman. In his mind, he knew that this was a woman who liked men. She was enjoying displaying herself. He was also enjoying looking at her charms. He asked Darren to tweak her nipples again, for art's sake.

Tom asked if Sheila was ready for the final stage of disrobing. She thought that if she was going to stop, now was the time. She slowly pulled her knickers down. She immediately used her hand to cover her little black triangle. Could she bear the powdering?

Darren soon popped over and started powdering, or rather caressing, her bottom. No spot was spared. His hand crept down to her private parts, and she clenched her thighs. She decided that she had reached the point where she was going to stop.

Suddenly, she was spun around, and Darren pushed her legs apart. He started to suck on her clit. It struck her that this didn't seem like the actions of a student, but they do grow up so quickly nowadays. She hadn't noticed at first that Darren was now totally naked. His huge thrusting member was coming towards her. Part of her wanted to scream 'rape,' but instead, she grabbed his cock and pulled it into her soaking wet pussy. It wasn't gentle. He fucked her like a beast possessed. He just pounded her and kept pushing her around the floor. At the same time, Tom was caressing her breasts, and Bill was playing with himself.

Darren fucked her and fucked her. She had multiple orgasms. He used her like a rag doll, putting her in many different positions. From the side, from behind and in every direction, imaginable. She felt that she now knew the full Kama Sutra. Suddenly, Darren came with a huge thrust. She had never experienced so much spunk before; it was everywhere. She felt exhausted. What would Wormy think of her now?

Before she could focus properly, Tom pushed her legs apart and entered her fanny. She thought that it was a bit cheeky of him as she hadn't given him permission, but then that was also true of Darren. Tom wasn't as big, but he clearly knew what he was doing. He slowly pushed his cock in and out, gradually building up tension. She could feel her body stirring towards yet another orgasm; she knew the signs. Tom was relentless as he very slowly increased the pace. Faster and deeper, faster and deeper and then he stopped. She may have shouted, 'No! I want more!'

Then he started again, slowly pushing his thick cock in her tight vagina and slowly pushing faster and harder. Faster and deeper; faster and harder. She had never been so wet before; her fanny was flooding. Faster and harder and then he stopped. She screamed, 'You fucking bastard!'

Tom laughed and entered her again. This time, he went for it—he just pushed harder and harder until she had the biggest orgasm of her life. He turned to Darren and said, 'That is how you do it.'

He pulled his engorged cock out of her love hole and sprayed her thighs and stomach with gentlemen's relish. Sheila thanked him like she had never thanked a man before—by sucking his cock. She wallowed in the salty taste. 'Thank you,' she said in her mind, 'thank you very much.'

She stood up; or rather, she tried to stand up. Her legs were wobbly. She used the chair for support. She noticed that spunk was everywhere.

Bill walked over with his cock hanging out of his trousers. Without saying a word, she bent over the chair. He quickly entered her; she certainly didn't need any lubrication. With a quick grab of her breasts and a few thrusts, he filled her up. She knew all along that he was a dirty old man.

She looked around for somewhere to wash, but there was nowhere. Sheila wiped herself down and got dressed. As she walked towards the door, Tom said that he would put the photos and the bill in the post. Now that would be a birthday surprise if Wormy found them. She wondered if Wormy would like some more photos for Christmas.

The Family Asset

Sheila had been invited to the wedding of her best friend's sister in Crete. She had to pay the airfare, but everything else was included. She knew that it was going to be hot as the wedding was in mid-July. Her best friend was coming over later due to work commitments, which gave Sheila some time for sunbathing.

She had met Anna, the future bride, once before. Even then, it had only been a brief meeting. She was a classic Cypriot beauty: dark-haired and slender with soft tanned skin and big brown eyes. Her fiancé was a lucky man, although he would have to be strong to cope with her very fiery nature. One wrong word and she was at your throat. Technically, Sheila was there as a handmaiden, whatever that meant.

Sheila packed her suitcase. All she needed to pack were some pretty summer dresses and some underwear. It was going to be far too hot for much else. She remembered her baby-doll nightie, her cosmetics and her sunscreen. She was ready to go. The flight took a couple of hours, and she was picked up from the airport by her friend's dad in an old and rusty Ford pickup truck.

She arrived late in the evening to find that most of the family had already gone to bed. There wasn't much else you could do in this heat. The temperature was still in the mid-thirties, and Sheila found herself sweating, which was rare for her. She ate some sardines on toast, which were delicious and so fresh. Sheila had a quick hand-wash, as the shower wasn't working, and changed into her nightie. She wished that she had brought something more modest as it didn't leave much to the imagination. At least she had some knickers on, and they were used to topless bathing here anyway.

The father couldn't help admiring Sheila's assets. She had a great figure, with a curvaceous bum and a pair of breasts to die for. Large but well-proportioned, they swung gently within the constraints of the almost see-through nightie. He had to fight the urge to grab them. In his younger days, he would have given in to the urge. Instead, he showed Sheila to her room.

The room contained a sea of beds. There was a large single bed in the middle of the room and four smaller single beds surrounding it. This was a room designed to hold one double bed, and even that would have been a bit cramped. There was no other furniture. If you put your hand out while you were in one bed, you would touch someone else in another. Talk about intimate.

It was also sweltering. There was an old fan in the ceiling that was struggling to rotate. It made an annoying, whiny noise—a bit like her husband, Sheila thought. The small, solitary window was barely ajar. It couldn't be opened much wider because of the mosquitoes, which were a serious problem at that time of year. To be honest, the room was worse than a prison cell in a small South American country. While this was probably an exaggeration, Sheila wasn't expecting to have a good night's sleep.

To make it worse, the room was too well-lit for her liking. The combination of a full moon and a nightlight meant that the room was cast in a blue tinge. Moreover, the room was fully occupied. The almost naked bride-to-be was in the centre bed, and three young men in boxer shorts were in three of the single beds. Sheila had to climb over one of the young men to get to her bed. She could see all three men looking at her breasts. She really should have brought a more discreet nightie, but she hadn't anticipated sharing a room with several young men.

The father said good night and closed the door. She was a bit surprised to see Anna on her back, more or less stark naked. She was playing with her pussy with the three men eagerly watching. Her masturbation was causing the room to smell quite musky. She had no shame and seemed to enjoy putting on this little show. Suddenly, there was a commotion coming from outside the room. Anna said, 'That will be Adam back from the pub; he always makes a lot of noise taking his clothes off.'

Into the room walked a slightly drunk, stark-naked man with a sizeable erection. He tripped over one of the single beds and almost landed on top of Anna. He started aggressively sucking her nipples, and at the same time, he managed to get his cock into her cunt. After a few strokes and a loud grunt, she managed to push him off. He soon entered the land of nod.

Anna got herself up onto her hands and knees and started wiggling her fine-looking arse. Sheila had to admit that it was a pretty bottom—well-rounded with a slit down the middle. The pussy was a bit puffed up, but it had a gaping hole in the centre that was ready for action.

One of the young men stood up—which wasn't that easy in such a crowded room—and pulled down his red boxer shorts. He exposed an admirable cock. Sheila didn't pretend to be an expert in such things, but she knew a good cock when she saw one. It was of a reasonable size and had a good girth, but what impressed Sheila most was its stiffness. You could hang a full line of washing on it on a windy day. Sheila wasn't too convinced that he would last that long.

Without any discussion, he walked over to Anna and put his cock firmly into her fanny. There was no foreplay, no chocolates and no flowers—just a good, hard fuck. He grabbed her slim buttocks on both sides and heaved away. Sheila wondered if it was the Cypriot way of doing things. Anna was making some encouraging sounds, but he just grunted and pulled out. Sheila was close enough to see the cum on his still-erect prick and all over Anna's cunt.

He returned to his bed, and a second young man stood up and pulled down his blue boxer shorts. He had a similarly sized erection, but Sheila thought that he might have had a bit more girth. What was particularly noticeable where his large, dangly balls. This young man climbed over to Anna and slid his full erection deep into her now very moist vagina. Again, there was no foreplay, although he did attempt to play with her large, dangling tits. He didn't make too much of an effort, however, as he was concentrating on the heaving. He certainly had to do more heaving than the previous lovers, who, it turned out, were his brothers.

Sheila was waiting for the grunt to come, and it duly happened. He quickly extracted his penis, which caused some of the spunk to run down Anna's leg. It didn't seem to worry her too much. She just continued wiggling her bottom. There are no prizes for correctly guessing what happened next. The young man returned to his bed, and the third young man stood up and removed his green boxer shorts. Sheila wondered if the shorts were colour-coded. He had the daddy of all erections.

He swaggered over to Anna. His cock was at least two

inches longer than those of the other two. What was scary was the girth. It was probably thicker than Sheila's wrist. Sheila was starting to feel a bit horny herself, with all the fucking that was going on, the smell of musk and other bodily fluids in the air and the look of lust in this man's eyes.

He followed the usual pattern and roughly entered Anna's fanny. Anna was clearly expecting it, as she had positioned herself for easy entry and maximum safety. This Adonis just treated Anna like a toy. He fucked, and fucked and fucked her. Anna was sweating profusely. He grabbed her buttocks, then her breasts and then her shoulders. He was devouring her—treating her fanny as if it was a railway tunnel. His steam engine just ploughed away. It was relentless. Sheila thought that no woman should have to put up with this.

Sheila suddenly realised that she was playing with herself while Anna continued to be fucked. Anna started screaming. Sheila wasn't sure if it was from pain or ecstasy, but it didn't seem to matter. A man on a mission was still using Anna's cunt. His mission was almost complete; and with two or three mighty heaves, he emptied his load into her willing receptacle. He pulled his monster cock out of her well-worn and clearly exhausted fanny. Anna had collapsed into a sleepy heap next to her husband-to-be.

The young man's eyes penetrated Sheila's, pleading for seconds. But Sheila was having none of it, and she turned over.

The next morning, nothing was said about the previous night's events over breakfast. All four brothers just sat there eating their croissants as if nothing had happened.

The next night, the entire process was repeated in almost exactly the same way. Anna was indeed a great family asset—especially when her future father-in-law took his turn.

Sheila's husband phoned to ask how her first day in Crete had gone. She said that she was struggling to sleep in such a hot room, but she knew that Anna was being well looked after by her in-laws. Wormy said to give her one from him. Sheila thought to herself that Anna would hardly notice his pathetic little todger.

The Family Asset: Part 2

Sheila's host, Anna's future mother-in-law, asked Sheila if she had slept OK. Sheila didn't really know what to say, as she had watched Anna being fucked by four different men the night before—one of whom was Anna's fiancé. Before she could answer, the woman said, 'I guess that you were a bit surprised to see Anna being fucked by other family members.' Sheila nodded. The woman continued, 'In Crete, it is tradition that the bride-to-be becomes family property at the time of the engagement, and all the male family members can use her until her marriage. Once married, she becomes the property of her husband.'

Sheila asked, 'What happens if the bridegroom dies?'

The woman said, 'She once again becomes the property of the family, and all male family members can use the facilities until she is married again. There are still two uncles that are planning to visit Anna before her marriage.'

Sheila asked, 'Don't the women mind?'

The woman replied, 'Yes and no. Naturally, there is some jealousy, but the whole process tends to bring a family together. When Anna first came here, she was a shy, timid thing. Look at her now.'

There wasn't much to do during the day except enjoy the sunshine, which was a welcome change from the weather in England. Meals were had, and there was a fair amount of drinking, laughter and joviality. It was soon time for bed. Sheila had put her nightie in the wash, but it wasn't ready, which meant that she only had a pair of knickers to protect her modesty. After last night, she wasn't too worried about it.

The bedroom was still hot and airless. It remained composed of a sea of beds with Anna stark naked in the centre. There was a slight difference in that while there were still three men in the room, only two of them were brothers—the third was Anna's future father-in-law.

Sheila was shown to the same bed that she had slept in last night. There was more interest in her breasts than there had been before, as they weren't covered, but mostly the men were fixated on Anna, who was playing with herself again. Anna's future father-in-law kept looking over at Sheila, which made her feel a bit nervous.

The events of the night before were mostly repeated, but not exactly. There was a lot of noise coming from the lounge, and in walked an inebriated Adam, Anna's fiancé, with a real stiffy. He once again attempted to suck Anna's breasts but failed miserably. He did manage to get his cock in her fanny, but he appeared to fall asleep during the process. To put it mildly, Anna was not amused. One of Adam's brothers approached and literally lifted Adam out of Anna's embrace. There was an audible 'plop' when the cock left the nest. Adam was dropped to one side, and the brother removed his red boxer shorts. Anna was once again positioned on all fours, ready for more action.

As before, Sheila was impressed with the size and stiffness of this new cock. He wasted no time in entering Anna, who was clearly ready for him. Sheila had to admire his stamina, as he had only had one day to recover. However, he wasn't really an attentive lover, as he didn't seem too interested in Anna's needs. He just heaved away until he came. He showed no great affection towards her as he withdrew, and then he wiped his cock on the side of her bum.

The second brother was soon naked and eager to sample the joys of Anna's cunt again. He was the one with the large, dangly balls. Sheila couldn't help watching them swing back and forth as he pounded away at Anna's snatch. The whole scene was somewhat mesmerising, as the balls seemed to synchronise their swinging with that of Anna's dangling tits. It reminded her of the chimes on a grandfather clock. Sheila was waiting for the sound of the grunt that usually signalled his orgasm. It duly happened, and Anna's bum was once again used to wipe the todger clean. 'Charming,' Sheila thought.

Sheila was then surprised to see Anna's future father-in-law stand up. He must have been in his eighties. The black shorts he was wearing came down to expose a genuine monster. His eldest son's penis was big, but his was ridiculous. His limp cock was at least ten inches long, and its girth was frightening.

Anna was wiggling her arse in a very seductive manner. She hadn't been satisfied by the previous three cocks, and now was the chance for her to take a serious ride. His cock was now almost fully erect. Sheila would put good money on it being impossible for any fanny to handle it. He lubricated his todger with a jelly-like substance, although it didn't look like Anna needed any more lubrication, as her pussy still glistened with his sons' semen.

He approached Anna, who was still on her hands and knees and positioned his cock in line with her fanny. You could see Anna steadying herself in anticipation of receiving a real pounding. She was almost pushing herself onto his cock. Sheila had never seen anything like it before—Anna was taking the initiative and gradually enveloping the monster. Sheila didn't want to think crude thoughts, but she couldn't help it. She decided that Anna's fanny must be huge to cope with that beast.

Anna rocked backwards and forwards. The cock just stayed firmly in her cunt. There was no movement from the elderly gentlemen. He just let her fuck him. As Anna continued, she started to orgasm. She made gentle little mousey noises at first, then guttural grunts followed by salacious screams. Two of the women from the next room, which included the man's wife, rushed in to see if there was a problem. They surveyed the scene, in which a gorgeous naked teenager had a huge phallus, which was attached to a geriatric gentleman, sticking out of her fanny.

Anna's future mother-in-law told Victor, her husband, 'Be careful with the young ones, you don't want to break them.' Victor then started to fuck Anna. Anna was sweating profusely as he gently edged his cock in and out. He knew that he couldn't get too frisky because of his size. His wife had always complained that it was his fault that her fanny was a bit slack. No woman could cope with a monster that size on a continuous basis.

Anna's future mother-in-law knew that Anna was going to need some help to get him off. She went up behind Victor and stuck one finger up his arse and used the other hand to fondle his balls. This seemed to do the trick, and Victor came explosively. Poor Anna was nearly shot across the room, but she had a genuine smile on her face.

Sheila was quite dumbstruck by the night's proceedings.

She had to admire Anna's fortitude, and she did wonder what a cock that size would feel like. Sheila turned over and was soon fast asleep.

Over breakfast, Sheila heard that Anna and Adam were off to the other end of the island to receive a blessing and wouldn't be back that night.

Sheila's husband phoned to ask how the previous day had gone. She said that she was still struggling to sleep in such steamy conditions, but really it was a family affair.

The Family Asset: Part 3

Anna's future mother-in-law asked Sheila if she'd slept OK. Sheila still didn't know what to say as she had watched Anna being fucked by her future husband, two of her future brothers-in-law and her future father-in-law. It really was a family affair. She still couldn't get over the size of Victor's cock.

Sheila tentatively asked the woman how she coped with the size of her husband's penis. She explained that she had had great difficulty at first, but she was fortunate in that he came quite quickly, particularly if she could get him over-excited. That was the trick: over-stimulation. Sheila asked if she minded him fucking Anna. The woman looked at Sheila and said, 'Yes, I do mind. I do get jealous, particularly when you look at her beautiful body, but then he always comes back to an old hag like me. It's just tradition, you know.'

Sheila then said, 'Isn't it really a form of abuse?'

The woman replied, 'Yes, of course, it is. But the young girls want it to carry on. That way, they can try out several cocks. It's a way for them to evaluate their future partner. Does Anna look like she is being abused?' Sheila had to concede that she seemed to be enjoying the whole process. The woman said, 'Anna had been looking forward to this for years.'

After another day in paradise, it was time for bed. Sheila washed and only put a pair of knickers on. It was too hot for any more clothing, and everyone had already seen her tits anyway. She was quite proud of them; they were much fuller and rounder than Anna's.

She was a bit surprised to see that she had been given Anna's bed to sleep in. The others were occupied by the two brothers, Victor and a teenager whom she hadn't seen before. It was strange being the only woman in a room full of semi-naked men. She was a bit nervous, to put it mildly, but she wasn't a family member, so she felt reasonably secure.

She was just starting to doze off when the first brother stood up and removed his red boxer shorts. He approached her bed and simply yanked her knickers off. He spread her legs apart and quickly entered her vagina. Like with Anna, there was no foreplay, no flowers and no chocolates—there wasn't even a discussion of any sort. She wasn't even sure if she had ever spoken to him.

He withdrew and lifted Sheila to position her on all fours. This was obviously the preferred family position. Sheila felt that she should be screaming for help, but she was enjoying being fucked. She eagerly waited for him to enter her again, which happened within minutes. He grabbed each side of her bum and heaved away in precisely the same way as he had screwed Anna. She expected him to fondle her tits, but there was none of that, which was a shame as they desperately craved attention. It wasn't long before he grunted and came. She waited for him to wipe his cock on her bum, which he duly did. She thought to herself, 'These Cypriot men do seem to lack imagination.'

Nonetheless, she wasn't complaining. His was a nice, hard cock with very acceptable dimensions. She knew that her body was now looking for relief, but then she had a horrendous thought, 'Is Victor going to fuck me next?' She wasn't ready for that. She assumed that the previous night's pattern would be followed and Mr Dangly Balls would have his turn.

She was right. The next brother entered her very moist vagina. She was surprised that there was no attempt at any foreplay. In no time at all, her tits were swinging in tandem with his balls. She looked at Victor and the youngster who were staring at her voluptuous tits. The brother reached down to grab them, which pushed his cock further into the depths of her fanny. This drove her over the edge, and she had her first gentle orgasm. She could feel the muscles of her vagina clenching his cock, which in turn caused him to come.

As per the family tradition, he wiped his cock against the side of her bum. 'What cheek,' Sheila thought. 'It's his semen, not mine.' Then she was surprised as Victor pulled down the young boy's yellow shorts and marched him over to Sheila, where they both had a good look at her cunt.

Sheila immediately covered her fanny with her hand and said, 'What do you think you are doing?' Victor looked mystified, and the boy seemed terrified. Victor shouted out for his wife as his English was not that good. She entered the room and asked what the problem was. Victor just made lots of gestures; clearly, he was very annoyed.

The woman turned to Sheila and said that this was the 'Making of the Man' ceremony. Sheila said, 'What do you mean?'

The woman replied, 'Tzmy turned eighteen last week, and consequently, he has the right to fuck Anna. And at the same time, he can declare his manhood. She is obviously not here, so as one of her handmaidens, you are required to fulfil her obligations.'

Sheila said, 'So, I'm expected to let this young lad fuck

me?'

'Yes,' said the woman.

Sheila had let the two brothers fuck her without a word. It was more or less rape, really, but then it wouldn't stand up in court since the tradition was so strong in Cyprus. Sheila removed her hand and wiggled her bum like Anna, as this seemed to be the way that consent was given. Tzmy had a long, thin cock with surprisingly dangly balls for his age. He took after his uncle. He didn't follow tradition, in that he started massaging Sheila's tits, which was very welcome. He had some experience as he knew just how to get the nipples hard. A gentle touch and squeeze here and there were getting Sheila going. Her nipples were as hard as they could get.

Tzmy then decided to concentrate on her fanny. He sucked and tickled her clit until she nearly came. He gently fingered her vagina, and then he added a second finger while pushing his thumb into her bum. She was on the edge of an orgasm again, when he slowly pushed his cock past her labia. He rested his penis just against the vaginal entrance. Sheila felt like a slut when she pushed back to force his entry.

Sheila soon realised that she was dealing with an expert. This was no boy. Tzmy still had his thumb in Sheila's bum. He pushed his penis against the thumb to create some friction. This excited both of them. Sheila had never experienced that before, and she was at the point of climaxing when she felt the boy's spunk hit the walls of her fanny. 'So close, but so far,' she thought. Thankfully, Tzmy didn't use her bum as a cleaning implement.

Sheila then wondered what she was going to do. Victor was removing his black boxer shorts. His cock looked bigger than ever. He intended to give her one as he was lubricating his cock. Fortunately, his wife was still in the room.

Sheila spread her legs as far as possible. Being on all fours did allow for easier entry, but she really wasn't sure if she could cope with this. She was tempted to do a runner. While she was contemplating a rapid exit, his massive todger entered her vagina. It wasn't yet fully erect, which is how he gained a relatively easy entry, but Sheila could feel it expanding inside her fanny as it engorged.

This was a somewhat unique experience. It was like putting a balloon in your mouth and then blowing it up from the outside. Every part of her fanny was fully occupied. She wasn't sure how she was going to get it out. It was locked in rigidly. There was no room for manoeuvre at all.

The woman said to Victor, 'What have you done to this poor girl?' Victor tried to withdraw, but he just pulled Sheila with him. The two brothers grabbed Sheila's shoulders to stop her from moving, but the withdrawal was still impossible.

They decided to lubricate her fanny. They even tried WD-40. Sheila felt like a machine being oiled as part of a maintenance routine. The woman suggested that playing with Sheila's breasts might help create some internal lubrication. The two brothers and Tzmy were soon on the case.

They then concluded that Victor needed to come so that his cock would deflate. So, his wife started sucking his balls, and the brothers began to move Sheila around in an attempt to loosen up her fanny. The woman continued sucking while Tzmy sucked each of Sheila's breasts in turn.

Rather ironically, Sheila could feel an orgasm rising in her loins. It might have made things worse as her vaginal muscles were clenching away. Victor was not looking well; this was not the sort of activity an eighty-year-old man should be doing. Sheila was worried that she might have a dead man trapped in her fanny. How would she explain that to her husband?

Victor's wife was making good progress as he began grunting. It looked like things were on the move. But from Sheila's perspective, it seemed that his cock was getting bigger. Perhaps it was the calm before the storm. Suddenly, and without warning, Victor heaved and grunted loudly. The force of his semen, leaving his cock pushed him out, and Sheila was free. Sheila reached down to feel her fanny—it had never been so extended before. She hoped that it would return to normal before she saw Wormy.

The whole family apologised to Sheila. The annoying thing was that Sheila still felt quite randy, but she couldn't face another cock. Well, not for a while at least.

Sheila's best friend, Jane, had finally flown over and joined Sheila for breakfast. Sheila asked if she had been the property of her husband's family before she was married. Jane asked what she was talking about. Sheila explained what she had experienced with Anna and Adam's brothers and father. Jane said, 'Sheila, my dear, you have fallen for an elaborate trick by Adam's family to get in your knickers. They have always been a randy lot.'

Sheila said, 'What about Anna? She was in on it?'

Jane said, 'She is more or less a nympho; she will fuck anything.'

Sheila said, 'You could have warned me.'

Jane said, 'Did you enjoy the experience?'

Sheila said, 'I did until Adam's father got involved.'

Jane said, 'Oh yes, his size is too much for any woman.'

Sheila's husband phoned to ask how her day went. Sheila said that last night she had discovered the limits of her capabilities. Apparently, bigger is not always better. Naturally, Wormy had no idea what she was talking about.

The Shoplifter

Sheila was not a shoplifter; she had never stolen anything in her life, but here was clear evidence of her crime. She had absentmindedly put the packet of batteries in her handbag rather than the trolley.

Jack had spotted her in the act and recorded it on his mobile phone. He had been secretly stalking her in the supermarket. He tended to follow all the pretty girls, and Sheila certainly fell into that category. Sheila had very attractive legs, which were showed off to her advantage in short skirts. Upstairs, she had a great rack, and many men admired her boobs.

A young man in an ill-fitting suit and tie approached Sheila and asked if he could have a word. He used a particularly stern voice when he said it, which immediately made Sheila concerned. He took her through to the back of the store into a dirty warehouse area and then into a small, tatty office which had a table and two wooden chairs.

He asked to see some identification, and Sheila showed him her driving licence. He said, 'Thank you, Mrs Allen. Do you know why I have asked you to come back here?' Sheila replied that she had no idea. The man stood and called for Jack. He was a young, geeky lad who still had far too many pimples. Sheila assumed that he wasn't that bright from just the way he looked and walked. He was all gangly arms and legs.

The manager asked Jack to connect his phone to the TV. 'Yes Bob,' he said, pushing the play button. It clearly showed Sheila committing the crime. She told them that it had been an accident.

Bob said, 'They all say that. You would be surprised how many packets of batteries disappear every year; it would appear that some people are obsessed with them.'

Bob said to Sheila in his very stern voice, 'In this store, we have a "Tough on Crime" policy. This has been encouraged by the Home Office and the local police service. I would imagine that you will get a custodial sentence of between three and six months.' Sheila looked horrified. She asked if there was any other way that she could make amends.

Bob said, 'Yes, Mrs Allen, there is something else that we could consider. It's obvious that you must be punished for your crime. We have learnt that if we just let people off, they re-offend. Our proposal is that you voluntarily have full sex with Jack and me.' Jack looked thrilled.

'No way!' Sheila quickly responded. 'What sort of woman do you think I am?' Bob replied, 'You are the sort of woman who is going to have a criminal record.' He picked the phone up to call the police.

'Stop!' Sheila said. 'What exactly would I have to do?'

Bob said that it was quite simple. 'You strip naked. Jack has sex with you. This is probably going to be his first time, so he will not want to rush things. Once that is done, I will then have full sexual intercourse with you. You get dressed and go home. Nothing said.' While all this was going on, Jack was nodding his head in approval.

Sheila asked if she could have some time to think about it. Bob said that he would give her five minutes. Sheila did think about it, but what choice did she have? A couple of fucks against six months in the clink.

Bob and Jack returned with a scribbled, hand-written document. It said, 'I, Sheila Allen, agree to be fucked by the shop staff.' She signed it, stood up and unbuttoned her blouse. She dropped her skirt and stood there in her matching bra and knickers set. Bob was impressed with what he saw. He had fucked quite a few of the shoplifters, but this one was the prettiest by far. Jack had been fortunate this time, but the rule was, whoever caught the shoplifter got the first chance to fuck them.

Bob admired Sheila's curves. His cock was responding in a most satisfactory way. The feeling of power the situation gave him always got his cock really hard. Jack was almost jumping up and down with excitement. Bob thought that he would have to help the idiot.

Bob looked at Sheila and said, 'Very nice. Please get the rest off.' Sheila wasn't going to make a show of it, so she quickly removed her bra and knickers. Bob turned to Jack and said, 'Look, you have got a naked woman for an hour. What do you want to do with her?' Jack just stood there gawping; he had never seen naked boobs or a fanny before.

Bob said to Jack, 'Probably best to undress and then let me know what you want.' Jack quickly stripped. He may have been gangly, but he had a fine-looking cock; large and rigid with a particularly impressive head. Even Bob was impressed.

Bob realised that he would have to help this lad. He instructed Jack to grab Sheila and start licking her boobs. He was like a bull in a china shop, and almost pushed Sheila over. Bob told him to do it a different way. He gently took hold of Sheila's left tit and caressed it, fondling the nipple gently but firmly. Jack was a quick learner; but then again, he was working on a great pair of tits. Sheila thought, 'What a strange world it is. I'm sitting here naked with two strangers sucking my breasts.' And to be honest, Jack was doing a good job. Sheila could feel the early signs of an orgasm coming. That always happened when her nipples were getting a good seeing to.

Bob told Jack that he had done very well. It was now time to play with Sheila's fanny. Bob instructed Sheila to lie on the table and hold her legs apart. She obliged. Her fanny had never been so exposed before. She was a bit embarrassed that it was already moist down there. Bob could tell that Jack found Sheila's naked pussy quite intimidating.

Bob said to Jack, 'Girlie bits are quite simple. Here you have the labia.' Bob was gently teasing them apart. 'At the top, you have the clit, and in the middle is the actual vagina. You will be sticking your cock in there soon.' Jack couldn't wait.

Bob grabbed Jack's finger and helped him rub the labia. He then moved his finger to Sheila's clit. Sheila visibly jumped as two men, or rather one man and a gangly boy of nineteen gently caressed one of her most intimate parts. Lastly, he took Jack's finger and pushed it into Sheila's pussy. Jack was so excited. He asked if he could put two fingers in, and Bob nodded. Sheila started to wonder whose body he thought it was.

The second finger entered. Bob suggested that Jack curl his fingers up so that he could feel the pubic bone from the inside. Jack wasn't too sure, so Bob showed him how. He explained that he should take two fingers from the right hand and put them in the fanny with the fingers pointing upwards. With a bit of luck and some practice, he should find the 'G spot.' The thumb would be free to flick the clit. Bob had done a great job demonstrating, and Sheila immediately climaxed, crushing Bob's fingers in the process.

'That,' he said, talking to Jack, 'is a woman having a climax. You have been a very lucky boy. I was thinking of a blow job next, but from the looks of you, I think we need to move on to the fucking stage.' In reality, he just wanted to get Jack out of the way so that he could fuck this little minx.

Bob asked Jack what position he wanted Sheila in. Since he had no idea, Bob suggested that he should go for the classic missionary position. Jack got up onto the table and simply laid on top of Sheila. Sheila could hardly breathe. Bob shouted, 'Stop!' He told him to put his arms on either side to support himself, and then Sheila grabbed his cock and put it into her fanny.

She wondered why she was helping. Partly, it was the fun of having a virgin, but it was also because she needed to get the job done. Jack started pumping away far too vigorously. Bob told him to slow down, which disappointed Sheila as Jack was hitting all the right spots. Sheila's boobs were jumping all over the place. Bob told Jack that there was no hurry and that he should savour his first fuck. Jack just ignored him and went for it. Sheila had never seen a man have such an intense climax. Jack's body went absolutely rigid and then buckled, moving Sheila all over the place.

Jack's cock popped out amongst what looked like gallons of spunk. He had obviously been saving it up for some time. Jack went up to Sheila, kissed her on the lips and said, 'Thank you.' Sheila felt quite emotional, but now she had Bob to contend with.

Bob said, 'Well, that was a revelation. I think we need to

get a move on, so I think I will have you from behind. Sheila was relieved to get up as the table was quite hard. Sheila bent over, exposing herself to him. Bob pulled his cock out and then rubbed it up and down her slit. He kept rubbing his cock against her bum hole. Without any warning, his cock was straight up her anus.

Sheila yelped. She had never had anal sex before. She'd often wondered what it would feel like, but she'd never really fancied it. Bob's cock was a lot smaller than Jack's, which was a relief. Bob pumped away until he shot his load up her bum. He withdrew his cock and wiped it against the side of her bottom. He then simply left the room without a word.

Sheila then noticed two warehouse lads looking through the window. They pointed at the security camera in the ceiling.

She decided to shop at Lidl next time. But since she still had the batteries, she guessed that it wasn't all bad.

The Debt

Sheila had become used to her husband being called "Wormy". Apparently, he was given that name as a young boy because he had a habit of eating worms. Sheila thought that it was a very appropriate name as it seemed to describe his character very well: pathetic, weak-willed, limp and dirty. He was a little man who thought that the world was always against him. Nothing was ever his fault.

Wormy was in serious trouble. He was a gambler. He had gambled on the stock exchange and lost. He had gambled on the horses and lost. And now he was gambling in an underground casino where the odds were stacked against you. He always thought that the next card would change everything. In this case, the next card meant that he owed the 'Club' over £50,000.

Sam, the club's manager, sat a shaking Wormy down and said that he wanted the money by that weekend or it might be Wormy's last. Wormy managed to blurt out that he didn't have it. There was no way he could pay. The manager asked if he had any assets, and Wormy shook his head. Sam said that he was wrong—he had a very pretty wife.

Wormy asked what he meant. Sam said, 'We've seen her in town in a little red patterned coat with a great set of pins and a fabulous smile.' He said that she could help pay off Wormy's debt. Wormy still wasn't sure what he was getting at. Sam said,

'Do I have to spell it out for you?' Wormy nodded.

Sam said, 'Well, me and my two boys would use your wife's assets as a way for you to pay off your debt to us.'

Wormy said, 'My wife hasn't got any assets either.'

Sam said, 'She certainly has an asset—she's sitting on it.'

It slowly dawned on Wormy what was being suggested. Wormy said, 'Are you saying that you want to make love to my wife?'

Sam replied, 'Well, I wouldn't put it that way, but yes, me and my two sons.'

Wormy said, 'I can't see Sheila agreeing to that.'

Sam said, 'In that case, Sheila is going to have to find herself a new husband, isn't she? I need to have your answer by Saturday morning as we will be ready and waiting Saturday evening.' Wormy was shaking as the manager helped him out the door. What was he going to say to Sheila?

Wormy arrived at his home and sat Sheila down. He suddenly burst into tears, which wasn't that unusual. Sheila comforted him and asked what the problem was. He explained that they had to sell their house to pay off his gambling debts. She asked how much it was, as they might be able to re-mortgage. When she heard that it was over £50,000, she was furious. There was no way they could re-mortgage with Wormy's pathetic wage. Wormy said that there might be another way to pay it off.

Sheila was all ears. Wormy didn't know how to say it, but with her prompting, he told her that the club manager and his two sons wanted to make love to her. Sheila said, 'You mean, three dirty old men want to fuck me?' Wormy nodded, with tears streaming down his face.

Sheila asked when this would happen. Wormy said,

'Saturday evening.'

Sheila said, 'But that's tomorrow evening.' Wormy nodded.

Sheila wasn't sure what to do. Say 'no' and her husband would be killed, which admittedly had some appeal, or say 'yes' and be treated as a fuck-toy. She told Wormy to send them around. In the back of her mind, she thought that at least she would get a good seeing to, which would make for a welcome change.

The day had arrived. Sheila had her best underwear on, and she had applied some fresh lipstick. Sheila was actually quite excited, but Wormy was terrified. He wondered what would happen if she didn't perform—probably a sharp knife to his guts. He could already feel the pain.

There was a very loud knock on the door, and three burly men entered. You could see that they were all related. They all had round, Eastern European-looking faces and were muscular and tattooed. They looked like pub bouncers.

They liked what they saw. Sheila was in a tight top that accentuated her boobs and a pleated mini-skirt that was hardly hiding two very sexy-looking legs. They were surprised that Sheila was smiling, but she liked men admiring her. She could see them undressing her with their eyes. Sam's sons, Tom and Jerry, were very keen to get her kit off and get the fucking underway as they were going on a pub crawl later that night. Sheila realised that this wasn't going to be a subtle affair.

Sheila suggested that they follow her upstairs to the master bedroom. Wormy said that he would stay downstairs and wait for them to finish. Sam said, 'No way. You are going to watch what's going on.' In the bedroom, the three men stripped off and told Wormy to remove his clothes. The visitors were naked in no time. They already had full erections. Sheila didn't know where to look, as she had never seen so much male nudity before. Wormy was taking his time when one of the boys just pulled his trousers and pants down to reveal his scrawny little chipolata.

Sheila had initially planned to do a striptease, but she could see that it would be wasted on them. She quickly undressed and just stood there; her fanny was starting to get excited. Tom got on the bed and gestured for Sheila to join him. She climbed on top of him, giving everyone a good view of her genitals. Tom, with no problem at all, turned her over so that she was resting face upon his body. She could feel his throbbing, erect penis resting between her legs. She knew that it wouldn't be long before the shagging would start.

Sheila thought that some lubrication might be useful and suggested so. Sam looked at Wormy and told him to get some. He came back with a bottle of moisturiser and tried to give it to Sam. Sam said, 'Come on, man. You can moisturise your wife.' Wormy patted some creamy fluid onto Sheila's vagina. He never really liked touching it; it always seemed a bit dirty to him. Sam grabbed the moisturiser off him and dropped a large dollop onto her fanny.

Sam had big, chunky hands, but he knew what to do with his fingers. Sheila's labia, clit and fanny were all being well lubricated. Fingers were massaging parts of her body that had never been touched by a man before. One of his fingers was well inside her anus. It was all a bit too much for Sheila. She could feel the early signs of an orgasm.

Without any warning, Sam grabbed his son's cock and rested it against Sheila's bottom. He told his son to push, and Sheila could feel the pressure against her arse. Sheila knew that something would give way eventually, and then he popped right in. Tom had his rigid cock up her bum. She hadn't expected that. Wormy tried to look away, but Sam grabbed his head and moved it so that his face was only two or three inches from Sheila's fanny.

Jerry took his engorged cock and rubbed it against Sheila's lips. She opened her mouth, and he was in. Sheila was never keen on blow jobs, as she was conscious of her teeth, but what could she do? Both Tom and Jerry were already teasing her with gentle thrusting.

Sam pushed her lovely legs slightly apart and gently pushed his cock into her well-lubricated fanny. For big men, they were all very gentle. She had assumed that she was going to get a hard, merciless shag, but that had not been the case thus far.

It was a very strange, but not an unpleasant feeling, to have a cock in her fanny and one in her rectum at the same time. She could feel the two penises rubbing against each other. They were only separated by the perineum, a thin piece of skin. It felt simultaneously dirty and exciting.

'OK boys,' said Sam, 'let's get this show on the road.' On the count of three, they each gently thrust and then withdrew. This gentle thrusting and withdrawing continued and continued. Sheila felt so many sensations from so many different parts of her body. They then slightly changed the tempo so that as one penis entered another withdrew. This went on for a while.

Sheila could sense that her climax was coming and so could Sam. Sheila thought, 'That man knows what he's doing.'

'OK boys,' Sam said, 'we are nearly there.' They upped their tempo and Sheila screamed. The three men also screamed. All four had come at the same time. Sheila was impressed—what a brilliant piece of synchronised fucking. But Wormy was in a terrible state—he was jealous and angry. His wife was enjoying the attention of other men. Men who knew how to fuck. He felt pathetic and useless, but then again, he was pathetic and useless. Sheila loved the fact that Wormy was being punished while she was being pleasured.

As Sam pulled out, his final spurt of semen covered Wormy's face. Sheila wasn't sure if that had been deliberate or not. Either way, she'd enjoyed it. Wormy tried to get up when Sam said, 'What are you doing? You don't think you are going to get off that easily, do you? You let your fabulous wife take a pounding from three strangers; you are pathetic.' Sam held his head down while Tom, who had always liked anal sex, stood behind him. Tom pushed Wormy's skinny, white buttocks apart and roughly entered him.

There was no lubrication, and Wormy was in a fair amount of pain. The hard, rough sex that Sheila was expecting had been reserved for him. Tom held nothing back, did the job and wiped his cock on Wormy's back.

The boys gave Sheila a very friendly cuddle and said that they would see her next week. Sheila waved good-bye and asked Wormy what they meant. He said, 'It's going to take some time to work off the debt, probably two years.' For that, Sheila kicked Wormy in the balls. Wormy had not had a good day.

Calendar Girl

Sheila hadn't wanted to be a calendar girl, but a good friend of hers had volunteered on her behalf. An animal welfare charity was looking for an attractive local model to spearhead a more daring type of calendar. Sheila was chuffed that Mary had thought of her, but she wasn't a print model or very interested in charity work.

She was meeting the producer and photographer at 14.00 in Brighton, near the lanes. She found the head office reasonably quickly and was invited in. Over a cup of hot coffee, they introduced themselves as Julie and Bob. Julie had executive control over the design of the calendar and Bob would be taking the photos.

Julie explained that most nude calendars had been designed to cover up the exciting parts of a woman's body. She wanted this one to be different. Julie wanted to be bold and daring. 'Let's ring in the new and display a vagina on the front page,' she said. She asked Sheila if she agreed, and Sheila nodded.

'Excellent,' Julie said. 'You are on the same wavelength as me. I'm fed up with these girls who are afraid of showing off their girlie bits. Well, let's get down to basics, we need to check your body out. Getting the right person to model is critical to the success of this project. So, off with your kit then.'

Sheila said, 'Do you want me to strip right here?'

'Yes, please,' said Julie.

Sheila said, 'But we are right at the end of an open-plan office. Won't it upset the staff?'

'Don't worry about them,' Julie said. 'Just get your kit off.'

Sheila felt compelled to comply and removed her blue skirt and patterned tights. This was followed by her silk blouse, leaving her standing there in her skimpy bra and panties. A couple of office workers stopped to look. Julie said that she looked great and gestured for her to take off the rest. Sheila slowly removed her bra and covered her tits with her arms. She tried to pull her French knickers down with one hand, but it wasn't easy. By then, she had attracted about ten onlookers and could see no point in trying to be modest, so she stripped off completely.

She put her hands up in the air and showed everything she had. The onlookers clapped. It's not every day that you see a naked pussy and a great pair of boobs in the office. Julie looked at Bob and said, 'What do you think?'

Bob said, 'From here, it is looking good: great pair of tits, flat stomach, cute little arse, a fine pair of legs and a very engaging smile. Let's try a few different positions.'

Bob grabbed Sheila and bent her over. He felt the firmness of her tits as they dangled in front of him. He stroked her arse and pushed her legs farther apart so that he could get a good view of her pussy. Bob told Julie that it was all looking good. However, he was a bit worried about the fanny, as it was hairier than he would have liked. He grabbed a small comb and brushed her bush so that the fanny was easier to see.

Sheila was just stunned. Here was a man manipulating her

naked body in front of an ever-growing group of bystanders. He was treating her like a man buying a horse. While she thought that, Bob played with her clit and put two fingers into her vagina. Bob called Julie over and said that this would make a good shot. He showed her the inside of Sheila's fanny, and Julie said, 'Come on, Bob, we are not doing porn.'

He said, 'OK,' and pulled his fingers out.

Bob said, 'Let's get started straight away.' Julie agreed and went to get her two assistants. Bob told Sheila that the charity shop was downstairs, and there was no reason why they couldn't get the draft shots underway. Sheila went to get her clothes, but Bob said she wouldn't need them.

Bob pushed her towards the stairs. They had to leave the office building to get to the shop across the road. Sheila's nudity caused a bit of a stir in the High Street, but she was soon in the shop. Mind you, the shop was still open to the public.

Julie's two assistants, Dick and Gavin, stripped off in the changing room and came out stark naked. Sheila must have looked surprised as Julie said, 'Hadn't I mentioned that it would be a mixed-sex calendar?'

'No,' Sheila thought. But they were two good-looking lads and not without talent in the trouser department.

Bob called Sheila over and said that he wanted some door shots. There was one with her opening the door. Another with her making love to the side of the door. One with her boobs pushed up against the glass. He then wanted one with Sheila leaning up against the door and Gavin standing behind her. Gavin grabbed Sheila's waist and then nudged his erect cock against the crack of her bottom. Bob asked Sheila to arch her back, which resulted in Gavin's cock easily entering her fanny.

Sheila was a bit surprised by this, to put it mildly, but all this public nudity had made her rather randy. Bob said that the pose was excellent and took some photos of it. He then grabbed Gavin's cock and moved it into different positions. He then separated them slightly so he could get a good picture of Gavin's cock entering Sheila's pussy. Sheila wasn't too sure if they could use these types of photos in a charity calendar.

Bob then dragged Sheila over to the till and made her bend over, which fully exposed her fanny. Two old blokes from the general public just stared. One said to the other, 'You don't see that every day.'

The other one said, 'That's the first one I've seen in thirty years. I wonder if they still taste as good.' Before anyone could stop him, he was stroking Sheila's fanny. Bob soon pushed him out of the way.

Bob called Dick over and asked him to place his thick cock at the entrance to Sheila's pussy. He then wanted Dick to enter her while he took photos every two seconds. Dick did as he was told, and it wasn't long before he was desperate to give her a good, hard fucking, but he wasn't sure if he would get the chance.

Bob then wanted Sheila to sit on top of one of the shop stands. It wasn't easy getting her up there, and once they did, it was certainly impossible for her to maintain her modesty. Bob asked the others what they thought. Should Sheila cover her pussy with her hand, leave it reasonably discreet or have her pussy fully on show? They tried all three positions several times. The men and women had different views. As far as the women were concerned, a little bit of modesty was more exciting than outright nudity. The men disagreed.

Sheila then laid naked on the cold floor with Dick on top of her. His cock was resting against her private parts. Bob had no shame. He grabbed Dick's cock and pushed it into Sheila's juicy fanny. It squelched as he forced the entry. Sheila was not expecting that. Dick started to grind his hips, but Bob told him to stop as photography was in progress.

Bob then got Sheila to stand in a clothes rack. A series of photos were taken with her legs and bottom sticking out. There was a pile of clothes with just Sheila's boobs on show. It looked a bit like a nest. At one stage, a bunch of flowers were protruding from her fanny. Both Dick and Gavin managed to enter her again as part of a pose, but their lust was never satisfied—well, at least not with Sheila.

The session came to an end, and Sheila was amazed by the finished product. It was a revolutionary calendar. It was much ruder than usual, but it was amazing what they achieved with Photoshop. If you looked carefully, you could just about see Gavin's cock entering her fanny.

Sheila's husband asked how her day had gone. She said that she had spent most of the day doing charitable work.

He said, 'Doesn't charity start at home?'

Sheila said, 'Not in this case.'

The Tent

Sheila had always been a keen music fan and had booked a three-day open-air rock festival with her husband. It would mean spending two nights in a tent. Not unsurprisingly, her hubby had decided that he couldn't make it in the end as his back was playing up. He was just a lazy, pathetic twat, but at least he was going to take her there and collect her when it was over. Because of that, she'd decided that she would still go, even if it meant her being on her own. She might even find a young man while she was there, she joked to herself.

The second disaster was that the car broke down on the way there, so she sacrificed some of her supplies and hitched a lift. By the time she arrived at the festival, she was knackered, but she was proud of the fact that she had made it. Sheila was one of the 50,000 people who were thoroughly enjoying the music. She loved Colin Bluntstone, Caravan and The Killers. She also took the opportunity to drink a bit more than usual; she wasn't drunk, but she was happy. It's what you do at these events.

As night-time approached, the wind started to gather. She struggled to find her small tent at first, as everything looked different in the dark. She found it by accident, washed quickly and put her rather short nightie on. She crept into her comfortable sleeping bag and was looking forward to getting a good night's sleep.

An almighty bang woke her up in the night. At first, she had to work out where she was—it's funny how the mind sometimes plays tricks on you. She unzipped the tent to see stuff flying everywhere: tents, sleeping bags, pot, pans and debris of all sorts. People were struggling to stand up. The noise was deafening and getting louder.

She quickly put a bath towel around her and got out of the tent. Without her weight to hold it down, the tent was airborne and flew away. She had never seen anything like it. The wind was so strong that it whipped the towel off her. She was struggling to keep her nightie on and was utterly unable to protect her modesty.

She didn't know it at the time, but she had been struck by the largest whirlwind ever to hit the UK. Many people were running down the hill and, rightly or wrongly, she joined them. Sheila had never heard the wind make noises like that before or felt the rain hit her so hard. She was soaked. She carried on running, slipped and (although it's hard to believe) fell through a hedge and onto a tent. It was much calmer on that side of the hedge as it made for a brilliant wind-break.

The three young men in the tent knew nothing about the windy conditions outside, but they had noticed a body landing on the canvas. Joe unzipped the tent to investigate. He was astonished to find a twister going by and a half-naked girl on the grass. Her body was naked except for some clothing wrapped up around her head. 'Boys,' he shouted, 'it's raining girls.'

All three men were standing there in their underwear, getting soaked but enjoying the view. On show were two perfect legs, a beautiful pair of tits and a naked fanny. Life couldn't get much better. They removed the cloth from around the girl's head and carried her into the tent. They all threw their pants to one side as they were soaked to the bone.

They rubbed Sheila's wet body down with a towel. All three of them took the opportunity to dry her boobs and fanny, which gave each of them massive erections. In fact, at that point, Sheila's fanny might have been the driest fanny ever. Danz, a Pakistani lad who had never seen a naked woman before, said, 'What are we going to do with her?'

Jack said, 'We need to keep her warm; we all need to get under the covers. Our body heat will help revive her.' Danz was worried that it might be an immoral act.

Nonetheless, it wasn't long before all four of them were under the covers in a two-person tent. To say that space was in short supply would be a massive understatement. Sheila didn't know which way to turn as naked men were pressing against her on both sides. She could feel two erections resting against her thigh.

Joe said to Andy, 'Do you think we need to massage her to help her get warm, as her feet are deathly cold.'

Before Sheila could say, 'They're always like that,' two hands were fondling her boobs.

Joe said, 'She can't be in such bad shape, as her nipples are fully erect.'

Danz said, 'Do you think we should be doing this?'

Joe said, 'It's OK, we are doing it for medical reasons.' Sheila was beginning to enjoy the medical treatment.

The boys were enjoying nibbling and sucking Sheila's fabulous breasts to get the blood flowing. It always got Sheila hot, and she could feel the warm, cosy tingling of an orgasm starting to develop. Andy decided that Sheila's fanny also needed some medical attention. He eased her clit out of its

84

little hood and started to play a tune. A tune that Sheila was thoroughly enjoying. Joe wanted in on some of the action and began to caress the inside of her fanny with one finger at first, and then two.

Sheila was squirming about in a tiny tent. She couldn't help rubbing her legs against Danz. He was tempted to grab a leg or a boob, but he knew that he shouldn't. Sheila was thoroughly revived, hot and eager for a cock in her fanny. She grabbed the nearest one and dragged it over to her pussy. Without any resistance, Joe entered Sheila and started fucking her for all he was worth. Sheila could tell he was young, as he thought that making love was a bit like mimicking a piston engine. To be honest, it was what Sheila wanted. The piston did its job, and Sheila and Joe both came.

Andy was worried that he would not get a go, but Sheila beckoned him over. Fucking in a small tent wasn't easy, but moving all the bodies around was the real challenge. At last, after much laughter and amusement, Sheila was ready, laying on her back with her vagina open and ready for the next young man. Andy crawled into position between her legs and gently edged his massive cock into her cute, little cunt. Sheila could tell immediately that he was much more experienced.

Andy gently stoked up the engine. He quickly, but steadily, moved from first to second, and then with a quick rub of her clit, he moved into third. Sheila wasn't sure if his engine had four or five gears, but she was going to find out. As he moved into fourth, the motor purring, Sheila could feel her oil level rising. Then he hit fifth, and there were two massive explosions. Sheila mentally and physically collapsed with exhaustion. It was a truly enjoyable driving lesson.

Danz had never seen a couple fuck before. He was

transfixed. His cock was aching for relief.

Joe and Andy laid on each side of Sheila, gently caressing her thighs and breasts. They were in a relaxed stupor. Sheila said to Danz, 'I could fit one more in if you were interested.' He was interested, but his upbringing was holding him back.

Andy said, 'Come on, Danz, this is your chance to make love to a beautiful woman. She's been the best fuck of my life.' Sheila found that to be very sweet.

Danz eased himself between Sheila's legs. He noticed that semen was still leaking from her fanny, but then again, she had been filled up twice already. With great hesitation, and after saying a little prayer to himself, he entered Sheila's fanny and came immediately. They all laughed. Sheila told him that things would get better over the next two days.

For the rest of the festival, Sheila and the three boys hardly left the tent. They just fucked and fucked and fucked. Sheila got a little bit sore, but Danz became a great lover.

At the end of the weekend, Sheila stood waiting for her husband to turn up wearing nothing but a blanket. He asked how it went. She said, 'Apart from the whirlwind, I had a fucking brilliant time. It was so relaxing just sharing time with fellow music lovers.'

Lady Godiva: Part 1

Not many people know that Lady Godiva came from Pershore in Worcestershire, which is where her life is celebrated at a festival in August. In Pershore, she is actually seen as a bit of a tart and is treated accordingly. Every year, the festival re-enacts the following events in the same order:

The trial (where she is found guilty);

The formal stripping;

The horse ride through the town;

The embarrassment of the stocks.

It is a major social event attracting thousands of visitors each year. Sheila had never been to the festival before, but she was quite chuffed that her name had been put forward as a candidate to play Lady Godiva herself, as she was a former beauty queen in Worcester.

Sheila was very pleasantly surprised to find out that she had got the role of Lady Godiva. What she didn't know was that the other five candidates, who were all from Pershore, had pulled out. They had read in the local paper that the rules of the festival had changed. For the first time, Lady Godiva would actually be naked. In the past, Lady Godiva had worn a flesh-coloured bodysuit which is what Sheila was expecting.

It had been decided that in modern times, female nudity was much more acceptable. However, the real reason was money. A beautiful naked girl riding through the town on horseback was bound to bring the punters in. Everything was carefully organised. Sheila had to do nothing but turn up on the day. It was not practical to rehearse.

She knew that she had to put medieval clothes on when she got there. She also knew that a man would even be riding on the horse with her, as she wasn't an experienced rider. Sheila was looking forward to it, as she quite liked being the centre of attention.

Sheila arrived early and went to the local theatre, which was strangely called Number 8. She was given a pair of white, drab drawers, a cloth to fasten around her ample breasts, and a large, multi-layered crimplene dress. It wasn't the prettiest outfit she had ever been in. She wondered when she was going to get the flesh-coloured bodysuit. One of the women in Number 8 approached her and said, 'You are so brave.'

She was introduced to the two guards who would be accompanying her throughout the day. They wore the full medieval garb with red tunics, tights, scabbards and swords. They both said that they were looking forward to her portrayal of Lady Godiva. One said to the other, 'This is going to be fun, looking after a naked lady all day.'

At the designated time, she ceremoniously walked into the court, which was actually the theatre. The two guards followed with their swords raised. She was surprised to see it was a packed house. She stood in the formal-looking dock with the guards behind her. The judge, who in history was also her husband, started the trial with a gavel hitting the bench. This woke everyone up, including Sheila.

She was accused of being a tart. She was accused of being a scold. She was accused of being an adulteress. Sheila had been told to admit to every crime, and she did.

The judge announced that she had been found guilty of all crimes and that they should proceed to the formal stripping stage. Sheila was still wondering when she would get the flesh-coloured bodysuit. The two guards grabbed an arm each and formally marched her outside to the accompaniment of a small brass band.

The crowd were laughing and enjoying themselves. There were many couples there, but Sheila was surprised by the large number of single men. Sheila was lifted onto a cross frame, and her legs and arms were gently tied to the four corners. She could still just about move, but there was no doubt that she was securely held in place.

She shouted out, 'When am I going to get the flesh-coloured bodysuit?' but no one could hear her. Apparently, the job of removing her clothes had been raffled off and turned out to be an excellent money earner. A middle-aged woman walked towards the frame and pulled off her dress. It had been designed to come off easily. The crowd cheered.

Sheila was tied to a frame, wearing a tatty pair of drawers and a cloth covering her breasts. The crowd were very impressed with her charms. She had a beautiful, curvaceous body with a superb pair of legs. Usually, she had a very pretty smile and sparkling eyes, but at that moment, she looked somewhat tense.

A young lad walked towards the frame and started to unravel the breast covering. It wasn't easy to do as it was wrapped around her. He had to keep leaning against her to release it at the back. Suddenly, her natural charms were exposed for all to see. The young lad grabbed each breast and attempted to suck them. One of her guards jumped down to pull the lad away, but it was a bit challenging as he literally had to pull the breast out of the boy's mouth.

The guard held Sheila's breast and stroked it, thinking that it might have been hurt. He then remembered that his wife was in the audience and quickly dropped it.

Sheila had beautiful breasts; they were ample, nicely shaped and well-proportioned with hard, erect nipples. They were certainly a handful, as the young lad had discovered. The crowd were thoroughly enjoying this spectacle. Some of the lads already had hard-ons.

An older man walked towards Sheila with a pair of scissors. Sheila felt herself trembling. She really didn't want her pussy exposed on Pershore High Street. The man cut up one side of the drawers, quite slowly, for maximum dramatic effect. He then slowly cut the other side. He then addressed the audience and said, 'Are you ready to see Lady Godiva's fanny?'

The crowd clapped, cheered and shouted 'Off, off, off, off!' With one hard pull of the knickers, Sheila's fanny was totally exposed. She wasn't sure if it was allowed, but the man continued to massage her pubes. He pushed against her pubic bone and flicked her clit. He was about to finger her fanny when the guard approached.

The man looked directly into the eyes of the guard and then pushed his finger into Sheila's vagina before he could be stopped. She couldn't believe it. Here she was in the middle of Pershore being fingered by a stranger. The guard asked the man if he had finished, but to his surprise and Sheila's, the man inserted a second finger into her fanny, clearly relishing the soft, silky texture within. Then the man walked away, and the guard apologised to Sheila.

The crowd enjoyed what they were seeing. It is not often

that you see a beautiful, naked woman tied to a frame. For some of the young people (obviously over the age of eighteen), it was the first time they had seen a fanny. The world would see a lot of Sheila's fanny as hundreds of photos were being taken.

The guards lifted Sheila down and walked her towards the horse. They managed to fondle the odd breast and pat her bum along the way, but that was nothing compared to what the crowd did. They pushed forward to get a closer look and a quick grope. The guards tried to push the hands away but to little avail.

Sheila was introduced to the horseman. He was standing there stark naked. The consensus was that it was only fair to have some eye candy for the ladies as well as the men. He was a good-looking young man with broad shoulders and an engaging smile. You could see that he fancied Sheila as his cock was already quite hard. He got on the horse, which did not have a saddle. They were going to ride bareback.

Sheila was lifted by the guards, giving them an excellent view of her fanny. In fact, one of the guards managed to stroke it as she landed on the horse.

Michael put his arms around Sheila and grabbed the reins. Effectively, her breasts were resting on his arms, and her nipples were being continuously rubbed, which was sure to start an orgasm. To make things worse, she could feel the end of his penis rubbing against her bottom.

Michael wasn't sure what to do regarding his penis, as it was gradually getting nearer and nearer to Sheila's little love hole. Sheila tried to make herself a bit more comfortable, which pushed his cock almost into the entrance of her fanny and regularly teased her clit. Her climax was getting nearer, which would be just too embarrassing to experience on Pershore High Street. The horse reared, and Michael's cock fully entered Sheila's vagina. The sudden shock pushed her into a significant climax.

The crowd were cheering and thoroughly enjoying the show. Little did they know that Sheila was riding a cock while riding a horse. She suddenly felt a sudden splash of fluid in her fanny. Clearly, Michael had come inside her. She couldn't blame him. He whispered an apology in her ear. She spotted some semen running down the side of the horse, but there wasn't much she could do about it.

They were approaching the middle of the town and turned down an alley towards the local supermarket. Michael helped Sheila off the horse, giving the audience a good view of her nether region. The two guards walked her over to some upright stocks in the middle of the car park. When she saw them, she started to struggle. One of the guards said that this was the last stage in the procession and warned her to behave.

Sheila was strapped in with her head and two arms firmly fixed in place. The sides were locked down; she couldn't get out. A man walked over with a pair of safety glasses and put them on Sheila. Michael approached and thanked her for the fuck. He had really enjoyed it, but he asked her not to mention it to anyone as it would upset his wife. Both the guards said goodbye as it was their tea time. Sheila felt very vulnerable.

The local supermarket had been very generous and were sponsoring this part of the show. Buckets of rotten tomatoes and dodgy fruit were provided to the crowd. Without any warning, she was pelted from all sides. Tomatoes hit her face, tits and fanny. They appeared to be the crowd's favourite targets. She was covered in a variety of squishy fruit and rotten vegetables.

The supermarket manager told the crowd to stop as he was going to wipe her down. With a dirty cloth, he cleaned her up. He particularly enjoyed cleaning her breasts and bottom. He even managed to extract some lettuce leaves from her fanny.

The pelting continued, and she was wiped down again. She asked how long this was going to continue. He said that it stopped at 18.00, so she only had an hour to go. He said that he had a call to make in the shop, but he would be back later.

One of the older lads in the group decided to get a bit nearer. He was throwing rotten fruit from only a few feet away. As no one stopped him, he rubbed a squashed tomato against Sheila's breast, enjoying the feel of her hard nipple against the palm of his hand. Other lads soon joined in and were playing with her more intimate parts. Fingers were everywhere. Sheila felt humiliated, but at the same time, she was enjoying the sexuality of it all. To be honest, the young men were being quite gentle, but it wouldn't be long before they would go too far.

The supermarket manager came out and shooed them away. He stood behind her where she couldn't see him. He was admiring the curvature of her arse. He liked the fact that her fanny was fully exposed. He whispered in her ear that he could let her out early if she would let him use the facilities. She nodded, and he walked her stark naked through the shop to his office. He bent her over his desk, pulled another lettuce leaf out and entered her sweet, little cunt.

After all, she had been through, she could not believe that her body was responding to his thrusts. They both came together. The manager organised a lift home for her in one of their home-delivery vans. The elderly driver said that she was the strangest and most beautiful delivery he had ever made. He could not help admiring her bum as she walked up the drive.

Then she remembered that she had read in the paper that the role called for full nudity. She wondered if they would want a repeat performance next year.

Lady Godiva: Part 2

Sheila had played the role of Lady Godiva at the Summer Festival. It had been somewhat embarrassing, as she had been stripped naked in Pershore High Street and abused by some of the locals. She had endured a long bareback horse ride during which her escort, Michael, fucked her from behind as they rode. She was then put in the stocks and had rotten vegetables thrown at her. Finally, she was molested by a group of lads and fucked by the local supermarket manager.

Despite all that, she had fond memories of the event. The local paper had been very complimentary about her boobs and bum. The reporter wrote that she was the best Lady Godiva ever based on the appearance of her breasts alone. Some of the photos were a bit near the mark, leaving very little to the imagination, but to be honest, no imagination was needed at all.

She was invited back to appear at the local Christmas ball as one of the star attractions. The mayor had personally invited her, mainly because he wanted to see her naked again. He was hoping to take things a little bit further this time. She wondered what she would be expected to do.

Then she saw a copy of the agenda:

Formal disrobing at Number 8 (the local theatre) in the afternoon;

Charity auction in the evening, men only;

The feast.

Sheila thought, 'At least I'm going to get a bite to eat.'

Sheila spent some time getting herself set up with some new sexy underwear. She had her hair and nails done. Sheila was all primed and ready to go. She arrived on time to see the cross frame being installed in the hall. 'Not again,' she thought, but she wasn't expecting to keep her clothes on for long.

Apparently, this time she was going to be wearing a lot more clothes so that more men—sorry, people—could take them off. Her two medieval guards from the last time reappeared. They said that they would be strapping her onto the frame. They had both previously enjoyed seeing her naked. She mentioned that they had taken advantage of her nudity before, and they both agreed that there was every chance that they would do the same again. It made Sheila laugh.

This time, Sheila was given two stockings, a pair of crotchless knickers, a pair of pantaloons, a long skirt and two tops but no bra. While Sheila was removing her regular clothes, the guards were having a good ogle. She said, 'Do you mind?' They replied that there was no point in her being shy as she would soon be naked; and besides, they had already seen it all before.

She noticed that there had been some innovations made. Her clothes had been designed so that they could easily be pulled off—no cutting was needed. The frame had been changed so that it could move in almost every direction. You could spin it around or turn it upside down. It didn't seem like any of it was intended to protect her modesty.

At 14.00, Sheila was tied to the metal frame, and the audience appeared. The guard called for the first official disrober to attend. He was instructed to go for the skirt, which was off in one pull. This displayed a beautiful pair of legs covered in short stockings and bright red pantaloons. There were raucous cheers all around.

The second disrober arrived. He was given the choice of her outer blouse or one of the stockings. He decided to go for the stocking. He placed his hands, on Sheila's thigh and asked the audience if he should move them upwards or downwards. The audience shouted upwards, but the guard stopped him. He slowly removed the single stocking and tickled Sheila's foot along the way, making her jump. Again, there were cheers all around.

The third disrober had decided to go for the outer blouse. He used the opportunity to discreetly fondle her boobs, flicking one nipple as the blouse was pulled off. The underlying blouse was much flimsier; you could see Sheila's erect nipples pushing against the material. This was starting to get the men excited, and there were only four items of clothing left.

The fourth disrober was instructed to remove the remaining silk stocking. He was rather cunning and stood behind Sheila, putting his arm between her legs. He moved his hand up towards her crotch when the guard told him to focus on the stocking. He patted her bum and pulled the stocking off.

The audience members were starting to get restless; they wanted to use their toy whips. Sheila had noticed some whips in the audience and wondered what they were for. The guard explained that they were harmless—not painful at all. They had been sold as part of the afternoon's entertainment. Everyone who'd paid could give her a whipping. Sheila was not looking forward to that at all. The guard gave her a quick whip to show her that they were harmless, which they were.

The guard called for the fifth disrober to approach. He was a very large, heavily bearded man wearing a dirty t-shirt. He had the choice of the pantaloons or the top. He went for the top, as he was desperate to get his hands on those gorgeous boobs that he had seen in the newspaper. He pulled off the flimsy top, exposing Sheila's breasts to great acclaim.

One of the boys in the audience asked why everyone was cheering. His mother explained that it was tradition. The disrober managed to fondle both breasts during the removal process. One of the guards tried to stop him and fell face first onto Sheila's boobs. Everyone cheered. The men in the audience couldn't help admiring the beautiful pair of tits on show. The mayor was particularly impressed. His hands itched to get hold of them.

It was finally down to the pantaloons and the crotchless knickers. The sixth disrober was a man in his sixties who was looking forward to carrying out his task. He wasted no time in standing behind Sheila and slowly pulling the pantaloons down. The guards initiated some clapping to mark the occasion. However, the man managed to pull the knickers down at the same time. A guard rushed over and held them up. He managed to accidentally rub his hand against Sheila's fanny in the process. The whole audience almost saw everything.

The pantaloons were tossed into the air to great applause. Then the audience started shouting, 'Off, off, off, off!'

The final disrober, who was the mayor, came over and stood next to Sheila. He stroked her left boob and said that he would like to thank her for being such good fun. He stroked her nipple and said that she has had to put up with a lot. He turned to the audience and said, 'What do you want now?'

The audience shouted, 'Off with the knickers, off with the knickers!'

'Before I do that,' he said, 'I need to show you that they are crotchless.' He put his hand down Sheila's knickers so that his fingers stuck through the hole at the bottom. On the way, he quickly caressed her clit, making her jump for the second time that day. The audience laughed at his fingers, poking through.

The mayor slowly pulled her knickers down, exposing her fanny to the audience. Everyone clapped. The whole session hadn't been dirty; it had been good, clean fun. Another little boy asked what the little black triangle was for. His mum said, 'Ask your Dad, but you might find that he has forgotten.'

The mayor stood next to Sheila, making idle chit-chat while stroking her bottom at the same time. His hand was gradually creeping towards her fanny when a guard decided to save her. 'Sheila,' he said. 'It's time for the whipping.' About a hundred whips had been sold. He pushed the frame into the middle of the room.

In typical British fashion, the whippers queued up politely, and Sheila was given a series of small, painless whippings. The worst were the young men, some of whom had bought several whips. Most of them focused on her bottom, boobs or fanny. They liked to see the boobs bounce, so they used their whips to lift them and drop them. The guards had to stop one young boy from poking her fanny with the whip end.

The whipping finished, and the guards helped Sheila down. This was their chance to give her a grope, and they did. They gave her the outfit she was going to wear for the auction: a see-through nightie and the crotchless knickers that had been ceremoniously removed earlier. They then walked her over to the restaurant next door.

She wondered what they were going to auction, and then she saw the sign announcing: 'Lady Godiva Goes All the Way for Charity,' but then that's another story.

The Retirement Home: Part 1

Sheila had been asked to help out at the local retirement home in Malvern by Help the Aged. She had always been keen on 'doing her bit,' although in this case, she wasn't sure what her bit was going to be. An appointment had been fixed for her to meet the entertainments officer at 15.00. She was almost there.

Sheila was very impressed by the scale of the retirement home and the excellent range of facilities available, which included restaurants, a gymnasium, swimming pool, cinema and a small theatre. She waited in reception for Tony, the entertainments officer, to arrive. He apologised profusely for being late, but he had just come off the phone to the mayor of Pershore, who sent his love.

The mayor had given her the most glowing reference. He'd said that Sheila had given two very commendable interpretations of the Lady Godiva story. Her contribution to the funding of the town's local charities had been world-class. He said that Sheila had sacrificed both her modesty and her body in the interests of the local community. Tony was particularly pleased about this, as she sounded like just the sort of woman they were looking for.

Tony thought that visually she looked perfect, with her very shapely legs and what appeared to be an ample bosom. She had the perfect smile for a Snow Queen, with large, sparkling eyes to match. Her long black hair with the occasional streak of colour provided an ideal backdrop for the face of this very pretty girl. He fancied her. In fact, he fancied her big time. He hadn't been too sure about it at first, but now he was really looking forward to the show—both the preparation and the show itself.

Tony said to Sheila that it would probably be best for her to strip before the committee arrived. Sheila asked what he meant. Tony looked horrified; obviously, she had not been briefed. Tony asked Sheila, 'Has anyone explained what we want you to do?'

Sheila replied, 'No, I was just asked to meet with you.' Tony's heart dropped. The committee would be there soon, and he probably wasn't going to be able to deliver.

Tony said that it was a bit embarrassing, but he would go through the requirements with her. He asked if she could wait until the end before she made her decision, as she needed to see the whole picture. He explained that this retirement home was specifically designed for men on the autism spectrum. They were all in their seventies or eighties and had varying levels of disability. Every year, the local retirement homes hold a Christmas tableau competition. This home's tableaux were infamous for always being a bit on the naughty side. That was where she comes in.

Sheila was taking it all in and could see where Tony was going—they wanted her for another Lady Godiva experience. She wasn't too sure if she wanted her bits on display yet again. Tony said that they needed a woman who would be willing to be the Snow Queen in the tableau. Sheila said that she couldn't see a problem with that.

Tony said that there was a minor complication. Sheila thought that there usually was. He said that the Snow Queen wouldn't be completely dressed. She asked if she would be wearing a bikini. Tony said that it would probably be a bit less than a bikini. Sheila said, 'How much less?'

Tony stuttered, 'Mostly naked, except for a fur hat.'

Sheila shook her head and got ready to leave. 'Same old story,' she thought. 'Men constantly want their pound of flesh; who do they think I am?'

Tony realised that he had lost her. There was a knock on the door from Miriam, one of the resident nurses. Tony beckoned her in. She explained that the men were very excited about seeing the model. They had seen her in reception and were impressed with her beauty. Tony told Miriam that Sheila wasn't available after all. Miriam's face dropped. She said that the men would be so upset and that they might have to drug them to keep them under control.

Sheila was a sucker for this sort of situation. She asked Tony what she would have to do. He said she would just have to stand on a podium with no clothes on. Sheila turned to Miriam and asked if she could unzip her dress. Miriam was so pleased that she kissed Sheila on the cheek and unzipped her zipper a few inches. Sheila asked if there was a place where she could change. Tony said, 'Not really; anyway, we haven't got the time.'

Sheila pulled her dress off over her head. Tony thought that if he were a gentleman, he would look the other way; clearly, he wasn't a gentleman. Tony admired her figure as she pulled down her tights. Sheila stood there in a yellow frilly bra and panty set. Even Miriam had to admire her figure. Tony thought, 'What a great pair of tits.' Tony was eager to see the rest. Tony said to Sheila, 'I think the lads expect everything off.'

Sheila reluctantly unclipped her bra and gave it to Miriam to hold. Tony almost whistled in admiration. He couldn't help noticing that her nipples were hard, just how he liked them. The panties were being edged over her curvaceous bum to expose her neatly trimmed fanny. Tony's erection was beginning to show. Both Sheila and Miriam noticed it, but neither said a word.

Sheila stood on the podium with one arm covering her breasts and the other covering her fanny. Tony asked if she could put her hands on her head. This was so he could have a good ogle. Sheila complied but wondered why he'd asked. Miriam said to Sheila, 'The committee are all good men, but they can be a bit rumbustious at times. They use their stage names: George, Paul, John and Ringo. They probably won't see you as a person at first, but as a thing—but don't worry about it.' She asked Tony if she should let them in, and he nodded.

The door opened and in rushed four old men. Well, in reality, three rushed in and one hobbled in on crutches. They went straight up to Sheila and said, 'Pretty, very pretty.' Hands were all over her in no time at all. Sheila's breasts were being examined. John had one and Paul had the other. They were being lifted up and down as if they were being weighed. The nipples were being tweaked and licked.

Another hand was stroking her bush while her bottom was being carefully massaged. Tony told them to be gentle; he wished that he was also doing 'committee work.' With no warning, a finger started playing with her clit. Sheila thought, 'Well, they can't be that autistic.'

George was saying, 'My turn, my turn.' And then he pushed his finger into her fanny, which startled her. It wasn't easy standing upright with all this going on.

Tony came over to keep Sheila from falling. Sheila could feel his erection through his trousers, but she was grateful for his assistance. There were at least two fingers in her fanny now. Ringo, the man on crutches, finally reached her and immediately started sucking her right breast. He was doing an excellent job of it. Sheila asked Tony if this was all part of the interview. He just laughed.

John asked Tony if he could fuck her. Tony said, 'Of course not.' Regardless of his response, John took off his trousers and pants to display a fine todger. Sheila was presented with a hard, erect penis with large, hairy balls. He started rubbing it against Sheila's leg. Miriam told Sheila that he was harmless and just to ignore him. Sheila thought that it was not that easy ignoring a seventy-year-old man rubbing his cock up and down your leg. The committee continued with the interview.

Fingers examined every inch of her body. Clearly, the inside of her vagina was a critical area to be checked out. As usual, Sheila found herself responding to all the attention. Her fanny was now very moist, and her heart was beating fast. She had always found being on public display to be a great turn-on.

It wasn't helping that John's todger was rubbing the outside of her bush and hitting her very sensitive clit. Surreptitiously, she manoeuvred her fanny so that John could enter her, and he did. At the same time, her mind reflected on the situation: she was standing naked on a podium with a man holding her up while a resident fucked her. Tony couldn't believe what was going on. He was finding it hard to hold Sheila up while John was thrusting away. John was acting like he hadn't fucked a woman in decades, which was probably the case.

The other residents were attempting to remove their trousers, but Miriam told them to keep dressed. However, like everyone else in the room, she couldn't help staring at John's old-man todger that was giving Sheila a right proper fucking. He certainly knew what to do. It was the merciless tempo that was surprising everyone. He was really going for it. Sheila had several small climaxes when John went for one last mighty thrust. Both John and Sheila screamed. The others screamed in surprise.

John pulled his spunk-covered cock out of Sheila's cunt. Clearly, he hadn't masturbated in a long time because the amount of spunk he'd produced was prodigious. Miriam wiped Sheila's fanny with a tissue and whispered 'Thank you' to her.

Tony was exhausted from just holding Sheila in place. He would have given anything to be John. 'What a woman,' he thought.

Miriam pushed the committee out the door. Sheila sat there naked and catching her breath. Tony asked her if next Monday would be OK for the dress rehearsal, and she nodded. Tony wondered if he would get a chance to fuck her, as it was an undress rehearsal. Miriam wondered if she would get an opportunity to fuck Tony. Sheila thought that it would be interesting to make love to Miriam.

Back at home, Sheila's husband asked how the day went. She said, 'It was mostly committee work, but it had its ups and downs.'

The Retirement Home: Part 2

Tony had been looking forward to the dress rehearsal of the Snow Queen tableau all week. He couldn't wait to see Sheila naked again. He had been fantasising about fucking her to the point that one particular part of his body was feeling quite sore. Miriam wondered if she would get a chance to play with Tony's trouser snake. Getting his attention was not easy with Sheila around, but then again, she knew that Sheila was married. Sheila was hoping that she could maintain her cool around the committee this time, but she also knew how weak-willed she was.

Sheila arrived at the small theatre in the retirement home and stripped off in the toilets. She was now wearing a large, fluffy dressing gown. Tony was a bit disappointed when he saw her, as he was hoping for another impromptu striptease. Tony and Miriam beckoned for Sheila to sit down and listen to the plan of action.

Firstly, Miriam said, 'We have got to paint you blue and white.' Sheila asked what she meant. Miriam said, 'As you are not wearing any clothes, we thought a covering of paint would go down well. We also need to put some sparkle dust on you. It would offset the effect of the total nudity and make the whole thing a bit more respectable.' Sheila couldn't help agreeing, but she wasn't looking forward to the experience of being painted.

Miriam then said that she was going to have a word with the committee when they came in to avoid a repeat of the last meeting. Tony thought to himself that he would like to see Sheila being fucked again—preferably by him. Sheila knew that she couldn't control herself if things started getting fruity.

Tony then asked Miriam, 'Have we got any overalls? I don't want to get my suit covered in paint.' Miriam hadn't thought about that and found she was in the same predicament. Sheila suggested that they both strip down to their underwear. Miriam said that she was too embarrassed to do that, but in her mind, she thought it would be an excellent opportunity to display her assets to Tony. Tony only thought it fair as Sheila had to strip.

Tony soon stripped down to his boxer shorts. He was a fine-looking man; it was no wonder that Miriam fancied him. With broad shoulders, a slim waist and long, strong legs, he could have been an athlete. Miriam didn't know that he was an amateur swordsman. Sheila liked his deep brown eyes and slightly unkempt hair. He was a relaxed individual that wanted things done correctly.

Miriam was nervous about stripping in front of an audience. Her nurse's outfit hid a slim figure with a bust that was possibly even bigger than Sheila's. Her hips were maybe a bit bigger too. Sheila subconsciously thought that they were perfect child-bearing hips. Nevertheless, Tony was quite impressed with the package, especially as the underwear set she was wearing was sheer. Tony was trying to work out if she shaved down below, but he didn't want to be caught staring— at least not too much.

Miriam opened the door to let the committee enter. They were surprised to see both Miriam and Tony in their underwear. They explained the problem of getting paint on themselves, and the committee agreed to strip down as well. Sheila thought that they weren't the prettiest of sights, but hey ho, everyone will get there one day. Sheila was in the unusual position of being the only one who was covered up.

Miriam called the older men together and explained that today they were going to paint Sheila and that she didn't want to see a repeat of last week. Two of the men complained that it wasn't fair because John had fucked the model, and the others had barely got a look-in. Both Sheila and Tony could understand where they were coming from. Miriam said that last week there had been unacceptable behaviour.

Miriam explained that Sheila would be lying on the table soon, totally naked. She said, 'She knows that she is going to be painted, but she doesn't expect men to be playing with her breasts and vagina all of the time.' Sheila was actually a bit disappointed. Miriam said, 'If you need to touch those areas, you will need to get Sheila's permission first.'

Miriam asked if everyone was ready. There was a general nodding of heads, and Sheila removed her dressing gown. Everyone stared as this beauty walked across the room to what looked like a massage table. Miriam looked at Tony's eyes, which were almost out on stalks. This irritated her to no end. Sheila was going to enjoy teasing the men—partly to annoy Miriam.

Sheila lifted her leg to get on the table in such a way that her fanny would be fully exposed. The men in the room just dropped their jaws. Sheila laid on the table on her stomach. Tony couldn't help admiring her buttocks; they were so cute. The men and Miriam stood around Sheila with their paintbrushes, but soon they found that it was easier to apply the paint with their hands.

Sheila had never had six pairs of hands massaging her at the same time. She knew that it would not be easy for her to stay calm. The silvery-blue paint that had a distinct sheen was being liberally applied. Tony had manoeuvred himself towards Sheila's buttocks. His hands were sliding towards the crack of her arse. Miriam looked at him and asked if he had asked Sheila for permission. Before he could respond, Miriam asked Sheila if she would prefer her to paint her bottom. Sheila replied that Tony could go ahead.

Tony smiled at Miriam and slid his hand into Sheila's crevice to start fingering her pussy. Miriam knew what he was doing; they could all see the effect it was having on Sheila. She was getting hotter and panting slightly. In an attempt to stop Tony's activities, Miriam suggested that Sheila got on all fours so that they could make sure that all the back parts were painted.

This actually made things worse. Sheila was now in a very seductive pose. Her glorious breasts were dangling for all to see. Her legs were spread apart, exposing her buttocks and fanny. Most of the men repositioned themselves to get a good view of her behind. Paul asked if he could paint her fanny, and Sheila nodded. He wasted no time covering her labia with blue paint. It wasn't easy because the area was so moist. He managed to finger both her clitoris and fanny in the process.

Ringo cheekily asked if he could put a finger in her fanny. Sheila nodded, and he soon inserted his index finger. Sheila hardly noticed as she was so aroused. Those of the other three soon followed Ringo's finger. Tony looked at Miriam and decided not to follow suit. He was sure that he would regret that decision for the rest of his life. Miriam noticed that Tony's erect penis was sticking out of the bottom of his shorts.

Miriam managed to move into a position so that Tony accidentally touched her almost bare backside. She bent over a bit more so that she could feel his cock just touching her buttocks. It sent an electric shock down the length of her entire body. He almost grabbed her before he realised what he was doing and stepped back, much to her horror.

Sheila's breasts were now bright blue. It was amazing how much painting they needed. Without warning, John, who had fucked her the previous week, stood behind her and fucked her again. The others protested, saying that it was unfair. Sheila didn't care as she was ready for another fuck, and John was the man. He fucked her like a dog. He held her hips and just ploughed away. There is no other way to describe it. He ploughed and ploughed and ploughed until he shot his seed. Sheila was almost ready to come, but she didn't quite get there as John had only thought about his own pleasure. He did make a mess of the paint job on her arse.

The room smelt of woman. It smelt of love juices and fresh spunk. It was getting Miriam even more aroused. She had had enough. She pulled Tony's shorts down and took his fully erect member into her mouth. He enjoyed the sucking, but what he really needed was cunt. He turned Miriam around, bent her over and entered her. Miriam was in heaven, but was he fucking her, or was he fucking Sheila in his mind?

Sheila did not attempt to stop Ringo from entering her from behind. He was not in the same league as John, but it was enough to push her over the edge. The job had been done: Sheila, Ringo, Tony and Miriam all came at the same time.

Sheila turned over so that the painting could be finished, but in all honesty, most of them were too knackered to continue. Some sparkles were added, and Sheila stood on the podium. Painted silvery-blue with sparkles all over, she wore nothing else but a fur hat and a big smile. She looked fantastic, except for the spunk running down her leg.

They were almost ready for the big day.

When Sheila got home, her husband (just like he did every other day) asked her how her day had gone. She asked, 'Do Snow Queens always get fucked?'

'Only in the winter,' he replied, as he never did listen to her properly.

The Pensioner

Sheila had always managed to find a few temporary jobs to take on to help the family budget and pay for a few extra goodies. This work included being a promotional services girl, doing market research, cleaning and cat and dog minding. It was mostly cash-in-hand work. One of her customers was Jim, a man in his eighties who enjoyed female company. It was supposed to be a cleaning job, but in reality, he paid her more for her company, since the house never really got that dirty. They often went to the theatre together.

Jim had always admired Sheila's shapely legs, bum and bust. She was very nicely put together. She was curvaceous and slim at the same time. Her well-endowed breasts turned many a head. Sheila knew this and enjoyed using her clothes to emphasise them. A pair of stunning legs supported her cute little arse. Well, it wasn't that little—it was just the right size to balance the size of her boobs. The overall effect was fabulous.

That was one of the reasons why she was in demand for promotional work at exhibitions. That and her infectious smile and large, sparkling eyes made her very popular. She was in many ways, a bit of a tease. She had always dressed well: smart and modern, but slightly flirtatious.

Jim really enjoyed her regular weekly visits. He enjoyed her company; she made him feel young again. If he'd been younger, he would definitely have proposed marriage, even though she was already married.

Likewise, Sheila was very fond of Jim. He was more than twice her age, but he had a young heart. He was always smartly dressed and regularly wore a three-piece suit and tie. Sheila imagined that he had quite the past as he had been married three times but was now single. Anyway, this distinguished gentleman was more interested in chatting than cleaning, which suited Sheila. The downside was that she had to contend with his wandering hands, but Sheila had got used to that.

Jim wasn't short of money and would often treat Sheila, which she appreciated. He acted more like her father than her father, which she also enjoyed. On one occasion, when she was short of cash, he immediately offered his help. So, in many ways, she owed him.

It was a scorching day in August and extremely hot in Jim's little flat. She removed her silky top and did the cleaning in her bra. It was all perfectly innocent, but Jim went wild. He couldn't stop staring at her well-proportioned breasts, which made her nipples harden. He followed her around the flat, looking for every opportunity to have an ogle.

Over coffee served in a china cup, Jim asked if she would be willing to do the housework in her underwear in the future. Sheila cheekily said, 'What do you mean?'

'Well,' he stuttered. 'I was thinking about how much I enjoyed you working in your bra today and wondered if we could make that the normal dress?'

Sheila asked, 'Are you saying you want me to do the housework in my bra and knickers?'

Jim hadn't been thinking of going that far, but he thought that it was an excellent idea. He immediately said, 'Yes.'

Sheila said that she would have to think about it but wondered if he wanted a quick look now. Jim nodded, and Sheila, being the tease, took off her pleated skirt. Jim just stared at the beautiful vision presented in front of him. Her knickers were slightly transparent, so he could just about see the black triangle of her pubes. Sheila mentioned that there would be an additional cost for such services. Jim said, 'Shall I pay you double what you normally charge?' Sheila was chuffed with that.

For the next few weeks, Sheila carried out the housework in her underwear. She took great care in choosing the outfits, employing a mixture of colours, sizes and different levels of transparency. Jim always wanted her to model for him. She got into the habit of sitting on his lap, but she never felt any movement in the trouser department. She assumed that he was well past it in his stage of life. Sheila looked forward to putting on her little shows as Jim appreciated them.

On one occasion, one of her well-rounded boobs unexpectantly popped out. Jim rushed to help her return it to its home. Both of them laughed, and Jim mentioned how much he'd enjoyed touching it. Without hesitation, Sheila took her bra off. Jim looked at her wide-eyed, then he bent down and gently sucked each nipple. He lifted each breast and gently caressed them one at a time. With all these distractions, Sheila couldn't get her cleaning work done—not that Jim minded.

From that day onwards, Sheila only wore a skimpy pair of knickers to do the cleaning. The amount of work she did declined dramatically, as Jim was more interested in her breasts than the dusting. They were regularly stroked, tweaked, tickled, licked and sucked. There were many times when she approached an orgasm. She tried to avoid it at all costs, as she thought it would embarrass Jim.

It was now a lot easier for her to choose her outfits as it was only a pair of panties. They had got steadily smaller and more risqué. This was in part due to Jim's comment that he liked them as skimpy as possible. Sitting on Jim's lap was also getting a bit more dangerous, as he would grab both of Sheila's breasts from behind and gently rub the nipples.

There were two or three times when she finished herself off later, climaxing in the car. She wondered what the neighbours must have thought. On one occasion, after Jim's extensive teasing of her breasts, her knickers were soaking wet. Jim must have noticed, but then again, he was in his eighties.

Sheila started to wonder if there might be some stirrings in Jim's trouser department, after all. She was going to test it out. She wore a thong to work for the first time. Her pretty bottom was totally exposed, and her fanny was only just being covered by a tiny piece of shiny cloth. She was finding it challenging to keep it in place.

Sheila arrived early to find that Jim was still in his pyjama bottoms. Being a gentleman, he apologised profusely for the impropriety. Sheila said that she didn't mind, and she sat on his lap as usual. Jim went wild; he had never seen a thong before, and he kept touching it. She told him that he was an old pervert and that he should keep his fingers to himself. But Sheila wiggled her bottom a bit, which made her thong move to one side. Now she could feel his erect penis. She moved her hand in such a way that it looked like she had touched it by accident. Neither of them said a word, but as Sheila stood up, her thong came off. She was now totally naked.

Sheila didn't put the thong back on and started cleaning

as usual. She paused to enjoy some breast groping, which again was getting her very hot. Jim's hand slipped down and started stroking the velvety hair surrounding her fanny. Still, not a word was uttered. Jim's finger gently caressed her clit. He knew how to handle one of those– after all, he had been married three times before. He gently played with the tender spot under her hood in a way that made Sheila's back arch, and she let out a small moan of pleasure. She had climaxed all over his hand. All he said was, 'Good girl.' Sheila grabbed her clothes and ran off in embarrassment.

Jim was worried that he had scared her off, but she turned up the next week as usual. Sheila stripped naked and started cleaning the oven. Her bum was sticking upwards in a most delightful way, fully exposing her moist fanny. He could clearly see her enticing little love tunnel. Her dangly breasts were swaying back and forth as she cleaned. She knew that Jim was behind her, admiring the view. She wiggled her bottom enticingly, almost begging for action.

For the first time in twenty years—with a little bit of help from Viagra—Jim took his stiff cock and entered a young woman's vagina. He savoured the feeling of silky skin against his wrinkled old cock. It was truly delicious. He withdrew entirely and then entered her again. He repeated this motion many times, each time increasing the pressure on her fanny— slightly at first, and then he increased the rhythm as time went on. He could tell that her orgasm was on its way. He wasn't so sure about his; he wasn't sure if he was still capable of achieving one.

Sheila suddenly came, arching her back for a second time. The muscles in her vagina squeezed his prick so hard that it triggered his orgasm. He was in heaven. He was just so happy.

Sheila cuddled him as his semen ran down her leg. 'The dirty old bugger,' she thought. She jokingly accused him of being a cradle snatcher.

When she got home, her husband asked her what sort of day she'd had. She said that she'd helped an old man get his rocks off. Her husband asked where she had put them. She said, 'Nowhere special,' but mentioned that she had fannied-around for a bit.

The Game

Sheila was not religious in any way, but she did occasionally help the local church with some charity work. The local vicar asked if she wanted to be a contestant in their local bake-off contest. She said she would volunteer if no one else was interested. Sheila was not a bad cook at all; her roast potatoes were just superb, a marvel of culinary excellence. But there were more classic chefs out there who could run rings around her.

However, the vicar had other plans. There was not a lot of interest in the bake-off contest, so he decided to make it a bit more interesting. He converted the competition into a 'Bake Off, Take Off' game in which there would be four rounds. After each round, there would be a judgement, and everyone but the winner would lose one item of clothing. An additional item of clothing would be removed if there had been an infringement of the rules. The other contestants were informed of this change, but he 'forgot' to mention it to Sheila. He desperately wanted to see her in the nude as he had fancied her for many years.

The contestants were told that they were only allowed to wear four pieces of clothing and their shoes. It struck Sheila that the dress code was rather strange, but she didn't think it would be a problem to follow: skirt, top, bra and knickers. She would miss her tights, but then it had been a hot summer.

Saturday night arrived, and Sheila prepared for the competition. She was a bit nervous, but apparently, the dishes were going to be relatively simple as there wasn't enough time for full-blown gastronomic delights. When she arrived, she found that one of the contestants was in a 'bit of a state.' She was a young woman in her late twenties called Sharon. She had a great figure and long, blonde hair. Sheila liked her immediately. Sharon said that she wasn't sure if she could cope if she lost.

She explained that her boyfriend had bullied her into participating. She wasn't an exhibitionist. Sheila said, 'You will start to like performing in front of a crowd after a while. I used to be shy, but now I'm up for anything. You don't know what you can do until you try.'

Sharon said, 'What about the embarrassment of losing?'

Sheila said, 'We all lose sometimes; that's the naked truth of it.'

Sharon said, 'But we will be exposed to the entire audience. Don't you mind?'

Sheila said, 'They will soon see that I'm not the best cook in the world.' Sheila thought that Sharon seemed excessively worried about a simple cooking contest.

Sheila surveyed the staging area. There were four separate cooking sections with ovens and microwaves and lots of different utensils. It was only a small hall, but Sheila was surprised how near the audience were going to be to the contestants. In her mind, she worked out that it was designed so they could see what was going on. The vicar had other thoughts.

The vicar asked Sheila to confirm that she was only wearing four pieces of clothing, apart from her shoes. She verified that that was the case, but he asked her to prove it. Sheila gingerly lifted her top to show that there was only a skimpy bra underneath. This got Simon, the vicar, rather hot as her breasts were quite tantalising. He then gestured that Sheila should repeat the exercise with her skirt. The only thing she could do was lift her skirt up. Simon couldn't help noticing an excellent pair of legs and the smallest pair of yellow polka-dot panties. Simon wasn't too sure if he could cope with the forthcoming events. Sheila wondered why he'd asked for evidence.

The four contestants, two men and two women, were lined up on stage. Both of the men were rather good-looking. Ben was in his mid-twenties, an IT specialist with a well-proportioned, muscular stature. Henry was quite a bit older but still in good shape. He said that he was a gardener, but in reality, he was a 'plant' set up by the vicar. His day job was as a professional chef. The vicar was determined that Sheila would end up naked on stage.

To make things worse, all three judges were close friends of the vicar. Two of them knew what the underlying objective was. They too were looking forward to seeing some naked female flesh.

Simon stood and welcomed everyone to the first-ever 'Bake Off, Take Off' contest in the world. Sheila thought that the game had a strange title. Then Simon explained the rules for the audience, which were as follows. There were four rounds of cooking. After each round, the losers had to remove an item of clothing. Sheila couldn't believe what she was hearing; no wonder Sharon was in such a state. She was tempted to leave, but now she felt that she couldn't let Sharon down. She gave her a look. Sharon was very nervous and almost at the point of tears.

Simon stated that the winner would be the one with the most clothes on at the end. Moreover, Simon carried on to say that if there were any infringements of the rules, then the judges could demand that an additional item of clothing be removed. Sheila could tell what was going to happen, especially as the audience was mostly comprised of men.

The first cooking task was to make a full English breakfast. The problem with cooked breakfasts is getting everything cooked and ready for presentation at the same time. Sheila had done a cracking job, but she was possibly a bit weak on the presentation. Both Sharon and Ben's efforts were acceptable, but Henry's breakfast was world-class; it was perfectly cooked and presented. None of the contestants were surprised to see that he was the winner.

Simon asked Ben, Sharon and Sheila to step forward for the disrobing ceremony. The audience were all eyes; they were keen to see a rather humiliating strip take place a few feet away from them. Sheila noticed that Sharon was shaking.

Ben stepped forward and removed his trousers to little applause. Simon then welcomed Sheila to come forward. He turned to the audience and said, 'What do you think she is going to take off? I happen to know that she is wearing the tiniest panties possible.' That annoyed Sheila; consequently, she removed her top. The audience was pleased to see a fine pair of boobs in a flimsy bra.

The vicar said, 'What a great pair of assets she has. I'm sure that we will be seeing more of those later.' That annoyed Sheila. Firstly, he was supposed to be a religious man. Secondly, he had already decided that she was going to lose. She suspected that the whole thing was a farce. At least the audience appreciated Sheila's assets.

Finally, Sharon came forward, sobbing. She shouted, 'Fuck the lot of you,' and ran offstage. Sheila was tempted to follow, but something held her back; it might have been the attention of the audience.

Then one of the judges shouted out, 'Point of order. We have a rule infringement.' Sheila assumed that it was to do with Sharon, but it was to do with her. One of the judges explained that Sheila had not washed her hands before making the omelette, which was critical as she had been handling meat just before. This was a serious infringement.

Sheila thought that this was all nonsense. Simon said that as far as he was concerned, it was all about spilt milk and cracked eggs. The judge insisted that it was an infringement. Sheila protested. Simon said, 'We will ask the audience.' He faced the audience and said, 'What do you think? Did Sheila break the rules? If so, this would result in her losing another item of clothing.'

The audience shouted back, 'Clear case of an infringement.' Sheila was still annoyed about the panties comment and decided not to show them. Instead, she unclipped her bra. She couldn't help playing to the crowd and slowly removed the bra to expose some of the most beautiful breasts in the Northern Hemisphere. Without going into graphic detail, her breasts were perfect in terms of their shape, size and firmness, and they were tipped by two beautiful nipples that were already hard. Simon put his arm around Sheila's waist as he escorted her back to her station. Was it an accident that he happened to touch her breast while doing it?

The second task was to bake a chocolate cake. Sheila enjoyed cake making, although her speciality was more cake design and decoration, rather than baking. Her sons had enjoyed masterpieces of graphic art on their birthdays, in terms of her cake modelling.

The second round started. Sheila hadn't realised how much a pair of bare boobs could get in the way. Half of the ingredients seemed to land on them: flour, sugar, chocolate, cream and cinnamon oil. As she rubbed the stuff off more seemed to appear. The audience was loving it. They shouted out encouragement and warned her when her boobs were in danger—and there was lots of risk. For a start, the food mixer's bowl had a dangling boob in it on more than one occasion. Luckily, it was removed in time; otherwise, it would have been in the cake.

The electric oven was a constant threat. The biggest problem was when Sheila bent down. It was difficult for her to see what was going on as her pendulous, fleshy orbs of delight swung backwards and forwards. No sooner could she move one out of the way before the other would arrive. If she tried holding them down, then she couldn't cook. She was anxious that her very stiff nipples would get burnt. Sheila wondered what she was doing on stage, topless, baking a cake.

Sheila and Ben had done an excellent job, but Henry's cake was fit for a wedding. Sheila wondered how he could bake such a great cake in such a short time. The winner was obvious. Ben and Sheila were brought to the front of the stage.

Ben removed his pants to display a very impressive and fully erect cock. It sprang to attention. The women in the audience gasped. The men just thought, 'Lucky sod.' Sheila couldn't help admiring it, but then she remembered her very skimpy knickers which were starting to get damp.

Simon put his pudgy arm around Sheila's waist again and

said, 'It looks like we are going to see those yellow, polka-dot panties now.' Once again, his hands were surreptitiously touching her breasts in front of the audience. Without warning, Simon pulled Sheila's skirt down, but in doing so, her knickers came down as well. The audience cheered as Sheila hurriedly tried to pull up her panties. Simon was embarrassed, but he had achieved his goal: he had seen Sheila totally naked on stage. In those brief, nude seconds, lots of photos were taken. Sheila was fuming.

The last contest was pancake making. The pancakes had to be flipped in the air. Since it doesn't take long to make a pancake, the tossing soon began. The audience enjoyed the bouncing of Sheila's breasts as they moved in all different directions. It was a truly glorious sight. Even Ben stopped to look. His cock got even harder.

While Sheila was exercising the frying pan, her knickers fell down—Simon had broken the elastic. The audience thought that this was deliberate, and they cheered and cheered. Sheila gave up all pretence of protecting her modesty and contorted her body and the frying pan into lots of rather erotic positions. If anyone in the audience had never seen a fanny before, then they were in for a real treat. Nothing was hidden, and many of the wives took their husbands home early in disgust.

The final three contestants were brought to the front of the stage: one fully clothed, but with an erection; one more or less naked with a full erection; and a naked woman. Ben was given a prize. Simon held Sheila's hand up and said, 'What a sport.' Sheila said that she had a present for him. Simon was surprised, but he was also chuffed. His state of mind changed when Sheila kicked him as hard as she could in the balls. He collapsed on the floor saying, 'Oh God, Oh God.' Sheila thought it unlikely that God would come to his aid.

Sheila couldn't stand being in the building any longer and pushed her way through the crowd. She was slightly manhandled in the process, but she had expected that. She flagged down a taxi and once again returned to her home in the nude. She quickly covered herself and paid the driver, who had a big grin on his face. From another room, her husband shouted out, 'How did your day go?' Sheila replied that she had been doing church work all evening, but that she had got a kick out of it.

The local paper said that an unknown contestant in that year's 'Bake Off, Take Off' contest had viciously attacked the vicar of St Marys. The vicar described the unprovoked attack as a 'sign of the times' and evidence that a man of God couldn't carry out his duties without serious risk to his testicles.

The Rugby Team: Part 1

Gavin was Sheila's son's best friend. He was a good-looking, muscular, twenty-five-year-old man. Sheila had known him since he was a young boy. She still went on girlie nights out with his mother. Unbeknownst to her, Gavin had a serious thing for her.

He fantasised about her shapely legs, her ample bosom and her sparkling eyes. There was many a night where he got his rocks off thinking about making love to Sheila. Often it would be on a desert island, or they were stuck together in a broken lift, where things naturally progressed as it got hotter and hotter.

Gavin was a very keen rugby player, and they were all looking forward to the local derby against Pershore. They were a stuck-up lot, and it was a chance to give them a real thrashing. He had been given the job of finding the post-match entertainment; a responsibility that he wasn't really suited for, but he had a cunning plan.

Gavin invited Sheila to the match and was thrilled when she accepted. Sheila liked watching rugby, but she was hardly an expert. She did enjoy seeing men playing sport. She loved to see their muscular thighs ripple in short shorts. The dirtier they got, the better.

Gavin picked Sheila up in his Mazda, and they drove off to Evesham Rugby Club. Gavin couldn't help noticing her bare legs as her short denim skirt rose up when she got in the car. He desperately wanted to ogle and caress them, but he had to keep his eyes on the road. Gavin left Sheila in the north stand as he went to change. He got a few pats on the back and comments like, 'You have done well there.'

The game had gone well, as they had beaten the 'toffs.' It was time for the team to celebrate. The atmosphere in the communal bath was very convivial, with much laughter and good cheer, and the beer was flowing. There were shouts of 'We beat them; we beat the bastards.'

Gavin invited Sheila 'backstage' to meet the winning team. She had to be a bit careful with her walking, as the prosecco had been flowing after the victory. She was suddenly presented with a large, square bath that could easily hold the whole team. It was full of hot, bubbly water and naked men. Gavin shouted out, 'Look what I've got for you, boys!'

Two of the hunky front row forwards came out of the steaming bath and grabbed Sheila, lifted her and plunged her into the pool. To say that Sheila was shocked would be an understatement. What made it worse was that her top came off in the process. The men cheered and chanted 'Sheila, Sheila.'

She tried to regain her composure, but it wasn't easy. She could see that her soaking wet bra was almost transparent. As she covered her breasts, one of the back-row forwards swam over and pulled her knickers down. To say that she was shocked again would not be an understatement. As she tried to retrieve her panties, her bra was unclipped. The only thing protecting her modesty was her skirt, but then she heard it rip as two players tugged at it. 'Sorry,' they said. And just like that, she was stark naked.

Sheila thought to herself, 'When you are an attractive,

naked woman in a pool full of dirty young men, things are not going to stop there.' The outside centre came over with some soap and started washing her back. In no time at all, he was giving her breasts a thorough cleaning. Her nipples were very erect, which was noticed by all.

She paddled towards the steps to get out of the bath when one of the prop forwards came up behind her, groped her breasts, lifted her slightly and entered her fanny. His hard member vigorously pumped in and out for a few minutes and he came. The other men were counting each stroke and cheered when he ejaculated. The prop said, 'Darling, I'm sorry that I can't spend more time with you, but I've got to go to my daughter's birthday party.'

The fly-half took his place and reached the count of eleven before he came. She learnt afterwards that they were allowed twenty strokes each. She thought that it put a fair amount of pressure on the lads, and in a twisted way, she felt a bit sorry for them. Then she realised that if she didn't get out of the bath, she would end up servicing the whole team—and what about the competition?

Sheila made another attempt to get out of the bath, but it was very wet and slippery and full of naked, groping men who took every advantage they could. She fell backwards into the lap of the scrum-half. 'Thank you, darling,' he said and pulled her onto his prick. The counting started, and when they got to twenty, he was pulled off her. He had not come and felt very frustrated. Sheila knew that he had cheated, as he had had at least twenty-two strokes.

This time, Sheila managed to free herself and get out of the bath. She ran towards an open door, trying to cover her tits and fanny, as girls do. There was a big cheer as she entered the locker room. At least twenty naked and semi-naked men were waiting for her. Towels were thrown up in the air.

She was lifted up and surprisingly groped at the same time. She could feel fingers playing with her erect nipples and soaking wet fanny. She was gently carried to the physio table where a soft towel had been placed. In no time at all, a dozen men were rubbing oil onto her body. No crack or crevice was left untouched. In fact, her fanny had enjoyed so much fingering that she was about to explode.

Then, without warning, her bottom was pulled to the edge of the table, and the tighthead prop entered her. Someone shouted, 'Give her a good fucking,' and he did. His engorged cock rammed home to success on the count of nineteen. He was patted on the back and said 'well done.' Apparently, the real trick was to come when the count hit twenty.

The fullback took his place and soon got into the rhythm of the count. Sheila wondered if he would make it before the count of twenty when she suddenly experienced a huge orgasm. It stopped the fullback in his tracks. They all cheered and seemed genuinely thrilled that Sheila had come. One of the men thoughtfully wiped her fanny, but not without giving it a little tickle.

They quickly agreed that it was only fair that the fullback should start again. It didn't make much difference, as he came on the count of three. Sheila knew why he was the fullback, as his semen went everywhere. There was much joking and laughter. Surprisingly, Sheila was really enjoying herself, as she revelled in male company. They treated her with kindness. She had got into the spirit of the game, but she was thinking that this had to end soon.

She lifted her head to see who was going to be between

130

her legs next. In front of her was one of the biggest smiles she had ever seen. Without a word, Gavin put his large cock into Sheila's tight, but slippery, little pussy. This was the climax of all his dreams. The count started, 'One, two, three ...' and Gavin was well into the rhythm. Sheila was not too sure where to put her face. Her son's best friend was giving her one. 'Four, five, six...' the count continued.

'Oh no,' she thought, as she felt her orgasm rising again. It was just too embarrassing. These men had already cheered for her first orgasm. 'Ten, eleven, twelve...' Gavin was doing a great job, hitting all the right spots. Sheila twisted her fanny in an attempt to stop the orgasm, but it just made things worse; she could feel the excitement in the pit of her stomach.

Gavin couldn't believe his luck. He was actually fucking the woman he'd fancied for ten years. She certainly wasn't a disappointment. He could feel that his orgasm was on the way. His tight balls were ready. He had learnt that you need to carry on pumping away until the very last moment.

'Fifteen, sixteen, seventeen...' Both orgasms were getting nearer. Sheila could sense that Gavin was holding back. She then realised that he was going for twenty. Then suddenly, on the count of twenty, both came with more force than she's thought possible. The world suddenly stopped turning for both of them. There were huge cheers in the room, and Gavin was dragged off to buy everyone a drink.

Sheila was left there naked on the bench and struggling to recover from one of the biggest orgasms in her life. Her fanny was still dripping when the referee came over. He was a bald man in his sixties. He very politely asked if there was any chance that he could have a fuck. Sheila thought, 'Why not? One more won't hurt.'

She gestured for him to carry on. He pulled his black shorts and pink flowery pants down and pushed his tiny, erect penis into her fanny. Sheila could hardly feel him. He jerked and pulled up his shorts. 'Thank you very much,' he said.

Sheila had no idea where her clothes were. She was too frightened to go back to the bathroom and wondered what to do. The referee asked if she wanted a lift home. She gladly accepted and sat in his car, naked as the day she was born. Sheila wondered how she was going to get from the car to her house without being seen by her neighbours.

The referee said that the team wanted to book her again because she'd been so much fun and so accommodating. Sheila asked what he meant. He said that most of the strippers wouldn't allow full intercourse. She didn't know where to put her face.

Later in the week, the post arrived, and Sheila got the match ball and a signed photo from the team, with her naked image in the middle. Apparently, there was a selection of indiscrete photos of her pinned to the notice board in the men's changing room.

Later, her husband asked if she had enjoyed the game of rugby. She said, 'Things got slightly out of hand in the scrum, and some were slightly too forward, but I am thinking of going back again. There were some outstanding tries and several conversions. Gavin was a particularly good exponent of the game, and he could well convince me to come again.'

The Rugby Team: Part 2

Sheila was well known at Evesham Rugby Club. In fact, she was almost legendary there, although she tried to hide her rather raucous past. She was a bit surprised when the club asked if she wanted to go on a rugby tour of Scotland, free of charge. All accommodation and meals would be provided at no cost. As she had always liked the company of men, especially young, fit men, she thought, 'Why not?' She was told that there would be a tour manager and that everyone had to follow the tour rules, but Sheila had no idea what they were talking about.

Sheila packed some of her prettiest clothes, not that she needed much help as she was a very attractive woman. Everyone admired her legs, and the young men particularly admired her boobs, which were firm, well-proportioned and certainly more than a handful. Pictures of her assets had been circulating around the rugby club for years. Some of the younger rugby club members were looking forward to meeting her—in more ways than one.

She arrived at the rugby club early to meet the other holidaymakers. There were eighteen hunky rugby players, three girls, including herself, and a bus driver. Serious quantities of beer and spirits were being loaded onto the bus. It wasn't going to be a "dry week". The weather was warm, the sun was shining, and everyone was looking forward to a great break.

Sheila chatted with the other two girls. They were quite a bit younger than her but not more attractive. Tina and Chloe were both dizzy blondes in their twenties. Tina was what you would call 'plump,' if you were being kind. Chloe was more attractive, but she had awful protruding teeth. They had both wanted to meet Sheila because of her "reputation". Sheila wasn't sure what they meant, but she was too much of a lady to ask.

Chloe said that she hadn't been too sure whether she wanted to come on the trip based on last year. Sheila inquired as to what had happened then. Chloe said, 'Let's say that there are eighteen of them and three of us. The odds are not good. What swung it for me was the free drinks; after a few pints, I'm anybody's.' Before Sheila could think about it, the holidaymakers boarded the bus, and they were off.

The fly-half, who was a natural leader, stood up and welcomed everyone on board. He said that he was the tour leader, and he had rules that must be followed, or there would be consequences. The first rule involved drink. When the buzzer went, everyone had to drink a pint of beer or knock back a shot. If this were not followed, the dissenting person would have to remove an item of clothing of their choice. There would be no exceptions.

The second rule was about mileage. Every thirty miles, the person by the window had to move back one seat, and the person in the aisle had to move forward one place. The aim was to ensure that everyone got to know each other properly.

The third rule was about luck. One person on the way there and one person on the way back would be stripped naked and left by the side of the motorway. The first person to pick an ace from a pack of cards would be the victim. Sheila had never been particularly lucky at cards.

The buzzer went, and Sheila was presented with a glass of vodka, which she managed to drink. Sheila had never been a great drinker. People would immediately assume that by that, she meant that she was not a great drinker of alcohol, but in fact, she was not a great drinker of any fluid. A couple of small coffees per day would be enough fluid intake for her, so this trip was going to be a struggle. She couldn't see herself keeping her clothes on for long.

After thirty miles, Sheila diligently moved back one seat. She was now sitting next to the tighthead prop. He was a big man by any standards—well over twenty stone but all muscle. They got talking, and he said that he had always wanted to meet her, as she clearly had no problems with props. She asked what he meant. He said that props were often seen as all brawn and no brain, but the photos of her were an inspiration. She was trying to think back, but it didn't make sense to her. He explained that when she was in the rugby club bath, the first man to fuck her was a tighthead prop. He said that the photos of her leaving the bath with a big cock in her fanny were the stuff of dreams. He had circulated the photo to everyone he knew on the internet.

The buzzer went, and Sheila just about consumed the second glass of vodka. The effects of the alcohol were getting to her, and she leant against the prop; or rather, he propped her up. He gently caressed her legs and held her hands. He was a true gentleman. However, another thirty miles had gone, and she had to move back one seat. She was now sitting with an outside centre.

He was a very fit-looking black man who must have been

well over six foot. His large hands helped her into the seat as her legs were not that steady. They chatted about his family and how he'd got into rugby. He was excited about having a break from family life and was hoping for some extra-marital romance. He was stroking Sheila's arms in such a way that Sheila felt that she might be the target of his desires. The buzzer went, and Sheila decided to remove a shoe. The fly-half collected it to stop any attempt at cheating.

The centre explained that the only experience he had with women was his wife. They had been sweethearts at school, and she knew very little about pleasing a man. He wanted and needed a more experienced woman. At this point, his hands started wandering. Sheila did not have the clarity of mind to stop him, but the buzzer saved her. A second shoe went, and then she had to move back a seat.

Sheila was suffering from the effects of the alcohol but in a nice way. She was slightly intoxicated, but she was still almost in control of her faculties. Her next seat partner was a hooker. He said that he knew her well. He had previously fucked her in the changing rooms at the club. Since that day, he had been looking for another opportunity to repeat the experience. He slowly pushed his hand up her skirt and encountering little or no opposition. He started tickling her fanny through her knickers. Sheila was planning on stopping him, but it all seemed too much effort. He managed to get his hand under the knickers' elastic, and he was gently probing her vagina. He took his finger out to show the lads. There was joviality all around.

The buzzer went, and Sheila decided not to consume any more alcohol. The fly-half asked what piece of clothing she wanted to remove. As Sheila couldn't decide, the coachload of men shouted, 'Knickers!' and the hooker gently eased them down. Her fanny was now fully exposed. A crowd of men clambered around to see this famous Evesham Rugby Club nude. She tried to pull her skirt down, but the men wouldn't have it, and the hooker pulled it off. The hooker also managed to lift her blouse over her head. She knew that this was cheating, as she had not heard any buzzer go off. She was pleased to escape to the next seat.

As she moved along the aisle, several hands stroked her pussy. She was, in fact, quite moist. The very early signs of an orgasm were there. She hoped that she wouldn't embarrass herself in a coach full of dirty young lads. She was now sitting next to the scrum-half, who immediately started stroking her bush. She moved her bottom so that he could get easier access to her fanny. She thought, 'Oh, I must be a tart. Why am I helping him?' Then she discovered why, as his experienced hands played with her clit. 'Oh no,' she thought. Her first climax was on the way.

Her whole body stiffened and then relaxed at the same time. Her fanny went super tingly and started to leak a sweet-smelling substance that smelt of musk. This had happened before, but now the aroma was much stronger. The whole coach had a musky smell. Everyone noticed it. If anything, it just made the men randier.

The other two girls were just sitting there, knocking back the vodkas. They were not helping the cause in any way; they were still fully clothed. All eyes were on the girl with the fabulous legs and a great arse. By then, all the lads had seen her charms but not her breasts—but that situation would resolve itself shortly as the buzzer had gone. The fly-half walked up to Sheila to collect her last remaining piece of clothing: her bra.

Sheila didn't need any assistance removing her bra, but help arrived anyway. Hands were everywhere, the bra was soon off, and her breasts were being massaged from every direction. Suddenly, she was lifted and gently laid across the back seat. The outside centre was now inside her. It happened so quickly; her legs had been lifted, and the centre had a try. His large cock was now experiencing extra-marital sex. It wasn't long before he converted.

The tighthead prop soon replaced him. He was a big lad, and the fit was quite tight. He certainly knew how to ruck. The blindside flanker also did his duty, followed by two wings, the fullback and the scrum-half. Sheila was thoroughly enjoying herself, but she needed a break when the eighth player, who also happened to wear the number 8, tackled her. She had experienced multiple orgasms, but the eighth one was a beauty.

The loosehead prop was in the line-up when the fly-half announced that they were at the halfway point. It was time to select a card to determine who was going to be ejected from the bus, totally naked. This had been a longstanding tradition of Evesham Rugby Club and many other rugby clubs. The pack of cards were shuffled, and Sheila was offered the first choice. It seemed impossible, but she picked the Ace of Hearts.

Many hearts were crushed. The loosehead prop was devastated. They demanded that the fly-half change the rules, but he was adamant that the rules were the rules. Sheila was ceremoniously walked down the aisle. On this "walk of shame", like the one in Game of Thrones, she was patted and stroked by most of the passengers. The driver said to her, 'Wait for the police.' They waved their goodbyes, and Sheila was left stranded on the side of the M1.

Sheila wondered how she'd got herself into this position. Fucked eight times and left stark naked on the hard shoulder of a motorway. She was hooted and waved at many times. Several drivers stopped to offer her a lift, but she waved them on. As advised, she was waiting for the police, who eventually arrived.

She got in the back of the police car. She could tell that they were not amused. Obviously, she was wasting their time. She asked for a blanket. They refused on the basis that since she had decided to be naked, she could stay naked. She noticed that one of the bobbies had adjusted the mirror so he could get the odd ogle in. Later, she asked for a cloth to wipe herself down. Again, she was refused. As she got out of the car, she thought, 'Serves them right; now someone is going to have to clean up that puddle on the seat.'

They arrived at the police station, where she was escorted across the car park to the desk. They did not attempt to hurry; they were maximising her humiliation. She was charged with indecent exposure and taken down to the cells. The jail door was opened, and she was pushed in to join five other cell-mates—all young men.

As it was a Friday, she would be spending a long weekend there. It was the end of her rugby tour but the start of another adventure. She had decided that she wouldn't go on another rugby tour.

Overall, the tour was a great success. The legend of Sheila grew, and even more, photos were circulated of her exploits.

The Brighton Raffle

Sheila had been volunteering at the Brighton Arts Centre for many years. In that time, she had helped with the teas and coffees, done a lot of ushering and sold thousands of lottery tickets. She had been very successful with the ticket selling, making a sizeable financial contribution to the fundraising. The Arts Centre certainly needed her help, as business had been weak. People didn't have the money to spend on the arts during a recession.

Sheila had always enjoyed selling. Her good looks and bubbly personality had certainly helped ticket sales, especially among the male clientele. Her usual banter was, 'Only a pound for a strip,' followed up with a very cheeky smile. The typical reaction was, 'That's cheap!' or 'How far do you go?' There were a lot of men there who would gladly pay Sheila for a strip as she had a great pair of legs and an ample bosom.

Sheila had found that a slightly risqué outfit helped to increase sales. She probably showed a bit more leg than she should have. She certainly showed a bit more cleavage than any respectable young lady should. Her boss, commonly called 'Sweetypie' by the other girls, made it very clear that he wanted to get in her knickers. He touched her at every opportunity. In fact, his touching was getting steadily more outrageous. Sheila had objected at first, but at least she was getting some attention. The old man at home hadn't touched her in years, although she had found other ways to entertain herself.

On Monday, she had a stinking row with her husband. He had lost another job due to continued lateness and insubordination. He was a total waste of time. The pressure was back on Sheila to get the mortgage paid. She wondered why she stayed with him. It would have been bearable if he was at least half-decent in bed, but he was just useless.

She was back at the Arts Centre that night. At least there she was appreciated, especially by Sweetypie, although she knew that he was just after her for a good time. She decided that part of the problem was that she had "unsatisfied lust". In other words, she wanted a good fuck. Then she told herself off for using that type of language in her thoughts.

She put on a slightly shorter skirt than usual with a tiny pair of knickers and a blouse that didn't entirely cover her bust. She knew that she was pushing her luck, but she wanted to annoy her husband on the way out. He looked up at her but said nothing. She expected him to say that the skirt was far too short or that she was showing far too much cleavage, but he said nothing. 'Well, that's his loss,' she thought.

She drove to the Arts Centre and received several wolf-whistles as she left the car. She immediately entered selling mode. Sales were going well. She was getting a lot of banter from her 'pound for a strip' quip. A party of footballers were showing her particular interest, especially when Sweetypie came up behind her, lifted her skirt and said, 'That's worth a pound.' She pushed him away but was strangely excited about showing her bum to complete strangers.

The footballers asked Sweetypie if Sheila would be interested in giving them a private striptease after the show. He said that he would ask, but he wanted to know what would they pay first. They came back with £100 each.

Sweetypie called Sheila over and said that there was a business opportunity that would pay her £250 and also raise £250 for the Arts Centre. She asked what she would have to do. Somewhat hesitantly, he said, 'Give a private strip show to the football party.'

Sheila said, 'You mean those five blokes we spoke to earlier?'

'That's right,' said Sweetypie.

Sheila asked how far she would have to go, but she already knew what the answer would be.

Sheila asked where it would take place. Sweetypie said that they would do it by the bar, which wouldn't be a problem as he had the keys. She was rather surprised that she accepted the offer. She told herself that she needed the money, which she did, but really, she was just excited about being naked in front of a group of lusty men. Sheila had seen the odd striptease in films, and in reality, she had no idea what to do, but she was sure that she would get the hang of it.

While she was watching the play, she was getting more and more excited. It was a mixture of nervous anticipation and fear. Fear that she would embarrass herself. She wished that she had put on a more decent pair of knickers. The pair she was wearing were more or less transparent—what would Sweetypie think? She was also worried that she couldn't do it, and she thought she might just do a runner. At the same time, she could feel her fanny getting moist.

The play finished and the audience left, leaving just Sheila, Sweetypie and five burly footballers behind who had clearly had a fair amount to drink. Sweetypie was certainly looking forward to it. He had gone home and got some music to play.

Sheila walked over to the bar and arranged six chairs for the men and one for her. The men took their seats amid much joviality and laughter. Sweetypie collected the money. It then struck Sheila that Sweetypie was going to get a free show.

Sheila started dancing to shouts of 'Get them off!' To be honest, there wasn't much to get off, but she needed to make the show last somehow. Her blouse came off to a round of applause and was followed by her skirt. She stood there in her bra and panties. Every man there just ogled her; she looked beautiful. Her breasts were just about kept in place by a lacy, tight-fitting bra. Her ample charms seemed good enough to eat, and Sweetypie was keen to give them a nibble.

Her panties just about covered her little black triangle of love. Her shapely stomach seemed to flow towards her crotch. Everything was just so well-proportioned. She should have been a Page 3 model. Her legs were a delight, topped by a tight and curvaceous little bum.

Sheila asked the first man to unclip her bra. He immediately started fondling her breasts, which made her nipples rock hard. He licked one nipple and then the other.

She moved on to the next man. Leaning on his knees, she rubbed her breasts against his face. He tried to catch her nipples in his mouth, but Sheila was too fast for him. She could see that he was getting an erection, so she moved her hand to touch it, which made him jerk. She laughed and went onto the next man.

She asked him to pull her knickers down. He couldn't believe his luck. He gently eased them over her bottom, and she kicked them away. She rubbed her boobs against his face while he stroked her arse. Sheila moved his fingers so that he could play with her clit. Before he could get too engrossed, she jumped up and went to sit on her chair.

She sat down and opened her legs. She couldn't believe just how sluttish she was being. She held her legs apart so that her pussy was fully displayed. Her moist vagina was aching for human touch. She invited the fourth man over and directed him to play with her fanny. He rather gingerly placed one finger in, then two. He stroked the inside silkiness of her cunt. Sheila moved his fingers so that he could play with her clit. 'Faster,' she said. 'Faster,' she shouted. An almighty climax hit her hard.

The man returned to his seat, and Sheila walked over to the fifth man. She unzipped his flies and pulled out his fully erect cock. She licked the glans and the shaft. She nibbled it like corn on the cob. Sheila started with a gentle stroke of his cock and gradually increased the intensity until it was too vigorous for him to bear. At the point of orgasm, she sucked it hard and swallowed his cum. Everyone cheered.

Sweetypie was starting to get excited and wondered what delights he was in for. He was distraught when Sheila returned to the first man. She unzipped him and took out a large, slightly bent phallus. He readied himself for a blow job when suddenly she turned around and sat on his lap—or rather sat on his cock—instead. With her hand, she moved his penis directly under her fanny. Sheila rubbed it against her clit and then suddenly dropped her cunt onto his cock. The pressure and tightness of her fanny made him come straight away.

She walked over to the chair and bent over so that they could see her spunk-covered fanny. She rubbed it in. Sheila called over the second man, pointed at her fanny and asked if he wanted sloppy seconds. He pulled down his trousers and entered her. He pounded away for a few minutes and then came with a mighty roar. 'Another happy customer,' Sheila thought to herself.

Sheila stood up and said, 'Gentlemen, the show is over.' The third man said that it wasn't fair as he hadn't had a fuck. Sheila said, 'You only paid for a strip; everything extra was at my discretion.' He took it well, and they applauded her efforts.

Sheila wandered off to get washed and dressed. On the way out, Sweetypie was waiting for her. He gave her £250 and said that he was a bit disappointed that he hadn't got any action. Sheila said, 'Did you pay?' and then walked away.

Afterwards, her husband asked her how the show had gone. She said that it was fine, but the afterparty was a 'fucking success.'

The Cancer Drug

Sheila had always done her civic duty. She had been a blood donor for many years. When she heard about the need for volunteers to help produce the ingredients for a new cancer drug, she signed up immediately. She had heard about it on TV. Apparently, women produce a chemical in pregnancy that inhibits the creation of cancers in babies.

The chemical had been identified, but so far, they hadn't found a way of producing it in the laboratory. As we know, human bodies are small chemical factories, but in this case, women have to be stimulated to generate this particular chemical. Everyone involved in the experimental trial had been honest with her: the extraction process was very embarrassing for the woman, which is why a generous fee was offered in exchange.

Sheila wasn't really interested in the money, but it would help pay for her holiday. For her, the important thing was all the good it could do. The new drug could almost eliminate most cancers. More importantly, it could operate as a vaccine. She would be saving lives, which made her feel good.

She arrived at the clinic at the appointed time. They asked her to undress and put on a dressing gown. Sheila loved the gown: it was large, fluffy and fresh. She felt warm and cuddly in it. At the same time, she was a bit nervous about the procedure, but she would find out more about it during the lecture.

Thirty giggly women were herded into the lecture hall. The tension in the room was palpable. Chris, the lecturer, welcomed them all and asked them to sit down. Drinks and nibbles were offered. Chris knew how important it was to get the women relaxed.

Meanwhile, Jack, who was doing his work experience, had been assigned Clive as his mentor. Clive completed the forms and checked his passport to ensure that he was over eighteen. Jack asked what the job involved. Clive said that it was a great job if you liked naked women. Basically, he said that Jack would have to connect them to the collecting apparatus. Jack asked what that meant. Clive said that he would find out during the 'on-the-job' training.

Jack asked why men were doing the work and not women. Clive said that initially all of the collectors had been women. However, the patients have to be stimulated to generate the chemical they are collecting for the trial. They'd found that good-looking young men helped create the right atmosphere. Jack said, 'So really, we are just eye candy.' Clive agreed. He then said that they had tried using gay men, but they were just not interested in the job, so that is why they had been recruited.

Jack felt quite excited about the work. His experience with girls had been somewhat limited, except for the odd fumble and the occasional grope of some breasts. He thought that he might have drunkenly lost his virginity at a party, but he wasn't too sure.

Back in the lecture hall, Chris had started his presentation. He looked at the audience to see that they were all sitting there demurely with their dressing gowns protecting their modesty. In a short period of time, the situation would be very different.

Chris explained how vital the drug was. It was genuinely a step-change in human medical research. He had done a great job, and the audience was captivated.

'Now ladies,' he said. 'I need to take you through the process. We have always been honest, and it is embarrassing to say the very least. We take you through the procedure to explain why it is done this way. No one is forcing you, and you are welcome to leave at any time.'

Someone from the audience asked how many volunteers come back again. Chris said that there was a very high retention rate.

Chris then went through the stages one at a time. He listed them:

You need to disrobe and leave the dressing gowns in this room.

You will go next door to the Collecting Centre.

You will be injected with a drug that stimulates your internal sex glands.

Your breasts will be connected to suckers that collect the chemical.

A stimulator will be put into your vagina that kicks off the process.

After 30 minutes, you will be disconnected, and hopefully, we will have collected the chemical.

We then provide prosecco, a good lunch, and we give you your fee.

The women looked at each other for group support. One of the women asked if there were any side effects. Chris said that it was very much an individual thing, but some women found that their nipples got slightly sore. Others had a slightly irritated vagina. However, the biggest complaint was that they felt exceptionally randy afterwards. Chris said that some of their husbands might be in for a good time later. This caused a lot of laughter.

Chris asked if anyone wanted to leave. No one responded.

Chris asked the ladies to disrobe and leave the dressing gowns on the chairs. Chris loved this bit: lots of bouncing boobs, giggling girls, round bottoms and a mixture of fanny coverings. He particularly liked the shaven ones. Chris stood at the front to make sure that he got a good ogle. He continued ogling while they queued for their injections.

Sheila wondered what she had got herself into. At first, she tried to cover her boobs and fanny with her hands but then thought there was little point. She caught Chris looking at her, which made her a little bit excited. Chris looked at Sheila with some interest; she had fabulous legs, a cute arse and perfect, bouncy breasts. He made a mental note to check her out later.

Clive and Jack were waiting for their patient. Clive said, 'It looks like our luck is in; we have got one of the pretty ones.' Clive had seen plenty of naked women in the last year, but he was still impressed with Sheila's body. He loved her sparkling eyes and the curve of her boobs with their fully erect nipples. Jack just didn't know where to look. He thought that he must be bright red with embarrassment.

Clive and Jack introduced themselves to Sheila. Clive had been trained to be caring and thoughtful. They were told to get permission at every stage and record it on a hand-held device. Clive walked Sheila over to his appointed collecting machine, gently patting her bottom on the way.

Clive said, 'Sheila, this is the collecting machine. We need you to bend over the bench with your breasts hanging down. Are you happy to continue?'

Sheila nodded, but Clive asked her to confirm, and she said, 'Yes.' Sheila leaned across the bench as requested, with her bottom up in the air. Her well-proportioned breasts were hanging over the edge. Clive asked Sheila to put her legs in the stirrups. He asked if she wanted his assistance, and she confirmed.

Clive gently lifted one leg into a stirrup and instructed Jack to do the other one. Jack had never seen a naked, exposed pussy before. He just wanted to stare, which amused Clive. Sheila wondered what the boys were doing, but then she guessed that they were probably just looking. Clive explained to Sheila that it was Jack's first day and that he would be taking him through the procedure.

Clive then said to Sheila that he needed to rub some lotion on her breasts to aid conductivity. He asked if this was OK, and Sheila nodded. He asked again if she could confirm, and she said, 'Yes.' Clive said that they would have a breast each. Both the boys sat down on a stool on either side of Sheila.

Clive said to Jack, 'Make sure that your hand is warm first. Then put the breast in your left hand so that you are holding it. Of course, this is not always easy with the flat-chested girls, but here it is no problem at all.' This amused Sheila. Clive continued. 'Take the conducting lotion, pour it on the breast and rub it in with your right hand. Continue rubbing in the lotion. Make sure that the entire breast is well oiled.' He asked if Jack was OK with that, and he nodded.

Sheila had never been massaged by two young men before. She could tell that Clive was very experienced. Jack was somewhat hesitant. Jack was worried that he might hurt the breast. Clive told Jack to be firmer and demonstrated how the breast should be massaged.

Clive then said to Jack that the nipples needed to be massaged next. He told Jack to take the nipple and hold it firmly. Then, he needed to gently stroke it so that it got as firm as possible, and then the lotion needed to be applied. Sheila had always had very sensitive nipples. This was almost beyond what she could bear. She could already feel her fanny reacting.

Jack just couldn't believe his luck. He was fondling the breast of a beautiful naked woman—could things get any better than that? Clive enjoyed Jack's reaction. He remembered his first day with pleasure; since then, he had lost much of his innocence.

Clive asked Sheila if it was all right to attach the collectors to her breasts. She had learnt to say yes instead of nodding. Clive showed Jack how the job was done. Remarkably, it was a fairly automatic process. The collector identified the breast and very slowly attached itself.

Clive asked Sheila if she was OK, and she nodded. Clive then asked Sheila if it was OK to put some lotion on her vagina. She said, 'Yes,' and Clive and Jack stood in front of Sheila's naked, fully exposed fanny.

Clive said to Jack, 'I assume that you have seen a vagina before?' Jack nodded, but Clive could tell that this was not the case. He knew that when he was eighteen, it was all a bit vague to him. 'Shall I take you through the various parts? It's important to place the stimulator in the correct position,' he said. Jack nodded eagerly. Clive apologised to Sheila and asked if it was OK. Sheila nodded.

Clive explained that the vagina was protected by inner and outer folds or labia. Technically, they are called labia majora and labia minora. He said that you need to move these out of the way to get to the vagina. Clive was holding them in his hand. He asked Jack to manipulate them a bit to get some experience. Again, Jack was a bit hesitant, but he soon got the hang of it. Clive made the point that they come in all sorts of colours and sizes. Pointing to Sheila's, he said that they were rather neat.

'At the top, we have got the anus,' Clive said, as he put his finger on the entrance, which made Sheila jump slightly. 'Then, we have the clitoris or clit. You will notice that it has a little hood protecting it. This, as you know, is one of the most sensitive parts of a woman's body.' Clive gently massaged it, which sent shivers down Sheila's spine. She could already feel the stirrings of an orgasm. She thought that it didn't usually start that quickly, but then she remembered the drug she'd been given.

Clive continued to massage Sheila's clit, enjoying the reaction it was having on her. Clive asked Jack to have a go. He grabbed Sheila's clit between his fingers and rubbed it a bit too hard, which made Sheila jump. Clive immediately apologised to Sheila. He told Jack that he had to be gentler. He told him to imagine that his fingers were feathers. Jack's second attempt was much more successful, and Sheila was squirming with pleasure.

Clive nodded at Jack to continue, and Sheila had her first orgasm. Clive asked if Sheila was OK, and she nodded. Clive gave Jack the thumbs up and patted him on the back. Sheila was still panting and trying to keep herself calm. Clive pointed out the urethral opening, which he said must be avoided. Jack asked why, and Clive said that if he attached the stimulator there, Sheila would be peeing for the next hour. Sheila said, 'Don't put it there.'

Clive carried on with his explanation. 'Obviously, the

opening in the middle is the actual vagina. That is where the penis enters during sexual intercourse.' Jack was grateful for the sex lesson, but what he needed now was some practical experience. Clive placed his finger in Sheila's vagina and moved it around. He told Sheila that he was looking for the best place to connect the stimulator. A second finger was inserted, and Sheila could feel her second orgasm approaching.

Clive withdrew his fingers and asked Jack to have a go. Jack couldn't believe his luck and prepared to pop his fingers in. Clive told him to be gentle. Jack slowly inserted his first finger, then his second. He was surprised at how soft and silky the fanny felt. He tried to imagine just how good his penis would feel in there. He gently caressed Sheila's fanny, and she had a second, much more violent orgasm. She was covered in sweat and actually shook.

Clive thought, 'We have got a real goer here.' Chris came over and asked if there were any problems. At the same time, he was taking a good look at Sheila's fanny.

Clive explained that he was training Jack and that they were debating whether to attach the stimulator to the vagina or the clitoris. Chris asked why this was a source of debate. Clive replied, 'Sheila has reacted positively to both areas.' Chris said that that wasn't unusual, considering the drug they'd used, but he felt that he should check for himself.

Chris warmed his hand, caressed Sheila's clit and put two fingers into her fanny. Sheila almost immediately orgasmed. She had never had such a high before. Chris looked shocked by the almost immediate reaction. His fingers were covered in Sheila's fanny juice. 'She won't need lubricating,' he thought. He kept his fingers in place and gave Sheila a smaller, gentler orgasm. That was Sheila's fourth.

Chris asked Jack to wipe Sheila down as things downstairs were somewhat damp. Jack couldn't believe that he was cleaning out a woman's pussy.

Clive asked Sheila if she wanted some balm on her fanny before the stimulator was inserted. She heard herself say, 'Yes.' Clive put the balm on his hand and rubbed it all over her labia and clit. He always made sure that he did a good job. Sheila, rather embarrassingly, could feel another orgasm rising, but she had ceased worrying about it. Clive handed the balm to Jack, who went for the clit, causing Sheila's orgasm to just explode. She heard herself say, 'Wow' out loud, which pleased Jack to no end.

Clive asked Sheila if it was OK to attach the stimulator. She said, 'Yes,' and attachments were connected to both her clit and inside her vagina. The device was switched on, and Sheila could feel a continuous buzz in her genitals. It slowly built up until she was feeling a constant low-key orgasm. This went on for about twenty minutes.

Sheila's body had reached the stage where it was just desperate for relief. She really needed a fuck; not just stimulation, but a real fuck. Clive came over to see how she was doing. She told him that she had never felt so randy and that she needed a fuck. Clive explained that this was a side-effect of the drug and that she would get over it. Sheila argued that she understood that, but she still wanted a fuck.

Clive explained that it was possible, but she had to consent. Sheila shouted, 'Yes!' Clive explained that he would need to get Chris's permission. Chris came over and said that it would be OK. He volunteered himself and asked if Clive and Jack wanted to assist. Clive said no, but Jack was very keen.

Chris removed his tracksuit bottoms and pants and stood in front of Sheila's well-oiled fanny. There was no point in any subtlety. She just needed a good fuck. Chris placed his large, throbbing cock into her cunt and just pumped and pumped away. He gave no thought to Sheila's pleasure, as the drug would handle that. He managed to hold on for a while to maximise his enjoyment, but then he came. This kicked off Sheila's orgasm, and her body convulsed with ecstasy.

Chris nodded at Jack, who immediately dropped his trousers. Before Sheila could calm down, Jack entered her. He just couldn't believe that he was in this beautiful woman's body. He felt her softness; he felt the curve of her fanny; he felt his penis entering and withdrawing. He could feel his orgasm rushing to take him over. He could feel Sheila's body responding to his. The pressure was too much, and he shot his spunk into Sheila's fanny. She felt it arrive and smiled to herself before yet another orgasm hit her.

Clive released Sheila from the frame and patted her bum. He said, 'Well done,' as she had produced a lot of the chemical they needed.

Sheila washed and dressed but was feeling quite exhausted. Chris came over and asked if he could book her in for another session. She nodded and booked another three dates.

The Anne Summers Party

Sheila wrongly had the reputation of being a good-time girl, but in reality, she enjoyed nothing more than being at home reading her book or watching a good film on the box. She liked being tucked up as snug as a bug.

Edel, one of Sheila's long-term friends, had organised an Anne Summers party but needed a couple of demonstrators. Edel approached Sheila, telling her that she wanted most of the products demonstrated and asking if she was up for it. She said that Sheila would get a share of the profits, so Sheila agreed.

It was against the rules, but Edel had also organised a male demonstrator because there was a large number of male-orientated products. In the past, she'd found that a lot of the women purchased items for their husbands in an attempt to improve their love life. Anyway, she thought it might be fun to 'sex' things up a bit.

She told all of her guests that a man would be attending. A few objected and pulled out, but it attracted some others. She forgot to mention it to Sheila, as she wasn't on the guest list.

Sheila wondered what she was going to be demonstrating; quite often, it was up to the guests to choose. Anyway, it should be a good, fun event for the girls. Sometimes, it's just nice to get away from the blokes.

Sheila arrived early at Edel's house to help with the preparations. She helped get the nibbles ready and prepared some drinks for when the guests arrived. She also carried in boxes of erotic demonstration equipment. She noticed that one was labelled 'Sheila' and the other was labelled 'Ben.'

There was a knock on the front door. Edel said that it must be Ben. In walked a black Adonis. He was one of the best-looking men that Sheila had ever seen: tall, muscular and debonair. It was apparent that he worked out. He had a cheeky smile and a very relaxed attitude. Edel whispered to Sheila that he had a cock to die for. Sheila was bowled over, but she also wondered what he was doing there.

Edel explained that he was a professional product demonstrator from the agency. Sheila said, 'I don't think the girls will like a man at an Ann Summers party.' Edel explained that the girls all knew in advance and were looking forward to it. Sheila was a bit miffed that she hadn't been informed, but that was typical of Edel. Anyway, what harm could it do?

About twenty guests turned up. Sheila knew quite a few of them from the school run. They were all offered drinks and nibbles. And after a lot of girlie chatting, it was decided to start the show. Ben was sitting in the lounge with the audience. He was only wearing shorts. He was enjoying lots of admiration and attention from the girls.

Sheila was next door in the kitchen. Edel had given Sheila some nighties to demonstrate. The first one was relatively tame: pink with teddy bears all over it. Sheila waltzed in and did a few turns while Edel was doing the commentary. Ben liked the look of Sheila and was hoping that the nighties would get a bit more risqué. He particularly admired her legs; he wanted to see more of them.

Sheila then returned in a fruitier silk number. She had taken her bra off as it wasn't appropriate for the outfit. She entered the room to clapping. She was the perfect model, slim but curvaceous, elegant but down to earth, sexy but with a girl-next-door look. She had always looked taller than she was. She had the magic ability to make almost any clothes look good.

Ben thought Sheila looked really beautiful. He couldn't keep his eyes off her perfect breasts with erect nipples. He thought to himself that this was going to be fun.

Sheila left the room. The next nightie was considerably more indecent. It was a lacy outfit that buttoned at the chest and then flowed outwards. Her breasts would be on show. There was a tiny pair of briefs that just about covered her fanny. She wondered what Ben would think of them. In she walked. Everyone stared at Sheila as she looked gorgeous. Most women appreciate a beautiful female body, but not as much as Ben. He was gobsmacked—those breasts were stunning. He was struggling to control his erection, which was starting to pop out the top of his shorts. He decided to go to the kitchen to get ready and also to ogle Sheila.

Sheila was getting ready to put on a baby-doll nightie that had no knickers with it. Ben was just staring at her. He said, 'Don't let me stop you,' and Sheila pulled her knickers down. She stood there in a totally transparent outfit. Nothing was left to the imagination. She spotted the top of Ben's knob sticking out of his shorts and smiled. She loved to see the effect she had on men.

Sheila walked into the lounge, did a twirl to Edel's commentary and left. She heard that Ben would be demonstrating a range of condoms next. Sheila thought that this would be worth watching and returned to the lounge in her baby-doll outfit. She deliberately sat with her legs slightly apart so that Ben could see her fanny.

Ben walked in naked, save for a coloured condom on his cock. The girls stared in awe. It was undoubtedly the largest cock that Sheila had ever seen. He invited the girls to feel the texture of the condom. There was no shortage of volunteers; hands were rubbing him up and down almost immediately. He told the girls to be careful because he had several condoms to demonstrate and didn't want to be premature. They all laughed.

Ben couldn't help noticing Sheila's naked pussy. She opened her legs a bit more to make doubly sure he noticed. She could feel her pussy getting damp. Ben's cock enlarged further because of the view, and it was beginning to ache with all the attention he was receiving. He asked if one of the girls wanted to put the next condom on. Mary volunteered and tried to pull the existing condom off, which wasn't that easy to achieve. Eventually, it came off, but Mary had bigger problems trying to put the new condom on.

Edel suggested some special Anne Summers lubricant, which was duly applied. It still wasn't easy putting a condom on such a large cock. Edel decided to move on to the vibrators and looked at Sheila to assist. Sheila was mouthing to Edel, 'Are you sure that you want me to demonstrate them?' Edel was nodding. Sheila thought, 'In for a penny, in for a pound.'

Sheila took her baby-doll nightie off and laid on the floor. She opened her legs for all to see. Ben's eyes were bulging. Edel had five vibrators to demonstrate. She easily popped the smallest one into Sheila's fanny. It was too small to be of use to most European women. The second one was larger, but it still didn't do much for Sheila. The rabbit came next, which tickled both the fanny and the anus at the same time. This was doing the job, and Sheila started to moisten up.

The next vibrator was almost too big. Sheila reflected on what she was doing. She was lying naked in front of twenty women, some of whom she knew quite well. She had exposed herself to a man with the biggest cock she had ever seen, and her friend was putting vibrators in her fanny. She wondered how she'd got herself into this position.

Edel managed to get the vibrator in and received a wild roar of approval. Most of the girls were straining to get the best possible view. Edel stated that she didn't think that Sheila could handle the largest vibrator.

Ben said; 'Of course she can,' and pushed Edel out of the way. He lubricated the large vibrator and then started to play with Sheila's labia. He told the girls that it's essential to get the whole cunt excited. He then licked and nibbled Sheila's clit, which got her very hot. She could feel her climax rising. She was resisting it, as it would be too embarrassing to come in front of her friends.

Ben's fingers were playing with the sides of her fanny, gently pushing every few centimetres. Her cunt was his to play with. She had lost all inhibition. Ben gently eased the largest vibrator into her vagina. Her love hole was full, but it was still just metal and plastic. She wanted a cock; she wanted Ben's cock. Ben could tell that her orgasm wasn't far off.

Ben said, 'Now ladies, shall I demonstrate the latest condom, or do you want to see a bareback encounter?'

'Bareback,' they shouted. Ben removed the vibrator and gently eased his huge cock into Sheila's fanny. He decided that this was not going to be pretty, as she was too near her orgasm. He decided to go for half a dozen powerful thrusts, which set them both off.

There were two world-class, simultaneous orgasms. Ben

pulled out his penis and spunk went everywhere. Edel said to the ladies, 'The Anne Summers tissues are excellent for cleaning up the odd spillage.'

Sheila knew that she had been "Benned". When she got home, her husband asked her how the party went. She said, 'Not bad. We listened to *Good Vibrations* by the Beach Boys.'

The Fluffer: Part 1

Sheila was reminiscing about one of her first rather embarrassing jobs. To be honest, it was far worse than merely embarrassing—it was downright shocking. She hadn't realised what it entailed at first. She had three young children and a husband who was always losing his poorly paid jobs. She managed to take on the odd cleaning job, and she took in some students, but she was being offered a job that paid £50 an hour for four weeks. She had told the children and her husband that it would pay for a lovely holiday.

A male friend of hers had recommended her for the job. Sheila was an attractive girl with a beautiful pair of boobs, a cute bum, a flat stomach and legs to die for. She had a friendly, bubbly personality that helped her make friends quickly and easily. Men liked both her appearance and her ability to tease them with her eyes.

At the interview, they explained that a fluffer's job was to get the men excited enough to perform onstage. The month-long show was Lady Chatterley's Lover, where there was a fair amount of nudity involved. Sexual intercourse was being simulated onstage. The gardener had to arrive onstage with a fully erect penis. Her job would be to ensure that the erection happened.

At first, this worried her, but then she thought that it couldn't be any worse than getting her old man's todger stiff.

It was just getting more and more difficult. She wasn't sure if it was his age, or if perhaps he had just lost interest in her. Thinking about it, it had always been her that initiated sex. Anyway, it would be a nice change to see another man's cock. She had never strayed. In fact, the only cock she had ever seen was her husband's. She wasn't too sure what was needed for her to succeed, but she thought that a hand job or a little bit of licking should be enough.

She signed the contract without reading it too carefully. They gave her a list of rehearsal and performance dates and some money upfront. She was so excited that she immediately booked the holiday. They were going to Spain in the summer. Her children couldn't wait.

She arrived at the first rehearsal, where she met both the actor and his understudy. They asked if she had done this sort of work before. She said, 'No,' but that she didn't think it should be too difficult. They said that it was an important perk as far as they were concerned and that they would be looking to take full advantage of the contractual conditions. Sheila wasn't too sure what they were talking about.

An hour later, the actors were waiting for Sheila to come to their dressing room. She arrived and was staggered to see two naked men. She looked at them, and they looked at her. Bill, the main actor, said, 'You have still got your clothes on.' Sheila looked bewildered. Bill said, 'We need to rehearse the fluffing; it is vital that we get it right.' Sheila still looked perplexed.

The understudy, George, asked if she had read the contract correctly. Clearly, she hadn't, and the manager was called. The manager asked Sheila if she had read the contract, and she nodded positively. The manager said, 'In that case, you would know that the actors can use your body to obtain an erection. It specifically says that they can use your hands, mouth, vagina or anus to get an erection. This is why you are being paid £50 an hour. In the industry, it's seen as a key perk for the actors in exchange for having to expose themselves onstage.' The manager stared hard at Sheila and said, 'Are you going to continue or not?'

Sheila wanted to go home. 'Sod them,' she thought. 'I don't want to be their whore.' But then what would she tell the kids? There would be no holiday. The manager said, 'Go to the loo, which is next door, give it some thought, and come back with your decision. But don't make it too long.'

Bill said to George, 'Pretty little thing, it will be rather fun taking advantage of her.'

George said, 'I hope she agrees to go ahead, as I would certainly like to give her one.' The manager was looking forward to seeing her nude too.

Sheila shed a little tear in the loo and unzipped her dress. She felt that circumstances had pushed her into an impossible position. Off came her tights, bra and knickers. She bundled her clothes up, put some lipstick on and left the loo. She knocked on the dressing room door and entered.

All three men looked at Sheila standing there in her naked glory. They admired her beautiful perky boobs, her perfect figure and her gorgeous pair of legs. George stared at her fanny and realised that he would be getting his wish granted soon.

'Well, gentlemen, how can I help you?' she said.

Bill gained his composure and said, 'I think I will use the fanny.' Sheila asked him if he wanted her on her back or should she bend over. Bill gestured for her to bend over. The manager, feeling a bit sorry for Sheila, pointed out that that the contract terms only covered achieving an erection, and it did not include ejaculation. He also pointed out that technically, Bill already had an erection, so, therefore, Sheila had done her job. However, as it was a rehearsal, he should probably continue.

Sheila bent over the settee and opened her legs to expose her fanny. She admitted to herself that she was starting to feel a bit randy. The only person who had seen her fanny before was her husband. Here she was being ogled by three strangers. The manager got a bit nearer to have a good look at her rather attractive, moist cunt. He could feel his cock harden.

Bill entered Sheila and gave her a serious pounding but pulled out before he came. Sheila was actually enjoying it. It was considerably more intense than her husband's pathetic efforts. Bill finished himself off on a hanky.

Sheila looked at George and said, 'And how can I help you, young man?' George said that he would also like the use of the fanny, but he would like her on her back. Sheila obliged by lying on the settee with her legs in the air. She used her hands to keep her legs in place so that George could get easy access. George took his throbbing, fully erect penis and gently pushed it into Sheila's cute little cunt. It felt so soft and smooth, like velvet. He desperately wanted to come. He had never felt so desperate, but he knew that he had to withdraw at the critical moment.

Unfortunately, during the withdrawal he came, spraying Sheila with hot spunk. It went everywhere—all over her pubic hair, stomach, boobs and face. They all burst out laughing. George was so apologetic. The manager explained that these things happened sometimes. He brought over a soft cloth and wiped Sheila down, focussing mostly on her boobs and fanny.

They all agreed that the rehearsal had gone very well.

There was another one tomorrow. The manager pointed out that ejaculations must be avoided. Otherwise, it would be difficult to maintain erections onstage. This made Sheila laugh as she now knew that she had power. The manager said that he would also be pleased to assist tomorrow.

All four turned up on time, with Sheila waiting in the dressing room stark naked. It was George's turn to go first, and he wanted a repeat of yesterday. Sheila got herself into position, with her legs up in the air and her fanny fully exposed. She thought it strange that there was no real foreplay, but then it looked like George was more than ready. She certainly was; her fanny was moist and eager.

George started slowly, gradually building up the pressure. Sheila could feel her orgasm rising as George fucked her. She realised what she had been missing all those years. George carried on, and suddenly Sheila climaxed. Her whole body just convulsed in pleasure. George's cock popped out, which was probably a good thing as he was about to come, and that was against the rules.

Sheila felt embarrassed as she had never climaxed in public before. What was she thinking—she had never been fucked in public before either. It was all so surreal. The manager looked exhausted, as he had been masturbating and came at the same time.

Sheila was trying to recover when Bill asked for a blow job. She had licked her husband's cock before, but she had never given a full-blown blow job. She thought it couldn't be that bad since he wasn't allowed to come. She knelt, took Bill's slightly limp cock in her mouth and sucked it gently, licking the glans at the same time. It wasn't long before it was fully erect. She wondered how porn stars coped with a huge cock because she was struggling to breathe. After a while, she could taste salty pre-cum and realised that it was the right time to remove his cock. Bill looked very disappointed, but she had done her job.

The manager stated that it had been another successful rehearsal, but tomorrow was the real thing. He needed to show Sheila where she would be positioned. She asked what he meant. He said that obviously, they couldn't use the dressing room since by the time the actors reached the stage, they would have lost their erections. No, she had to be positioned next to the stage to do her magic.

Sheila got dressed, and the manager showed her where she would be positioned by the stage. She couldn't believe it. She would be on show to all the backstage staff. There would be no privacy whatsoever. She was going to be fucked in public. The manager also said that she had to be ready on time. The actor would come offstage, strip and she would have minutes to get him erect, literally minutes. The manager made one last point, saying 'There are three people on your contract: the two actors and the stage manager. He will probably contact you on stage tonight, as he works evenings.'

Sheila was not looking forward to practically being fucked on stage and by a third man. But then again, the show must go on, and she needed the money.

Sheila returned the next day and stripped off. She wasn't allowed a dressing gown as that would slow things down when the timing was critical. She walked to the stage area stark naked except for a pair of shoes. It was funny how many men happened to be there as she walked by, including most of the office staff. It was strange how many men found an excuse to talk to her by the stage.

The play was already underway, and her big moment was nearing. She lubricated her fanny to ease the actor's entry, as the whole process was going to be very quick. She bent over and opened her fanny, ready for action. George came offstage, stripped, rushed over to Sheila and entered her. His penis was fully erect in no time at all. George withdrew and rushed back onstage with his large, erect cock swinging backwards and forwards.

A man then came over and introduced himself as the stage manager. Sheila said that she had been expecting him and asked how she could help him. He said that he would have the same as George. She bent over again, and he entered her already very moist vagina. He was a big boy who knew what he was doing. He pumped away with a strong, steady rhythm that started to spark off her orgasm. As he pumped, she could feel herself coming. Suddenly, he let out a long moan and filled her up, which pushed her over the edge.

He gave her his hanky to wipe herself down. He thanked her and walked off. Sheila thought that she wouldn't mind a bit more of that. Then she looked up to see that at least thirty people had been watching. She went bright red with embarrassment.

She carried on doing her duty when the manager approached with a colleague. The manager said, 'I would like to introduce you to the stage manager.' Sheila then explained what had happened. The manager said that she'd fallen victim to an old trick. 'Some people will do anything for a free fuck.' The stage manager then said that he would be knocking on her door the next day since he couldn't do it tonight as it was his wife's birthday.

Sheila walked back to the dressing room with the manager. On the way, he said that he knew a way of adding a few more hours to her contract. She entered the room and said to the manager, 'And how can I help you?'

The Fluffer: Part 2

Sheila walked back to the dressing room with the manager. On the way, he said that he knew of a way of adding a few more hours to her contract, but there would need to be a slight contractual change. A new clause would add him to those who could use her fanny without restriction. As she entered the room, she said to the manager, 'And how can I help you?'

He said, 'Well, I think I would like you to bend over so that I can admire that fine arse of yours.' Sheila bent over and assumed one of her regular positions. He gently pushed Sheila's legs apart so that her pussy was fully exposed. He caressed her labia, stroked her clit and put two fingers in her vagina. Sheila felt that she was just his plaything; just a rag doll. He could do whatever he liked, and he did. He took his hard, fully erect cock and rubbed it against her clit.

He now knew what made her come, and he was determined to give her an orgasm. He constantly rubbed his cock against her little clit. Back and forth until the tingling sensations were getting just too much for her. At the right moment, he entered her entirely, but he carried on using his fingers on her clit. She suddenly exploded; she saw amazing stars, bright lightning and tantalising, bright lights. This was followed by half a dozen smaller orgasms.

The manager was delighted with his performance; he'd always enjoyed giving a woman an orgasm, especially a beautiful woman like Sheila. Now it was his turn to enjoy himself. He pushed his cock into Sheila as far as he could. He moved his hands around her side to grab both of her tits. He had enjoyed watching them swing about earlier, but now he wanted to play with them.

His cock was very sensitive. He thoroughly enjoyed the feeling of his cock rubbing against the soft skin of Sheila's fanny. Hers was a beautiful fanny that seemed to grab him and hold him for a few seconds before letting him go. As he pushed and withdrew, he could feel his semen rising. He looked forward to the relief he'd feel when his balls were emptied. At the same time, he was tweaking Sheila's hard, extended nipples. He loved breasts; he loved the feeling of the hard nipple against the soft tissue underneath. Without a doubt, squeezing them was the best stress reliever in the world.

He was almost there, and he pulled out so that he could come all over Sheila's bum. His semen ran down the crack of her arse. It covered her fanny, which glistened in the light. He then plunged back into Sheila's cunt for a final time to get that last ultimate sensation. He withdrew again and enjoyed the sight of his spunk running down her legs.

He patted Sheila's bum and said that she had done a great job. Without thinking, she said, 'Thank you.' He said that the next day there would be a rehearsal and another live performance in the evening. Sheila got up, showered and dressed.

When she got home, her husband asked her how work had gone. She said that it was fucking hard work. He said, 'You don't usually use language like that.'

She replied, 'Well, it was one of those days where I got well and truly fucked.'

Sheila wasn't too sure about the work, but it was somewhat surprising that she had seemingly transformed from a shy, demure housewife to a wanton slut. She thought that slut was a hard word, but over a matter of days, she had been fucked by six men, and on one occasion, she'd had an audience of at least thirty. What was worse was that she quite liked having the men want her. Part of her even enjoyed being naked onstage. Perhaps 'slut' was too harsh; 'tart' might be more fitting.

She spent a bit of time in her wardrobe, choosing some sexy underwear. She wasn't sure why she bothered because it wouldn't be on for long. She looked at her schedule and realised that it was going to be a hectic day—she would have two men to service during the rehearsal, probably the manager as well, and then there was the live performance and the stage manager. 'That's five,' she thought. 'My poor little fanny is going to be sore by going home time.'

She arrived early and noticed that while the girls in the office were giving her the cold shoulder, the boys were very attentive. Lenny was particularly useful and wanted to help her with her bag. He was an enthusiastic, gangly, ginger-headed boy. He looked to be about fifteen or sixteen, but he was probably much older than that.

She sat in the dressing room, waiting for the actors to arrive. The manager turned up first. He said that the other two were on their way so she might as well undress. She slipped her dress off and stood there in her skimpy bra and panties. He had to admire her body. It's always good to see a woman naked, but sometimes less was more. Her breasts looked magnificent and were held in place by a couple of patches of fabric.

While he was ogling her, Bill and George turned up. They were also impressed by Sheila's near nudity. George asked if he could take her knickers off, and Sheila nodded. George bent down and slowly, very slowly, pulled her panties down. He gradually slipped them down over the rump of her bum, exposing her naked fanny. There was just enough hair to make her pussy interesting. He couldn't resist giving the fanny a little stroke, slightly teasing her clit.

The manager walked over and unclipped Sheila's bra, releasing her two beautiful tits. He couldn't resist lifting them one at a time. He was surprised at how heavy they were and how quick the nipples became hard. Both men were now gently massaging her body. George gradually worked his way towards Sheila's vagina, and after teasing the labia to one side, his finger entered her inner sanctum. She was already quite moist and aromatic. Bill said, 'Now come on lads, it's my turn to go first.'

Sheila asked Bill for his preference, and he said that he would like her on her hands and knees with her bum in the air. 'Good choice,' the manager said. Sheila obliged, and Bill stood facing her bum with his hands on her hips. He bent down and started licking her clit and fingering her vagina. His licks got harder and more intense until it reached the point that he was almost biting her. Sheila had never experienced anything like that before, and she started to come. Her orgasm was like a series of concentric waves. The followed one after another with varying levels of intensity. While she was squirming and moving her bottom about, Bill entered her quickly and then decided to pull out in case he came.

The manager was relieved since Bill was performing that night and would need to get an erection. He said to Bill, 'At first, I thought you were going to come.' Bill said that he was almost at the point of no return and it was so bloody frustrating because he felt that he was missing out on the joys of a hot, juicy pussy. The manager explained that Sheila was only there to give Bill an erection; she wasn't there to give him a good time. George was eagerly awaiting his turn.

Sheila asked George for his preference. He decided to go for the same treatment as Bill. Sheila wiggled her bum to tease him. George quickly grabbed her hips and inserted his todger deep into her gaping vagina. There was no subtlety; he was just desperate to give her one. He established a reasonably fast rhythm which made her tits swirl violently. The manager came to the rescue, holding them both down.

George then remembered that ejaculation was not allowed and slowed down. He was still enjoying the silkiness of her cunt when he decided to withdraw. He then asked the manager if he could come in Sheila, as he was only the understudy, and since Bill was there, he wouldn't be needed on stage that night. The manager explained that it was Sheila's fanny and that George needed to ask her.

George asked Sheila if he could fuck her again and come in her fanny. She shook her head. He pleaded with her, saying 'Pretty please?'

Sheila enjoyed the power of the situation and said, 'No, I'm not a tart, you know, I'm a fluffer.' Sheila was relieved to stand up as her back was beginning to ache finally.

The rehearsal was over, and Sheila was preparing to go home when the manager said that he had one more job for her. She looked down and saw that his erect cock was poking out of his flies. She bent down and started to lick and suck away. He lost control and shot his load straight into her mouth. Sheila had read that nice girls swallowed, and she did her duty. Well, that's three out of five done. She still had the wall of shame tonight and two more fucks.

Lenny walked her to the bus stop, chatting all the way. He was starting to get quite irritating as he always wanted to talk about her and kept asking lots of personal questions. She was back later that night and stripped as usual. She was preparing herself for the long walk to the stage. She wasn't sure why she couldn't cover herself for the walk, but they were adamant about the rules.

There were more men about this time, taking every opportunity to view her nakedness. A few photos were also being taken. She was slightly more confident than before, holding her head up and making the most of her assets on display. She even bent over at one point to tease the onlookers.

The action followed on from the previous night, with Sheila bending over at the appropriate time to allow Bill quick access. Bill entered her and whispered that he was going to fill her up at a later date. He was soon out of her cunt and back on stage with an impressive erection. After two nights of performances, she wondered why they even needed fluffing rehearsals, but it was not for her to question.

The stage manager wobbled over with his cock hanging out. He said that he wasn't feeling too great but that he might as well use the facilities. Sheila bent over once again. The stage manager put his heavy hand on her back to stop her from moving and roughly inserted his old, wrinkled cock into her somewhat juicy fanny. It was all over fairly quickly. Sheila was surprised that there was no audience this time. Later, she learnt that no one had wanted to upset the old, cantankerous stage manager. He could be a right bastard.

The next day was going to be a lot easier as there were no rehearsals and the managers were off on a training course. However, Sheila was somewhat perturbed to discover that Lenny was going to be the acting stage manager and he'd inherited the contractual rights to her fanny for the night.

Lenny met Sheila at the theatre door and walked her to the dressing room. He said that he was really looking forward to fucking her later that evening. It was hardly subtle. He explained that as the managers were away, things backstage would be a lot more relaxed. She asked him to leave while she prepared herself, which was a bit of a joke since she only had to strip and put some lipstick on.

As she left the dressing room, she could tell that the atmosphere had changed. Most of the staff were waiting for her along the corridor. As she walked by them, they stroked and caressed her. Her nipples were tweaked, and a finger even managed to enter her fanny. It was a horrible experience, but she was determined to continue.

She carried out her theatrical duties diligently. Bill entered her and withdrew to finish the scene, and then came the part she dreaded.

Lenny walked over with most of the staff, both men and women. A mattress was thrown on the floor, and several stage lights were erected to fully illuminate the area. Sheila managed to say, 'How can I help you?' Lenny said he wanted her on her back. Sheila obliged, but she made no effort to hold her legs apart. However, two of Lenny's associates agreed to hold them, and just like that, Sheila was fully spread-eagle. She had never felt so exposed before. At least forty people were enjoying watching her predicament.

Lenny removed his dressing gown to expose his very

impressive manhood. At first glance, he looked like a gangly youth; but in the trouser department, he was all man. He asked for a pillow to be put under Sheila's bum. One of the girls put the pillow in place and then lubricated Sheila's fanny, not that it needed it. She rubbed oil all over her. Sheila heard someone say, 'Start the video camera.'

Lenny bent down and slowly inserted his very manly cock into her love hole. This was going to be the biggest cock that she had ever experienced. She wasn't sure if she could take it. He slowly pushed his way in. Sheila was glad of the additional lubrication. It was a very tight fit; every inch of her cunt was filled by his cock. There wasn't any room to move, but move he did.

Lenny very slowly pushed in and out. He gradually increased the speed and at the same time teased her clit. Lenny was in no hurry. The crowd were egging him on. Half of the men were tugging at their pricks. One girl was giving a blow job. Sheila was worried that this could quickly turn into an orgy. She was also concerned that they were a bit too near the stage. She could hear the actors perform, so there was every likelihood that they could hear them too.

Lenny built up the rhythm steadily, and Sheila could feel an orgasm rising. The crowd was counting the strokes. They cheered when he passed the one hundred mark. Lenny continued increasing the relentless pressure, and at the two hundred mark he stopped, withdrew his cock and lifted Sheila. He was a strong man indeed. He turned her over so that she was now on her hands and knees. They had moved even closer to the stage.

In no time at all, that big cock was back in Sheila's fanny. In that position, he had much more leverage, and he could give

Sheila a bit of a pounding. Unfortunately, each stroke pushed her and the mattress forward slightly. Sheila was enjoying it, but at the same time, she was struggling to keep her orgasm under control. As no pussy could cope with that much pressure, she thought 'When it comes, it's going to be a monster.'

Sheila gave in and had the loudest orgasm ever. In an attempt to quieten her, someone managed to pull the stage curtain down, and the entire theatre audience could see Sheila stark naked, on all fours with a huge cock up her fanny. There was a raucous cheer, and a hundred cameras clicked at once.

That was the end of Sheila's career in the theatre, but the photos commemorating the occasion are still selling well on the internet.

The Fluffer: Part 3

Sheila had never been so embarrassed. It had been the most embarrassing day of her life. She had been put on full display, surrounded by bright lights and fucked by one of the largest cocks she had ever seen in front of forty people. Strangely, it was being watched by the women that was the hardest to bear. They just saw her as a slut, but at the same time, they were jealous; they wanted to be in the same position. They wanted the attention that she was getting.

In her mind's eye, she could see the women, some of them still in their teens, egging Lenny on. 'Go on, fuck her,' they said. She could hear them shout, 'More, more, more!' The men just enjoyed seeing a huge cock entering her tight little fanny and watching her boobs bounce as if they were dancing. They both followed the same pattern, moving faster and faster as the fucking got more intense.

Then came the big finale when she was fully exposed onstage in the theatre in Croydon. She was naked with a magnificent cock up her cunt. There was no hiding anything. The lights behind her made everything totally visible. The flashes from the cameras in the audience blinded her and made her jump up. This freed Lenny's cock from her fanny, and to add to her embarrassment, he chose that exact moment to let loose a steady stream of spunk.

Some of the photos caught the semen travelling through

the air. Sheila's back and bum were just covered in it. She ran offstage to clapping and cheers and found her way back to a locked dressing room. Fortunately, she had brought her car with her that day and managed to get home safely.

Her fanny tingled as she thought about that night. She decided that she had a strong exhibitionist streak. She missed the whole experience. She missed being fucked by men who knew what they were doing. She enjoyed feeling desirable and being wanted. Now she was back to the odd fumble with her prematurely ageing husband: what a waste of time he was.

Purely by accident, she ran into Ken, the theatre manager, in the Whitgift Shopping Centre. She said how sorry she was to hear that he had lost his job. He said that those things happened in show business. In a rather shy way, he asked if she wanted to continue their arrangement of £50 per hour. Sheila smiled but said, 'No, I'm not a prostitute.' She had carried out her duties because the job demanded it. They both laughed. Then Ken asked her if she had ever thought of performing onstage.

He explained that he was working with a team that was putting together an X-rated pantomime. With her looks and attitude, she would be perfect. He asked if she wanted him to organise an audition. She nodded. To be honest, part of her had wanted to say yes to Ken's previous offer as well.

The following week, she received a call asking her to attend an audition at Thorton Heath. She spent a lot of time on her hair and make-up and more time than usual, making sure that she had a colour coordinated outfit that looked stylish but sexy. She arrived on time to find a rather seedy-looking building. It was a private club that could seat about two hundred people.

A good-looking man in a well-cut suit met her in reception, introduced himself as Chas and took her to a meeting room. There, she found two other young men, both of whom were probably younger than her eldest son.

They organised a coffee for her and started the audition process. It was amicable, and she was quite relaxed. They asked if she had appeared naked on stage before, and she nodded. One of the young men asked if she had ever simulated sex onstage before. She took the opportunity to say that she had gone one step further and had engaged in full sex onstage. She explained that it had been accidental, but these things sometimes happened in show business.

The men were slightly shocked as Sheila looked far too innocent. Her sparkling eyes and infectious smile were captivating. Chas emphasised that she would be nude on stage and that some simulation work would be required. She explained that it wouldn't be a problem. Chas always found it a bit embarrassing, but it had to be done, and he asked Sheila to strip so that they could assess her assets. Sheila said, 'Oh, you want to see if my boobs and bum are up to the job?' They all laughed.

Sheila stood up in what was a tiny room. The lads made a bit more room for her. Sheila knew that it wasn't a striptease, but in reality, it was an audition. She asked Chas to unzip her dress, which he did. Once the dress was off, Sheila posed in her lacy bra and knickers set. They had been carefully chosen to show the right amount of flesh while at the same time, being somewhat demure.

Sheila could tell that they were impressed. Her recent theatre experience had given her a lot of confidence in her body. She continued to pose, highlighting her bum and boobs.

She asked them if she should remove her bra now. The men eagerly nodded.

She unclipped the bra and let it gently slip off. Her hands immediately covered her boobs to make the show more entertaining. Her hands then held her boobs up and released them. Her ample charms bounced in a little dance to the delight of the men. She walked over to Chas and asked him to tweak her nipples to make them hard. He went bright red but grabbed both breasts and expertly squeezed them. She was hard in no time at all.

She couldn't help noticing the lump growing in Chas's trousers. She did a little dance to show the movement of her tits. One of the men complimented her on her rack. She smiled and asked if it was time to remove her knickers. They all agreed that it was.

Sheila stood in front of them and grabbed the sides of her panties. She very slowly pulled them down. It might have been the slowest removal of a pair of knickers in history. The men were presented with a naked, but slightly moist, fanny. The aroma of Sheila's fanny was apparent to all, but no one mentioned it.

Sheila kicked her knickers off her feet and turned around to show them her cute, well-proportioned bum. Chas wanted to caress it; in fact, he was desperate to bite it. She wiggled her bum to their delight. Sheila loved this and realised that she was an exhibitionist. She asked if they wanted to see her fanny. They grunted, which she took to mean yes.

She gently pulled her labia to one side so that the boys could get a clear view of her vagina. She was totally exposed to them.

Sheila stood up and bowed. The men clapped in unison.

Chas said that she had passed that part of the audition. However, they needed to make sure that she could cope with the simulated sex. Sheila thought, 'Here we go, this is where they are going to use their position to take advantage of me.'

Chas could tell from Sheila's reaction that she was concerned. He explained that he wasn't after sex or anything, but in the past, it had turned out that one of the applicants couldn't stand anyone touching her. They just wanted to make sure that it wasn't the case with Sheila. Sheila smiled and said, 'Touch me anywhere you'd like.'

Chas walked over and started fondling her tits, focusing on the nipples. He then gently caressed her bottom and stroked her little black triangle. While staring Sheila in the eyes, he flicked her clit and popped a finger into her fanny. Sheila said nothing. Chas continued stroking the inside of her cunt and said, 'I think that was very satisfactory.'

Chas turned to the other two and said, 'Sheila has passed the audition. We need to think about the contractual terms.' He then turned to Sheila and said, 'We will leave that to Ken to sort out, but I hope you will offer similar terms to those of your previous appointment, as I'm one of the actors.'

Sheila said, 'It should not be a problem,' and bent over to pick her knickers up off the floor. The men couldn't help admiring the view.

Sheila left, thinking, 'What have I done?'

When she got home, her husband asked her how the audition went. Sheila said that they had been remarkably thorough and penetrating. No stone was left unturned.

My Three Friends

Sheila got a call from Ken, the old manager at the theatre. He said that he hadn't got the go-ahead yet for the new pantomime, but he did have another opportunity. He had thought of her first, as he knew that things had been relatively tight since she had lost her job. He had been asked to organise some entertainment for a stag night and wondered if she'd be interested.

Sheila asked what was involved. Ken said that full nudity was a requirement, along with some physical contact. Sheila asked how much physical contact. Ken said that, to be honest, it was going to be a stag night. Things often got out of hand, but the pay was good. She would take home £1,000.

Sheila said that the money was very tempting, but she didn't want to spend all night onstage being shagged by a series of randy, drunken lads. Ken said that it was to be a very up-market affair. They had booked five girls, and there was going to be several sexy games. Edel, who Sheila knew, was organising it. However, Sheila wasn't sure if Edel's involvement was a good or bad thing as she was known as a "good-time girl".

Ultimately, Sheila needed the money to pay her gas bill. Later that week, she made her way to Addington to find the slightly run-down nightclub. It was the classic sort of seventies club with the dance area in the middle and tables and chairs all around the edge. It even had some large, sparkling balls hanging from the ceiling that were used to reflect and deflect light. In her mind, she was playing old Bee Gees numbers.

On arrival, she was directed towards the changing room. She was glad to get inside the building as the evening air was starting to get quite chilly. Inside the small, tatty room, she found four other girls in different stages of undress. They were all new to her. She introduced herself as Sheila and got positive, friendly responses.

There were naked boobs and fannies everywhere. Clothes were hanging up, legs were being moisturised, hair was being brushed, and lipstick was being applied. One girl was asking another girl what the itinerary for the evening was. She said that she wasn't too sure, but she knew that Edel had organised at least three sexy games. Then she said that they were not going to get away without some serious fucking since it was a stag party and they were paying the girls £1,000 each.

The other girl said, 'I can't do that. I just got married, and my fanny is for his use alone.' The other girls laughed.

Sheila was starting to think the worst. If she hadn't needed the money, she would probably have done a runner. This was her husband's fault for losing his job once again. He was at home with her boys watching Match of the Day. He wasn't there preparing to display his genitals to all and sundry. It was just so unfair.

Edel entered the room with their costumes. Well, they could hardly be called costumes—they consisted of skimpy pairs of panties. Edel explained that the first game was quite simple. They would each put a Cox's apple down the back of their knickers. The contestant would have to take a bite out of the apple and then pull the knickers down with their teeth. The five contestants had already been selected, so the girls were expected onstage in five minutes. Edel added, 'By the way, I have some masquerade masks if you want to protect your identity.' Sheila immediately grabbed one.

The girls quickly put the knickers on and placed an apple down the back. Sheila found the apple quite cold; it made her fanny tingle. She wondered, once again, what she had got herself into. She looked at the other girls and thought that she looked pretty good in comparison. She easily had the fullest bosom and the best-looking legs.

The five scantily-clad girls were soon onstage with the odd-looking protrusions sticking out of their knickers. Edel introduced each girl to a round of cheers. She described the game in detail and then said that the contestant to finish first would get to fuck his girl. Sheila just hoped that it wasn't going to be her. The girls were placed around the disco floor, and the contestants came forward.

Sheila recognised her contestant as her best friend's husband, Jeff. What was he doing there? She didn't think he recognised her because of the mask. They all got into position, and the buzzer went. Jeff was quick; the apple was bitten, and her knickers were down. They had a clear winner; none of the other contestants had even got past the apple-biting stage.

Edel jumped up, screaming, 'We have a winner, we have a winner!' A small bench was put in place, and Sheila was arranged so that everyone could see her pussy. Additional lights were organised, and a camera displayed her charms on the big screen. Sheila had been embarrassed several times, but this was about the worst. On the screen, everyone could see her pretty little cunt about ten times its normal size. Edel came over and prised her labia apart so that the entrance to her vagina was fully exposed.

Edel told Sheila to wiggle her bum, and everyone cheered. Jeff removed his trousers and pants and walked towards the stage with a huge erection preceding him. Edel said, 'It's all yours,' pointing at Sheila's fanny. He rested his cock against the entrance to full dramatic effect.

The audience started shouting, 'Fuck her, fuck her!' and Jeff obliged.

Jeff did his job in a workmanlike way, but he pulled out at the last moment. His spunk covered Sheila's arse and fanny. Clearly, he had been storing it up for a while. Sheila was just worried that he might have recognised her. But he shouldn't have been there cheating on his wife anyway.

To Sheila's amazement, Edel shouted out, 'Is there anyone in the audience that would like to clean Sheila up?' There were lots of volunteers. Edel chose a young man with a large moustache. He asked if he could use his tongue, and Edel said, 'Why not.' His face was soon between Sheila's buttocks, licking away at her clit and fanny. She wondered why someone would want to lick up someone else's semen.

The young man was doing a great job. He knew where and how to lick a woman's body. He cheekily bit her clit, which made Sheila tingle all over. He nibbled her clit and bit it for a second time. 'Oh no,' she thought. A climax ripped through her body that almost knocked the young man out. Everyone cheered and stamped their feet while Sheila ran off the stage in a daze.

Jeff got dressed and found his seat. The other two lads congratulated him on his performance. 'To be honest,' he said, 'I was thinking of Wormy's wife, Sheila, at the time, and it got me hard and randy.' All three had fancied Sheila for some time.

They often went out as four couples, although none of them liked Wormy. Wormy was Sheila's husband's nickname. They did everything they could to leave him out. James said, 'Thinking about it, she does look a lot like Sheila, and she has the same name.' They all laughed at the impossibility.

Raz said, 'Sheila is too much of a lady to even think of going to a nightclub.'

Sheila sat down in the dressing room and had a quick cup of coffee. The other girls were all congratulating her on her performance. Sheila thought that there wasn't much she had to do, just let an ageing bloke fuck her onscreen and let a teenybopper lick her out. Nothing to it. She was just so glad that Jeff had not recognised her.

Edel entered the room and said, 'OK, ladies. Time for the second game. I think the audience enjoyed the first one.' They all looked at Sheila. Edel said, 'The second game is musical chairs with a difference. Five men from the audience will strip off, and you girls will be attached to them face to face. '

Jenny asked, 'What will we be wearing?'

Edel said, 'Your birthday suits. You will then play musical chairs as normal.'

The five volunteers were easily found. The men stripped off and paraded themselves around the room to much cheering and banter. Sheila was amazed to see how different their todgers were: big, small, long, limp, slightly erect, etc. Then she recognised one as James, 'Not the todger,' she laughed to herself, but the man. He was another friend of her husband's. She wondered if Raz was also there, but she couldn't spot him in the audience. She didn't think it was his sort of thing.

The tying together was hilarious. Leather straps were used to push breasts and chests together. Male and female genitals got to know each other quite well. The contestants had to work out how to walk together. Couples were falling over everywhere. The men in the audience were just killing themselves laughing. Sheila was not that amused because her partner was James. She thought, 'What are the chances of that?' She could already feel his erect penis resting against her thigh. She was worried that the mask might come off in the melee.

The game started with five chairs and five contestants dancing, or rather hobbling, around the room to the sound of Queen's 'Another One Bites the Dust'. One chair was removed, and the music stopped. Sheila and James managed to grab a chair, but in the process, James's cock entered her fanny and stayed there. Sheila looked at James through the mask, but what could she say? The music started again, and they got up. James lost interest in the game and just wanted to fuck Sheila. He pretended to play, but all his attention was focussed on one thing. He got his way and filled her little cunt up with sperm. They lost the game, but James won.

Edel helped them remove the leather straps and pulled James's cock out of Sheila's fanny, saying, 'Sheila, you are a very naughty girl.' Then she smacked her bottom. Sheila dashed upstairs to get cleaned up. James returned to his seat with a massive grin on his face.

The other men said, 'Why are you so happy, you lost?'

James replied that he'd won all right, and with a wink, he said, 'I gave her fanny a good seeing to.' They patted him on the back. James leaned back in his chair and said, 'She does remind me of Sheila, but it can't be.' They all agreed that it couldn't be the Sheila they knew.

The girl that had just got married won, and she received

the full video treatment. Her fanny was getting a heavy pounding from a slightly drunk biker who looked like he hadn't washed in months. He impressed everyone by drinking a pint of Guinness at the same time.

The last game was just a chase. The five girls would run around the disco floor naked, and whoever captured them could take them back to their table for dessert. After what she'd been through, Sheila didn't have much running in her, and Raz easily captured her. Sheila thought, 'Well, what do you know? He is here, after all.' Raz carried her back to his table and gently placed her on top of it.

Without saying a word, James and Jeff each grabbed a leg and pulled them slightly apart. Sheila's vagina was on view for everyone to see. Raz pulled his trousers and pants down to display a real man's erection. He outclassed both James and Jeff in length and girth. He spat on the end of it and entered Sheila, who could hardly breathe due to the size of it. It didn't take much pumping before he shot his load. They left Sheila there sprawled across the table. Edel came over, wiped Sheila's fanny and helped her back to the dressing room.

On the way back home, the boys discussed what a great evening they'd had. They were all very impressed with Sheila's body, which made going home to the wives a bit of an anti-climax. James said, 'I hope that Mary is not feeling randy tonight. Well, to be honest, I hope that she never feels randy again.'

Sheila got dressed and found her car. Once again, she had let the situation get the better of her, but she knew she enjoyed the limelight. The newly married girl was standing by her car, crying. She turned to Sheila and said, 'What have I done? I've let my husband down big time.'

Sheila said, 'He will never find out.'

The girl replied, 'I'm not so sure of that—that was my father-in-law who fucked me on stage!'

When Sheila got home, her husband asked her how it went. Sheila said, 'It was OK. I met up with a few old friends and had a fucking good time, although I think they may have taken advantage of me.'

A few days later, she met up with the wives of her recent lovers. One of them was complaining that her husband was no longer interested in sex. Apparently, he couldn't get it up if the Queen of Sheba had walked in stark naked. Sheila sat there thinking, 'If only you knew.'

Snow White: Part 1

Ken, who had previously been the manager of the Croydon Theatre, now had the job of producing a new X-rated pantomime being organised for the Christmas season at a club in Thorton Heath. He had previously employed Sheila as a fluffer and had used the opportunity to sample her charms on several occasions. He was eager to sample them again.

Sheila had passed the audition for a role in the production. She had no idea what part it was or how much she was going to get paid. All she knew was that it was X-rated, which generally meant that she wouldn't be keeping her knickers on for long. But after losing her previous job, she desperately needed the money. It wouldn't have been so critical if her useless husband hadn't been sacked as well. She also knew that there would be no way that she could keep Ken from fucking her. It had already happened quite a few times, and anyway, he certainly knew what he was doing. Her fanny started tingling just thinking about it.

Ken invited Sheila into his office. He couldn't help admiring her figure, with those fabulous legs, slim waist and gorgeous boobs. He knew Sheila's body well; he knew how to give her an orgasm. Just the thought of sliding into her soft, silky fanny was enough to provide him with a raging erection. They kissed each other's cheeks, and Ken organised some coffee for her in a bone china cup. Sheila appreciated the proper china cup and saucer, as she was a lady.

Ken turned to Sheila and said. 'I have a surprise for you. We would like you to play the part of Snow White.'

Sheila immediately said, 'But I don't have the skills or experience to play that sort of part.'

Ken said, 'With your bubbly personality and good looks, you won't have a problem. Anyway, half the audience will just be there to see you naked. We want to promote you as "The Girl Who Was Caught Onstage." We are, of course, referring to that unfortunate, but amusing incident, where you were naked on all fours, with one of the largest cocks I've ever seen, up your fanny.'

Sheila blushed because it had been so embarrassing. It wouldn't have been that bad if not for the photos. They were everywhere—in the papers and on TV. Even though they had been censored, it was still obvious what was going on. Sheila had seen one of the videos on the internet that showed everything in a fair amount of close-up detail. She probably had one of the most famous fannies in the world.

Sheila said that she wasn't sure if she could act the part. Ken said, 'Agree to the job, start the rehearsals and if it doesn't work out, you can leave without any penalties. I will make sure of that. Anyway, you need to know the fee structure before you decide.'

Sheila said, 'OK, give me the lowdown.'

Ken explained that there would be several contractual conditions but offered the following as a good outline:

£1,000 per week during rehearsals; there would be five shows per week for four weeks.

£2,000 per week for live shows; there would be five shows per week for eight weeks.

All expenses paid.

Full onstage nudity would be a must.

Conditions apply.

Sheila was speechless, which had never happened in her lifetime. The remuneration was serious; she had never been offered that sort of deal before. As far as she was concerned, it was life-changing. Sheila asked what the conditions were. Ken said, 'At the theatre, you carried out several personal services, and we would be looking for a similar range of services provided here.'

Sheila said, 'And who would receive these personal services?'

Ken said, 'Me, Chas, who is the club owner and also one of the actors, and a rota for the other actors if they are interested.'

Sheila said, 'The answer is no. I'm not a whore; it's just unacceptable.'

Ken said, 'We are here to agree to the terms, so let's negotiate. You have had sex with me on several occasions before, and that didn't seem to bother you too much.'

Sheila said, 'Well, Ken, I understand where you are coming from, but fluffing was different. I had to excite the actors so that they could perform on stage. Here, it is just straight sex for money.'

Ken said, 'That wasn't true regarding my position; you paid me in kind for finding you a job and for paying you a bonus.'

Sheila said, 'Well, to be honest, it just felt wrong leaving you out. I felt sorry for you.'

Ken said, 'It's the same situation here; I got you the job, and I fancy you so much, and of course there would be an extra payment every time someone entered your vagina.'

Sheila said, 'I'm still not sure, but exactly how much extra would it be?'

Ken said, '£200.'

Sheila said, 'And how often would you like to have sex with me?'

Ken said, 'Every day.'

Sheila said, 'Sorry, I meant how often would I have to do it with you?'

Ken said, 'How about once a week?'

Sheila's resolve was weakening, as the standard package would be £20,000 plus the contribution from Ken. Sheila asked if this would be for the full twelve weeks. Ken said it would. Sheila worked out that the new total would be £22,400. It was getting harder to resist.

Sheila realised that the whole deal hinged on this condition. The "little angel" on one shoulder said, 'Don't do it,' but the "little devil" on the other said, 'It's not like you have been as pure as snow.'

'More like "slush,"' she thought to herself. She was worried about how she would see herself in the future. How would it affect her self-esteem? But she had already fucked Ken a few times anyway, and it had all seemed innocent then.

While she was thinking about it, Ken said, 'And there are the other two conditions you need to think about. Firstly, there is Chas. He is the one you did the striptease for at the audition. You also let him finger your pussy. It's going to be hard saying no to him. If you don't agree, then the deal is probably off.'

Sheila asked how often she'd be expected to have sex with him. Ken suggested once a week. Sheila worked out that it would increase the total to £24,800. Ken could see that Sheila was wavering. He had a budget £40,000 for the star, so he still had room to manoeuvre.

Sheila asked who the other actors were. Ken said that there would be seven in total. He suggested that over the twelve weeks, each actor should have sex with her just once. If she agreed to more at a later date, then she would be paid more. Sheila worked out that a further seven would bring the total to £25,200. Her outstanding mortgage was £30,000. In her mind, she thought that if she could put up with this challenging situation, then she could get her mortgage paid off. Ken asked what her thinking was.

Sheila replied, 'I'm not sure. I'm happy to fuck you, and I'm reasonably happy to fuck Chas, as he was pretty good-looking, but I'm not sure about the others. It seems so clinical.'

Ken said, 'Let's ask the question differently. How much would it take for you to agree to go ahead?'

Without hesitation, Sheila said, '£30,000.'

Ken smiled to himself. He deliberately took his time to respond. He said, 'I'm willing to offer you £32,000 on the condition that I can interview your fanny now.'

Sheila stood up and pulled her knickers down, asking, 'And where would you like the interview to take place?' Ken said in the McDonald's across the street.

They caught the lift down, but Ken seemed to think that the lift controls were under Sheila's skirt as he kept pushing her little button. By the time they'd reached the bottom, Sheila's bottom was ready for action. They walked briskly across the road to McDonald's. Sheila could feel a draft around her private parts. They ordered two Big Macs.

Ken found a quiet corner, pulled his erect penis out of his trousers and beckoned Sheila to sit on him. Sheila was mortified, but she did what she was told. With a little bit of difficulty, she managed to force his cock into her tight little fanny. It was an awkward position to be in to try and get any real movement going, but Ken was enjoying the feeling that his 'cock had been captured.' His cock was being held firmly in place by one of the strongest muscles in Sheila's body—her vagina.

Sheila took some bites out of the burger and did her best to fuck Ken at the same time. In fact, she managed to synchronise the burger biting and the fucking. She was beginning to enjoy the situation, but she also wanted to get it over quickly before they got caught. They had already had some strange looks, especially from a young lady who was wiping the tables down.

Sheila increased her biting and was thinking that she might have to start on Ken's burger when two young lads walked by and said, 'We know what you are doing.' Sheila tried to close her legs as they started looking under the table. Sheila took decisive action and forcefully pushed herself up and then down very hard. She did this twice. The second one did the job as she felt an intense ejaculation in her fanny. She quickly stuck a burger in Ken's mouth to keep him quiet. They very quickly made their exit.

The moral of this story is that a burger in the mouth is worth two in the bush.

Sheila was excited that she'd won a role in the pantomime and that their mortgage would be paid off, but her fanny was going to take a bit of a bashing. At home, her husband asked how her day went. She said that she thought she'd been burgered.

Snow White: Part 2

The day of the first rehearsal soon came around. Sheila wasn't sure what to expect, and she wasn't really too sure what had sparked it off, but the day had already started badly. Every now and then, Sheila would have the loudest sneeze imaginable— very loud. People had taken shelter in the past, thinking it might have been a bomb. Imagine the loudest sneeze you have ever heard, quadruple it and then add some.

Sheila arrived at the small, seedy club in Thorton Heath in her best clothes. As a 'star,' she wanted to make the right impression, and she did. Chas was there to meet her, and she was as beautiful as he'd remembered her from the audition. Chas was looking forward to using the facilities, but he needed to make sure that his wife was out of the picture. Sheila thought it strange that sometime this week, this man, who was a stranger, would be inside her. She thought, 'Isn't life strange?' as they entered the dressing room.

Sheila was introduced to Hazel, who was a stunning blonde. She was playing the part of the Evil Queen. Sheila wondered if she had the same contractual conditions. Would Chas be in her fanny later today? Sheila felt strangely competitive. The first scene was going to be the one where the Evil Queen asks, 'Mirror, mirror on the wall, who is the fairest of them all?'

Chas explained that as it was going to be the first scene in the pantomime, he wanted it to have a strong visual impact. Both girls would be stark naked on different pedestals on the stage. Hazel would stand in front of the mirror and deliver the famous line. A spotlight would flash from one actress to the other, and eventually, it would land on Sheila. Hazel would then appear to be furious. Sheila would have no idea what had just happened.

Sheila asked if the area would be cleared for the scene. Chas looked at her and said, 'No chance, this is a working club. The staff here are used to nudity. Just get on with it. Now please get undressed as we are waiting for you.' The two girls unpeeled. Chas stayed to watch. Sheila was soon in the buff, displaying a great pair of legs, an ample bosom and an adorable little bum. Chas thought that she was definitely the right choice for Snow White and the right choice for him. He was certainly looking forward to giving that pussy a bit of a seeing to.

Hazel was also a very pretty girl. She had a great figure. Her stomach seemed to flow nicely into her hips, highlighting her fanny. Sheila also noted that she was a natural blonde. She wondered if Chas preferred blondes or brunettes. Again, she was having competitive thoughts. 'I bet I'm a better fuck than her,' she thought.

They were soon on the pedestals at different ends of the stage. There had been several wolf whistles and a few attempts to pinch her bum. Both girls stood there stark naked, showing off all their charms. Chas asked them to turn, to put their hands up, to bend over, etc. It was partly to add effect but mostly to titillate the audience. All of the crew, including Chas, were titillated. The spotlight flashed back and forth and ended up on Sheila, as per the plan. The bright light meant that no part of her body was hidden, especially not when Chas asked her to bend over.

Hazel was duly furious. She, as the Evil Queen, ordered the Huntsman to take Sheila out to the forest and kill her. She told him to bring back her underwear as proof that the job had been completed.

Chas congratulated the girls on a job well done and said that Hazel could go home as she was not needed anymore that day. The next scene involved the Huntsman, who was going to be played by Chas. He had to take Snow White into the forest. The Evil Queen had instructed him to kill her and bring back her clothes, but as this was an X-rated pantomime, he planned to take her clothes, rape her and then kill her. It's not that the Huntsman was evil; he just thought it would be a waste not to take advantage of her as she was going to die anyway. Of course, in the end, he can't kill Snow White, and Sheila escapes in the nude.

Chas explained that onstage, he would chase Sheila around, gradually ripping her clothes off. He would then pin her down and simulate a rape. Afterwards, he would feel so guilty that he would send her away. Chas asked if she had any questions. Sheila asked in what position she was going to be raped. Chas said, 'Let's see how it goes; we might have to test out several positions.'

On the stage, the Huntsman was marching Snow White through the forest. Sheila was wearing special "easily rippable" clothes comprised of a dress, panties and bra. She was struggling to keep them on. The Huntsman turned to Snow White and said, 'Take your clothes off.'

Snow White said, 'Sorry, Mr Huntsman, I couldn't do that. I'm a good little girl.'

The Huntsman said, 'Take them off now, or I will do it.'

Snow White said, 'My Mummy said that I mustn't let a man take my clothes off unless I'm married to him, and even then, only in the dark.'

The Huntsman said, 'This is your last chance.' Snow White ran around the stage.

The Huntsman lunged at her, and her dress came off. Snow White was screaming, but it was hopeless. The Huntsman was far too strong, and after some pretend chasing and fighting, Snow White was soon nude. Sheila was quickly on her back, and the Huntsman was between her legs. Sheila was egging him on to fuck her, but Chas was holding back. Sheila manoeuvred her fanny in such a way that it was nearly impossible for him to miss. His cock was at her enticing entrance, but he withdrew before any contact was made.

He quickly picked Snow White up and turned her around so that she was on all fours. Snow White was ready for the taking. Chas made sure that his cock went over the top of Sheila's fanny or underneath it, but not inside. Sheila was getting more and more frustrated. Perhaps he doesn't fancy me, but his cock is saying something else. It was hard and already leaking pre-cum. Chas suddenly said, 'Well, I think that pretty well covers the rehearsal for today.' He then explained that at that point in the show, Snow White runs offstage and eventually finds the dwarfs' house.

Sheila and Chas walked back to the dressing room stark naked. Sheila opened the dressing room door only to be confronted with seven naked dwarfs. Sheila screamed in surprise as they were all running around. They each had a voucher to fuck her once, which they brandished. They thought that they would wait for her and get the job done.

Sheila thought that it was a bit like a scene from Time Bandits, except they weren't wearing any clothes. Sheila noticed that they were little men, but their wedding tackle certainly wasn't. She had never seen so many erections in one room before, including Chas's.

Chas said, 'Gentlemen, I am the owner of this club, and consequently, I have first dibs.' He looked at Sheila and said, 'Come here, you little minx,' and kissed her on the lips. 'Now, lie on the bed face down.' Sheila complied and laid on her stomach with her legs slightly apart. Her breasts were being squashed and pushed sideways so that only the edges were on display.

Sheila half assumed that he was going to take her anally. Chas turned to the dwarfs and said that he would like some privacy. The dwarfs each asked if they could stay and watch. Chas reluctantly agreed. He couldn't waste any more time as he had to get home to his wife.

Chas liked his women in this position. It made him feel dominant. He had no intention of going for the anus; he was strictly a fanny man. The other advantage was that penetration was deep—very deep. He could get some serious todgering done.

He put some lubricating gel on his penis and sat on Sheila's bum. He admired her curves and the softness of her skin. He had been looking forward to fucking her for some time. He couldn't believe how hard she had got him on stage; he'd nearly come then.

Chas prised Sheila's lovely buttocks apart to expose her inner sanctum. The folds of her labia were gently pushed apart, and he positioned his cock at the entrance of her vagina. He then relished the prolonged entry into her opening, almost centimetre by centimetre. He gradually eased his entire engorged cock into that little pussy. He savoured the smoothness, suppleness and silkiness of her most private part. In many ways, he was a romantic at heart. He'd always appreciated the fact that a woman was allowing him to enjoy her body.

Chas, in many ways, was too gentle. Sheila desperately wanted a good, hard fuck. She wanted his cock to really todger her. She was going to be disappointed as Chas came on his second thrust. He came so hard that he wondered if he could maintain consciousness. Chas withdrew, patted Sheila's bum and left.

Sheila laid there feeling quite frustrated and surrounded by five gaggling dwarfs. She wondered where Sneezy was. Then she found out. His cock was suddenly deep in her pussy. She thought, 'Cheeky little bastard.' But actually, it was just what she needed—a hard, vigorous, no-nonsense fuck. However, at the same time, she could feel two things stirring: her orgasm and one of her massive sneezes. She wasn't sure which was going to come first.

For a small man, Sneezy knew how to fuck. There was no holding him back. Then it happened—Sheila had a delightful orgasm, and all the tensions of the day disappeared. Then it happened—Sheila had her almighty sneeze. Sheila's vaginal muscles contracted in unison with the sneeze. Sneezy literally flew into the air with a trail of semen following him.

Apart from the bruises and mild concussion, Sneezy thought that it was the best fuck of his life.

Sheila thought it was somewhat ironic that Sneezy suffered the 'big sneeze experience.' Sheila told the other dwarfs that they would have to wait for another day. That made

Happy grumpy, but Grumpy just carried on being grumpy.

When Sheila got home, her husband asked her how her day went. She said that there had been a few small problems that she had to fix, but that most of the staff whistled while they worked.

Snow White: Part 3

Sheila turned up for the second day of rehearsals. She wondered what joys that was going to bring. On the first day, she had spent much of her time walking around the club stark naked to a cacophony of wolf whistles. She was displayed under a spotlight, suffered the indignity of a simulated rape on stage, had sex with the club owner and was then ravished by a dwarf. 'All in a day's work,' she thought, and then her waste of skin husband had the audacity to ask how her day went.

Wormy, her husband, was in bed when she left to go to work. He wasn't even making an effort to find a job. Here she was, giving everything to put a meal on the table. She felt annoyed about everything and decided that she was going to kill her husband if he asked her tonight how her day went.

Chas was waiting for her. He gave her a quick peck on the cheek. Sheila thought that that was a change from the day before when he'd had his big cock up her fanny. She was also annoyed with him, as he had made no effort to look after her needs. But then she thought, 'Why should he?' She was just meat to put on stage for his pathetic pantomime. She decided to move on and smiled broadly, which lit up the stage. She told Chas that she was really looking forward to the rehearsal.

Chas said, 'We have got to the point where Snow White has been left in the woods by the Huntsman. She has been raped but not killed. She was fleeing when she found the dwarfs' cottage.' He turned to Sheila and said, 'We need you to strip off and go into woods.' As practically everyone had already seen her naked, she stripped off by the stage. She still managed to create a bit of an audience. There was ogling from all quarters.

Chas decided that he wanted a bit more of that, but he needed to make sure that his wife was out of the way. Sheila managed to get on the stage with the help of a passing handyman, who had a very close look at her bits and then patted her bum. Sheila ran around the stage with her boobs bouncing everywhere, and surprise, surprise, she found the dwarf's empty cottage.

Sheila went in and ate some of the tiny meals and drank wine from some tiny glasses. As per the script, she found one of the tiny beds, which wasn't so tiny, and fell asleep. Then seven naked dwarfs walked across the stage singing, 'Whistle While You Work.' They weren't entirely naked; they had hard hats, boots and pickaxes, and in some cases, a hard erection. They discovered that their food and drink had been consumed. Then they found a beautiful naked woman in their bed.

Snow White woke up to lots of jumping and hysterical dwarfs. She thought it was a classic case of over-acting, but then their cocks weren't acting—they were armed and ready. Sheila could see what was going to happen next.

Snow White explained her predicament. The dwarfs said that she could stay with them in return for providing them with certain services. Sheila knew what they wanted, but Snow White didn't. Snow White said, 'Gentlemen, I could cook, clean and sew for you all.'

Grumpy said, 'We know, but that's not what we want.'

Snow White said, 'I could do the gardening, make the

beds and do your washing.'

Happy said, 'We know, but that's not what we want.'

Snow White said, 'I could do the ironing, make scrumptious pies and read you bedtime stories.'

Doc said, 'We know, but that's not what we want.'

Snow White said, 'Well, what do you want?' Sneezy said that men, even small men, have certain needs. Snow White said, 'Like food and drink?'

Sneezy said, 'In a way, but these are more personal needs.'

Snow White said, 'The Huntsman said that he had needs as well. He pulled my knickers down and put his truncheon into my private parts. Are you saying that you want to do that as well?'

Seven dwarfs nodded in unison. Snow White said, 'Well, I don't think that should be a problem,' and the seven dwarfs jumped on her. She was covered in a sea of dwarfs. They were licking and chewing every bit of Sheila's body. Both nipples were being enthusiastically sucked, and her bottom was being lifted. Doc took his glasses off and entered Sheila's fanny. It felt like a fine cock, but should he be doing this onstage in a rehearsal?

Chas walked over and said that while he appreciated the authenticity, he didn't think they should be doing it now. Sneezy said, 'Well, you had her yesterday.' Chas motioned for him to be quiet as his wife might still be around. Doc just continued with his fucking of Sheila. She was finding it hard listening to Chas with all the squelching noises. That generally meant that she was quite wet and not far off an orgasm.

Doc came noisily and said, 'By gum, I needed that.'

While Chas was still talking, Happy jumped on the bandwagon. Well, he jumped on Sheila. Her legs were still wide open from the last encounter. Happy didn't mind sloppy seconds, and he was soon on the job. Sheila could tell that he wouldn't last long. She wasn't far off herself. It was a competition to see who would come first. Happy won. He had a massive smile on his face and said, 'Thank you, Sheila,' and jumped off.

Chas said to the dwarfs, 'We can't have this sort of behaviour onstage. We may be an X-rated pantomime, but this is taking things too far.' Sheila was still on her back, listening to Chas when she felt someone pushing her from the side. They were small men, but they were strong. Bashful had a cute, rosy face with a small, shy smile. He had manoeuvred Sheila into a position where he could enter her from the side.

And enter her, he did. He may have been bashful, but he had a large cock. He was soon ploughing away to the point where the bed started moving. Chas gave him a filthy look, but Bashful just carried on. Sheila was sure that he was whistling 'Off to Work We Go.' It might be work for Sheila, but it was undoubtedly pleasure for the little dwarf. Sheila's orgasm was growing again, but Bashful proved that he wasn't, and he filled her up. She could feel the force of his ejaculation.

Sheila had reached the stage where she needed finishing off, but who was left? In her mind, she worked out that it was Dopey, Grumpy, Sneezy and Sleepy—not the best of the bunch. Sneezy wasn't showing any interest, but he probably hadn't recovered from the day before.

Chas said, 'After the simulated gang-bang, you dwarfs, go off to work again. The Evil Queen then does her "Mirror, mirror on the wall" routine and finds out that Snow White is still alive. She comes into the forest and sells Snow White a poisoned comb. Are you all listening?' It was clear that they weren't. They were watching Doc.

Doc, who was the leader, was pushing Dopey towards Sheila. He told him that it was his chance to lose his virginity. Dopey was pushed onto the bed. He sat in front of Sheila's legs and was trying to build up the courage to approach her when he suddenly came. A huge spurt of cum covered Sheila. Doc was very apologetic. Dopey just ran off.

Sleepy rushed over with a towel to help clean Sheila up. Sheila thought, 'What a nice guy,' but then she noticed that he was spending far too much time cleaning her boobs. She felt that she might as well get it over and done with and opened her legs wide. Sleepy rightly took this as an invitation and entered Sheila's cute little pussy. He was still on the job when he rested his head on her boobs. He had fallen fast asleep with his cock still in her pussy. 'The shame of it,' she thought. To be honest, it wasn't the first time that had happened to her. Wormy had nodded off on more than one occasion.

Chas came over and picked Sleepy up. Sheila could feel the 'plop' as Sleepy's cock departed from her fanny. Sheila looked at Grumpy, who looked grumpy. He cried, 'I can't get it up,' and ran off. Suddenly, they all knew why he was called Grumpy.

Chas said that it was lunchtime, and the dwarfs left the stage. Chas apologised for the dwarfs' behaviour and said that it wasn't planned in any way. He asked Sheila if she was OK. She said that she was fine, but she desperately needed an orgasm. Chas said that he could help her out there. He pulled the curtain across the stage and pulled his cock out of his flies.

Despite all the dwarf action, Sheila looked fantastic. She was lying down with her arms holding her slightly up. Her fanny was fully exposed but very moist. Her gorgeous legs were just so welcoming. He couldn't help noticing the curvaceous nature of her body, and especially her breasts. He was going to enjoy fucking this beautiful woman.

He crept towards her and gently entered her sweet-smelling cunt. Sheila was ready and came immediately. A large, hard cock from a real looker was too much for her. She convulsed and contracted, extracting every last inch of pleasure. What a day!

Then Hazel appeared and said, 'Is this how you incentivise your staff?'

Sheila thought, 'What nerve.'

Hazel started crying and said, 'That is no way to treat your wife. It's only been a few weeks since the honeymoon.'

It was ultimately decided that Sheila wasn't the right person to play the part of Snow White after all—Hazel was. She got some compensation before being let go, but not enough to pay off her mortgage.

When Sheila got home, her husband asked her how her day went. She said that seven dwarfs had fucked her. Her husband laughed, but he soon stopped laughing when she attacked him with a baseball bat. He survived the ordeal, but only just.

Snow White: Part 4

Ken, the theatre agent, asked if Sheila could come to his office the next day as he had a proposal for her. This was quite exciting news as she desperately needed the money. It was even more urgent now that Wormy had left her for a friend of hers. It had been a terrible surprise—more of a shock really—but in some ways, she was now a free agent. She had been so loyal to him; she had looked after all his needs for years. Well, she thought she had, but life does throw some curveballs at you occasionally.

She put her sexiest underwear on, as there was every chance that Ken would want to take advantage of her. That was one of the downsides of having an agent like Ken. It cost you a lot to get a job. She arrived on time, as she always did, and a young secretary shuffled her into Ken's office. The secretary's skirt was so tight that she could hardly move her legs. Ken was there waiting for her. They kissed each other's cheeks, and Ken managed to squeeze her breast in the process. 'Dirty bugger,' Sheila thought, but she had been expecting it.

They sat down on each side of the desk, and Ken said, 'There is a strong possibility of you getting your old pantomime job back.'

Sheila said, 'Do you mean the part of Snow White?'

Ken said, 'Yes, that's right.'

Sheila said, 'But I thought, Hazel, Chas's wife, was now

playing that part.'

Ken said, 'That's true, but it hasn't gone well, and she wants out.'

Sheila was all ears. 'Tell me about it.'

Ken explained that the sales figures were not doing too well. The usual crowd was turning up to see a naked girl on stage since it was always a crowd puller. And Hazel was a very attractive girl. Sheila had to agree; she was a real stunner. Chas was a lucky man. But Hazel didn't have any stage presence, which is hard to quantify. She was not the type of girl who was caught being shagged on stage at the Croydon Theatre. They both laughed as they could now see the funny side of it.

'Ken said, 'So, that's the first problem. Chas thinks having you back in the role will bring the crowds in.' Ken said that he happened to agree. He was looking forward to seeing Sheila naked again.

'The second problem is that Hazel doesn't like having all these dirty old men leering at her onstage, especially when it comes to the Huntsman scene where Chas is raping her. Obviously, they don't have to hold back as they are husband and wife. So Chas is giving her one in front of five hundred people. Apparently, it is affecting their sex life, but I haven't heard Chas complaining. Thirdly, it is the dwarfs. They have taken advantage of Hazel on several occasions.'

Sheila said, 'But that is their job.'

Ken said, 'Well, so far Sneezy, Doc and Happy have accidentally put their cocks in her fanny.'

Sheila said, 'That can easily happen when you have lots of naked people on stage.'

Ken said, 'Well, Hazel wants to avoid having all seven— she thinks they are playing a game to achieve that.' Sheila thought that was probably the case. 'Chas now has the moral high ground. He fucked you accidentally.'

Sheila said, 'It was hardly an accident!'

Ken said slowly, 'You don't understand. It was an accident—wasn't it?' Sheila cottoned on and nodded her head. 'Now, Hazel was accidentally fucked by three men. From Chas's perspective, that is three to one. But Hazel argued that the dwarfs only counted as one and a half men. Anyway, Chas and Hazel are prepared to offer you your job back on the same terms, except that you must agree not to fuck Chas.'

Sheila said, 'In that case, do we remove the clause that gives Chas the right to fuck me?' Ken said that Chas wanted it left in. 'And will you still be requiring my services?' Sheila asked. Ken said that he would, but today he thought a little suck would be enough as his secretary had already relieved him. Sheila thought, 'What a bitch.' She needed a good seeing to after Wormy's departure.

Sheila pulled her knickers down, lifted her skirt and sat on Ken's desk. He approached Sheila's side of the desk and started licking away at her fanny. He knew how to perform cunnilingus. He started slowly licking all her private parts before focussing on her clitoris. Ken imagined that her clit was an ice cream cone and licked up one side, spent a fair amount of time on the hood, then licked down the other side. He repeated this over and over again; he knew that women's bodies liked steady stimulation.

Sheila's body was responding well. Ken knew the signs. Sheila was gently moaning, her thighs were pressing against his head, and her hands started pulling his hair. Sheila was getting very damp, and her hips were beginning to gyrate. Ken knew that it was time for penetration. He slowly inserted his finger into Sheila's fanny, and at the same time, he started to suck her clit. He then used strong, firm strokes, pushing his finger in and out of her fanny.

Sheila's body went for it. Her orgasm ripped through her body, making her back arch in abandonment. That was just what she needed. The secretary who had brought some coffee into the room clapped and said that she would like some of that. In all honesty, it was Ken's skill at love-making. He was the best.

Sheila thanked Ken for his good deeds. Ken said that he had heard that Wormy had left her for another woman. Sheila said that she couldn't understand why, as she had been so faithful for all these years. Ken intimated that she had not been that faithful, as he had fucked her quite a few times. Sheila looked at him, aghast. Sheila said, 'Ken, you are confusing work with life. I may have had the odd cock up my fanny, but that was business. Here we are talking about an affair; an act of deceit.' She didn't think Ken understood. Ken had no idea what she was talking about.

It was arranged for Sheila to go to the Pantomime venue the next day to meet Chas and Hazel. Sheila was nervous for obvious reasons. Chas met her at reception, but he shook her hand instead of kissing her on the cheek. Sheila understood, but she was still a little hurt as they had shared so much in the past. Hazel soon joined them, and they discussed the way forward over a cup of coffee. It was nice that Sheila was given a bone china cup and saucer, as she was a lady.

In some ways, they managed to patch up their differences. Hazel didn't want to be Snow White, but mostly she didn't want Sheila and Chas to have sexual intercourse. She didn't mind them carrying out a simulated rape as long as the

Huntsman didn't enter Sheila's fanny. It was as simple as that—the show goes on but no todgering. Sheila was happy with that.

Chas said, 'It will be difficult during the rape scene to avoid our two sexual organs touching each other.' Hazel said that she didn't mind touching, but she objected to full penetration. She asked them both if they understood. Both nodded, but Chas said, 'I understand the principle, but it would be very easy for penetration to happen by accident, it's what nature intended.'

Hazel said, 'That is why we are going to have some practice sessions now to see how it can be avoided, aren't we?' Both nodded.

Sheila and Chas stripped off. Chas couldn't help admiring Sheila's naked body. She certainly had that X-factor that Hazel lacked. He really wanted to fuck her again. Sheila couldn't help noticing Chas's erect chopper; the fact that it was out of bounds made her want it even more. She decided that she had to behave as she needed the job. There were already several members of staff who just happened to be passing by while ogling them at the same time. This included a number of new starters. She thought that one of them looked a bit like Wormy.

Sheila laid on the stage floor, which happened to have a mattress built into it. Hazel told her to open her legs wide, which she did, exposing all of her charms. Hazel then told Chas to get on top, which he was quite happy to do. Hazel told Chas to make sure that his cock maintained a vertical movement, effectively going up and down. It would rub against the outside of Sheila's vagina but not go in. She told Chas to practise this movement, and he lifted himself up and down.

Chas's prick was sliding down Sheila's body, hitting her clitoris on the way, and stopping just past her anus. It was effectively going vertically between her legs. Sheila was rather enjoying it as it provided a lot of clitoral stimulation. Hazel then told Chas to start the raping. As soon as he started simulating it, his penis was pushed forward towards Sheila's fanny. Hazel grabbed his cock just before penetration was achieved. Hazel gave Chas a dirty look. Apparently, he wasn't trying hard enough.

Sheila suggested that she could wear flesh-coloured knickers. Hazel said that they couldn't do that because it was an X-rated show. This time, Hazel told Chas to push under Sheila's bum during the rape scene. They started with the vertical approach first, which was now over-stimulating Sheila's entire vagina. Things were getting very damp and musky. As things were getting a bit fruity, Hazel decided to put her hand over Sheila's fanny to stop any penetration.

Chas was pushing his cock against the back of Hazel's hand and then towards Sheila's bum. Sheila wasn't interested in anal sex, but she could see it happening if things carried on as they are. The pressure of Chas's todgering was pushing Hazel's fingers into Sheila's pussy. Sheila thought that was rather strange. She had the wife's two fingers in her fanny while the husband was rubbing his cock against the back of her hand on a journey towards anal penetration. She thought, 'I bet that Wormy has never tried this.'

Hazel wasn't going to let Chas anally fuck Sheila, so she turned her hand around. Hazel was now effectively holding her husband's cock in her hand; but unfortunately, the pressure of Chas's todgering caused the tip of his cock to enter Sheila's cunt. Chas wasn't too sure what was going on and who was doing what to whom.

Hazel managed to retrieve her husband's cock and said nothing about penetration having been achieved. Hazel then suggested that they should try a different position. Sheila got on all fours. In this position, she could see the crowd of admirers watching. One of them definitely looked like Wormy, but his hair was different.

Chas stood behind Sheila with his large, erect cock proudly displayed in front of him. Sheila couldn't help wriggling her bum as it made the crowd cheer. Hazel said that his cock needed to go over the top of Sheila's bum or way underneath. Either way, he must miss the fanny. Hazel asked if he understood, and he nodded.

Chas walked up to Sheila. His cock was already touching her bum. He aimed and pushed forward. Sheila's whole lower region was slippery, and his cock slipped and buried itself deep inside Sheila's little treasure chest. Hazel shouted at him to get it out. He gave Sheila two or three small thrusts and withdrew. Hazel was not a "happy bunny", which amused Sheila. Sheila thought, 'If looks could kill, then Chas would definitely be dead by now.'

Chas took a second run at it. What are the chances of scoring a second bull? Hazel just screamed, 'You bastard,' and ran off. Chas decided that since he had started, he might as well continue, but then he thought better of it. He withdrew and ran after Hazel.

An elderly man came over and offered Sheila his hanky. She said, 'Thank you, Wormy. You look different with a wig on.'

Wormy said, 'I didn't expect to see so much of you here.'

Sheila said, 'Well, I need a job now you have gone. I need

something where I can express myself.' Wormy asked if they could have a coffee sometime.

The moral of the story is: "The early bird catches the Wormy".

Snow White: Part 5

Sheila wasn't too sure if she still had a job or not. She had promised Hazel that she wouldn't have sexual intercourse with her husband. It certainly wasn't her fault that Chas, Hazel's husband, took advantage of Sheila, and not for the first time. She decided that the consequences would become clear later on that day.

It was also embarrassing that Sheila's estranged husband had seen her having unrestrained sex onstage, in multiple positions, while a large audience looked on. It would have been better if she hadn't egged the crowd on by wriggling her bum. What if he tells the children?

She also wondered if she was going to get paid for the day. If Hazel had her way, then there was no chance of that happening, but Sheila had done exactly as instructed. She decided that she needed cheering up, so she got dressed and went off to see her seven little friends.

She knocked on the dressing room door and entered to find seven naked dwarfs. She wondered if they ever wore clothes. She was dragged in, and within seconds, her skirt was off, and her knickers were down. The little men had not wasted any time. As she stood there, Happy was licking away at her fanny. He was just the right height to get the job done. At the other end, Doc was rubbing his cock up and down the crack of her arse.

Sheila said, 'Now, come on. I've popped in to see you. I'm not here to look after your sexual needs.'

Doc said, 'Since you have been away, we have been celibate.'

Sheila said, 'I heard that three of you fucked Hazel.'

Doc said, 'Not really; we were playing a game to see who could fuck the bitch first.'

Sheila said, 'You don't seem too keen on her.'

Doc said, 'Not really; she is a jumped-up stripper who used to throw it about a lot. She is such a snob now. She made it very clear that she had no time for us. As far as she is concerned, we are scum. So we decided to get our revenge.'

Sheila asked, 'What did you do?'

Doc said, 'As you know, during the house scene, it's absolute bedlam. Snow White is lying on the bed naked. The dwarfs come home and find her. After some banter, we all jump on top of her. She was fighting us off, but one of us accidentally entered her fanny. We did an excellent job of making it look accidental—well, we are actors, you know. I got in first.'

Sheila said, 'You usually do, but then again, you are the leader.'

Doc then said, 'Happy managed an unfortunate accident the next day. She seemed to be enjoying it at first, but then suddenly she ejected him. Sneezy also had a successful penetration. It has been good fun, although it looks like it has finished if you are coming back.' Sheila said she wasn't sure if she still had a job or not, and that it was probably down to Hazel.

Doc said, 'There is every chance that you will keep the job as she doesn't want another dwarf up her. It's Bashful's turn next.'

Sheila said, 'You are all very naughty dwarfs, but it sounds like you had a lot of fun.'

Doc said, 'Bashful was wondering if he could have sex with you instead.'

Sheila said, 'It is tempting, but I can't just have sex with anyone who wants it. If it were part of the act, then it would be a different matter. I don't want to be seen as an easy lay.'

Doc said, 'You had sex with Ken, and you had sex with Chas. Are you saying that you don't want sex with Bashful because he is a dwarf?'

Sheila felt that she was being pushed into an awkward position, so she just said, 'OK,' and laid on the sofa with her arms in a welcoming embrace. Bashful was the smallest of the dwarfs but not in the trouser department. He shyly crept around the sofa and gingerly got on top of Sheila. She wasn't sure what to expect, especially as he did not attempt foreplay. While he was doing his business, there was a knock on the door.

In walked Wormy with his toolbox. He just stared at Sheila being fucked by a two-footer with a nine-incher. That was about three and a half feet shorter than him and seven inches longer. He couldn't believe that he had seen his wife being fucked by two different men on the same day. He wondered how long this had been going on.

Bashful carried on fucking regardless. To be honest, Sheila was beginning to enjoy performing in front of her audience, well Wormy, and she laid it on thick. She moaned and groaned, gyrated and convulsed. She shouted, 'Bashful, you are the best.' This gave Bashful a lot of confidence, and he started performing better. Wormy just stood there looking flabbergasted.

Bashful started fucking like a stallion—hard, forceful and relentless. He was a satyr. Sheila's body was genuinely reacting; her orgasm was growing, and the room had a strong musky odour. Everyone in the room was impressed by a couple who knew how to copulate. Sheila could feel that Bashful was almost there, and she wanted it to be a particularly good show to spite Wormy. Sheila contracted her pelvis and pushed hard against Bashful's cock, which was far too much for him. Sheila hadn't orgasmed, but she pretended to. There were shouts and screams; the dwarfs all clapped.

Wormy said to an exhausted Sheila, 'Don't forget that it would be good for us to have a coffee together.'

The other dwarfs asked Sheila if they could have some love. Sheila looked at them all and said, 'No.'

Doc said, 'You had sex with Ken, and you had sex with Chas. Are you saying that you don't want to have sex with us because we are dwarfs?'

Sheila smiled and said, 'That line only works once. I'm off the clock. I've got to find a job.'

However, Sheila couldn't find her skirt or knickers. In disgust, she walked out of the dressing room as she was. She thought it was only a short walk to the car. On the way out the door, Chas shouted after her, 'Where are you going?'

Sheila said, 'I assume that I'm no longer required.'

Chas said, 'Come over here,' and he gestured for her to sit on his lap. She obliged, even though she was knickerless. He said, 'I've had a word with Hazel, and she agrees that you were innocent in today's events. To be honest, she just can't handle those dwarfs. I'm not sure if you know, but they tried to rape her. If it weren't for the money we have invested in the show,

I would sack them all.'

Sheila said, 'Does that mean I've still got the job?'

Chas pulled his plonker out of his trousers and lifted Sheila slightly so he could ease it into her fanny. Sheila didn't object as she was still waiting for an answer. Chas said, 'I'm still thinking about it.' Sheila knew precisely what he meant. She lifted herself and lowered herself down so that his cock was as far into her cunt as possible. She lifted herself again and used all her weight to fall hard onto his todger. He found it slightly painful but exhilarating.

Sheila continued lifting and lowering. Halfway through, Chas said, 'It is looking like you have still got the job.' Sheila clenched her vaginal muscles and pushed hard against his stiff todger. It was too much for him, and he shot his load. Wormy walked over for the second time that day with a hanky in hand. Chas said, 'Sheila, you are Snow White, and walked off with the hanky.

Wormy said, 'Sheila, do you want these?' Sheila took her knickers and skirt back. Wormy said, 'Shall we have that coffee now?' Sheila drove Wormy around to the local coffee house.

Sheila looked at Wormy and said, 'How could you have an affair with Glennis?'

Wormy said, 'I can't explain it; perhaps I was having a mid-life crisis.'

Sheila said, 'At your age?'

Wormy said, 'I know. Anyway, how can you talk? You have been fucked three times today—once by a dwarf!'

Sheila said, 'What have you got against dwarfs?'

Wormy said, 'Nothing; but it doesn't matter. The important thing is that I love you, I miss you, and I want to come home. I really can't carry on without you.'

Sheila said, 'Glennis has thrown you out, hasn't she?'

Wormy said, 'Yes.'

Sheila said, 'Sorry, Wormy; you are on your own. You can fuck off.'

Sheila skipped on her way back to the car; she had a job, she could pay her mortgage off, and she had got rid of the tosser she was married to.

Sheila now had a 'Wormy-eyed view of the world.'

Snow White: Part 6

Sheila had finished her Christmas season as Snow White to rapturous applause; it had been a great success. She had a relatively realistic view of life and knew that the acclaim had less to do with her great acting ability and more to do with her pussy. There was no doubt that a large part of the audience came just to see her being fucked on stage. That was never her original intention, but at least her mortgage had been paid off. Things were looking up.

She had a meeting planned with Ken to agree to the final payment. She pretty well knew that she wouldn't get out of his office without a good seeing to. It seemed to be the way that business was done, and she was looking forward to it anyway.

Sheila arrived at Ken's office on time, as usual. They kissed each other's cheeks, as usual. Ken managed to stroke her bum as part of the process, as usual, and they got down to business. It was the last two weeks that needed sorting out as some bonus payments had already been paid, but not enough.

Ken said, 'Let's go through the contract details for the personal services rendered. It says that Chas and I can use your vagina once a week and that there would be a rota for the dwarfs; is that correct?'

Sheila nodded and said, 'That's right, but it's not how it turned out.' Ken suggested that they look at each clause separately, and Sheila agreed.

Ken asked, 'Did Chas use the facilities in the last two weeks?'

Sheila answered, 'Yes, seventeen times.'

Ken said, 'Never.'

Sheila said, 'It was definitely seventeen times; he fucked me during every performance—that's fourteen times.'

Ken said, 'Are you saying he entered your vagina onstage every night in a row?'

Sheila said, 'Absolutely. He liked to bend me over this large artificial stone, he then spread my legs as far as possible so the audience could get a good look, and then took me to huge applause.' Ken asked if he came. Sheila said, 'Every time.'

Ken asked about the other three penetrations. Sheila said, 'Those three were during rehearsals; he liked to be as realistic as possible.'

Ken said, 'Didn't Hazel mind?'

Sheila replied, 'At first she did, as you know, but she was pleased to get out of the play, and that was the price she had to pay. I think she worked him hard to stop any additional extra-curricular activities.'

Ken said that he admired her professionalism. Sheila said, 'That is nothing compared to the dwarfs -they took me over forty times.' Ken said that it wasn't possible. Sheila said that she was probably underestimating the number of times. Ken asked if she could provide some more details.

Sheila went through the routine. She shared a dressing room with the seven dwarfs. Actually, she had little choice in the matter as it was the only dressing room they had. When she arrived in the room, they stripped her. There was no debate or discussion; they just took her clothes off. Sheila said, 'There was no point in dressing up too much, as I would be naked in less than five minutes. Two minutes later, I would be bent over the arm of the sofa and Doc would be humping me. When he finished, Bashful would take over. And I must say, he always did a good job; although he would never look me in the eyes.'

Ken asked if she minded. Sheila said, 'It just became a routine; I was going to be fucked onstage later, so it seemed a bit prim to object to being fucked in the dressing room.'

Ken said, 'Did they come?'

Sheila said, 'Every time.'

Ken said, 'Was that the end of it?'

Sheila said, 'Oh no. Once I was on stage, I was more or less gang-banged. You know the scene where I was sleeping on the dwarfs' bed? I was taken by two or three of them every night. I don't know who did what, but they all seemed happy!'

Ken asked if she kept any records. Sheila said, 'It was an impossible task; I would say they were all involved, except Grumpy.'

Ken said, 'And you think it was about forty times?' Sheila said, 'If you take fourteen days and multiply it by five dwarfs, that comes to seventy, so forty is a conservative estimate. Besides, I don't want people to think I'm a tart. And if you add Grumpy, that's forty-one.'

Ken said, 'Can I ask what the situation was with Grumpy?'

Sheila explained, 'To put it simply, he couldn't get it up. So I suggested Viagra, and after getting some, he couldn't get it down. I'm not sure if he should have taken a full adult dose or not, but I've never seen a cock be so stiff for so long. As I was the one who'd suggested it, I had no choice but to help him out. For two and a half hours, he was pumping away at my poor little fanny. I got quite grumpy and sore. We went through a whole tube of K-Y gel.'

Ken said, 'I hate to ask, but did you get the job done?'

Sheila said, 'Yes, eventually. It was the first time he'd come in twenty-seven years. He proposed marriage afterwards and has been chasing me for the last few days. As far as I'm concerned, that's taking acting a step too far.'

Ken said, 'Let's sum it up. You had Chas seventeen times and the dwarfs forty-one times, but probably nearer seventy. You have certainly done your duty, but in both cases, you have exceeded the contracted allowances.'

Sheila said, 'True, but I did it for the show.'

Ken said, 'Is there a figure that you had in mind?' Sheila was hoping to get £5k, although it should be nearer £15k.

Sheila answered, 'I need to leave it to you, as I see you as my agent.'

Ken said, 'I'm pretty sure that I can get you £10k, but there would be one condition.'

Sheila stood up and was preparing to remove her knickers when Ken said, 'No, keep them on. I want to feel my cock rubbing against the knicker elastic as I fuck you.' He wanted Sheila on the desk. She was soon on her back with both her legs in the air. Ken's desk was the perfect height to facilitate easy entry. Without any foreplay, he eased the knicker elastic on the leg to one side. His large, engorged cock passed by the elastic and easily eased into her cunt. He got as much as he could in, and then his secretary walked in.

His secretary, Stella, said, 'Sorry, I didn't realise that you were busy, but I have a call for you.' Ken said that he would take the call. Stella asked how Sheila was, and they got to chatting about babies, holidays and shopping. Ken continued to fuck Sheila as he was discussing business opportunities on the phone. Ken quite liked being in a situation where sex was treated like an everyday activity rather than something romantic.

Sheila asked Stella if she had a napkin as she thought that Ken was going to come soon. Ken didn't know that he was nearly there and he wondered how Sheila knew. Stella said, 'Has he got to the point where his cock feels extra hard and a bit more aggressive?' Sheila nodded, and Stella, who had been fucked by Ken a few times, said 'I doubt if you have got two minutes then.' Ken wondered how Stella also knew he was going to come.

Then, within the next two minutes, his cock just exploded, and he withdrew. He shouted something into the phone while his cock was being wiped down by two attractive women. Stella took Ken's cock and gently cleaned it with her mouth. Ken apologised to the person on the other end. Sheila attempted to wipe her knickers down. It had all been a bit frantic.

Ken got his way, Stella got a promotion and Sheila got her money. Ken said to Sheila that he might have another job for her and that she should come and see him next week.

Sometimes it takes two to clean a cock horse.

The Circus

Sheila had fixed a date to meet with Ken, who was now effectively her agent, as he possibly had a job lined up for her. Such meetings usually ended up with her being naked or worse. At the very least, Ken would take advantage of her, but then she usually looked forward to that part because he was a great lover.

Sheila arrived on time, as usual. They kissed each other's cheeks and, as usual, Ken managed to caress her bum. Ken couldn't help trying to remember how many times he had fucked this beautiful woman. He had always admired her free spirit and willingness to go that extra mile. He just loved her zest for life and her great sense of fun. He quickly stopped himself from reminiscing since there was work to be done.

Sheila started the conversation by asking, 'What sordid job have you got for me now?'

Ken said, 'That's a bit unfair.'

Sheila said, 'Well, let's consider the facts: I've been fucked by seven dwarfs on multiple occasions, I've been raped onstage, I've been ravished three or four times in public at the nightclub and to top it all, I appeared naked on the front page of the local paper.'

Ken said, 'That's quite the CV. It would seem that you have all the qualifications required for your next opportunity.'

Smiling, Sheila said, 'Go on, give me the dirt.'

Ken said, 'This new job does require some nudity—well, quite a bit, really.'

Sheila said, 'Go on.'

Ken said, 'It's a new type of circus where they want some nude performers.'

Sheila said, 'What type of performer?'

Ken said, 'The job spec says, "assorted tasks depending on skills", but it would undoubtedly include some clowning. It starts this Monday in Redhill. Are you up for it?'

Sheila said, 'Do I need to go for an audition?'

Ken said, 'No, they trust my judgement.'

Sheila said that she would be there.

On the train to Redhill, she wondered what she had let herself in for. She arrived at Redhill Station and then had to get a taxi to the circus site. On arrival, she was met by the ringmaster. He explained that she would have to carry out several tasks, starting with the grope box, and then move on to more advanced clowning activities. He was a very stern man, and Sheila didn't feel that she could question him too much.

He said that he thought he recognised her. He asked if she had ever performed at the Thorton Heath Theatre. She replied that she had. He then asked if she had ever had live sex onstage there, and Sheila had to admit that she had. He simply replied, 'That's interesting, very interesting.' That was not a route she wanted to go down. Sheila was asked to report to the make-up department.

There, she met Paul, who headed the make-up department. He had a clipboard with Sheila's details on it. Paul said, 'Morning, Sheila. Welcome to the Everyman Adult Circus. I hope you enjoy your time here. We have you down as a nude clown, so I would appreciate it if you could strip off.'

Sheila replied, 'Do you want me to strip here?'

'Yes, please,' replied Paul. Sheila was concerned that it was almost a public path, but then if she was going to appear nude anyway, it didn't matter that much.

Sheila removed her skirt and blouse and then hesitated. There were some wolf whistles in the background. Her bra and panties followed, leaving her stark naked under a giant circus tent. Paul said, 'Very nice. Great tits, and I particularly like your arse. We need to make sure that we keep you as naked as possible. You will go down really well with the punters. The first thing I need to do is to find you some boots. He asked her what size shoe she wore.

He went off in search of boots, leaving Sheila standing there naked for all to see. She certainly attracted some interest. The ringmaster had heard that she was naked and decided to take a look for himself. He was certainly impressed with what he saw. He walked up to Sheila and asked if she would bend over. Sheila wondered why, but she obliged anyway. That gave him the chance to have a good look at her fanny and check out the cut of her boobs.

Paul returned with some boots. The ringmaster asked him what he thought of Sheila. Paul said, 'Not bad; not bad at all. I like her large, bouncy breasts and the cut of her arse. I haven't seen her fanny properly, but it looks pretty good to me.' The ringmaster asked him how firm her tits were. Paul said, 'Let's find out.' They grabbed a tit each. Paul said, 'Heavy, firm, nicely rounded but very soft to the touch.'

The ringmaster said, 'I like the way that the nipple gets hard very quickly.'

Paul said, 'Yes, that's always very useful.'

The ringmaster said, 'The legs look pretty good too.' He

stroked one almost up to her bush. Paul followed suit. The ringmaster said, 'My eyesight is not so good nowadays; can you see her clit?'

Paul said, 'Yes, it's there all right,' and he bent down to stroke it, which made Sheila twitch. Paul said, 'I think we are onto a winner here.'

The ringmaster said, 'I've checked her references; it appears that she has been fucked onstage over a hundred times, not counting the dwarfs.' Sheila did a quick calculation in her head, and thought that was about right, and felt rather disgusted about it.

Paul said, 'What dwarfs?'

The ringmaster said, 'Sheila appeared in the adult version of Snow White at Thorton Heath. Every night, she was fucked by two or three of them.'

Paul said, 'I guess she isn't very bashful, then!' Which he thought was rather funny. In both their minds, they had Sheila down as a tart. Paul said, 'Well, we'd better get the make-up sorted. Sheila was assigned a large, red nose, a white-and-red face and a bright ginger wig. She was issued a large pair of gloves that matched her boots. Sheila looked in the mirror to see a naked woman with coloured bits all around the edge. It somehow emphasised her boobs and fanny.

Paul said, 'Now, for the last job. We need to paint your minge red.' Sheila looked horrified. He told her to get onto the chair and open her legs wide. Sheila did as she was told. Paul combed her pubic hair so that it was all facing one direction. He squeezed her labia together to stop them from getting in the way. Sheila was embarrassed as her fanny was starting to respond to his touch. It was starting to get wet.

Paul applied the water-based paint. He then brushed the

hair the other way and applied some more paint. He painted each side of her fanny to create an even effect. To get it right, he had to poke and twist the vaginal area quite a bit. There was nothing Sheila could do to stop her fanny from juicing up. Paul looked Sheila in the eyes and said, 'You have got to learn to control yourself.'

'Sorry,' she said.

Paul used a brush to apply the final touches. The brush accidentally touched Sheila's clit, which immediately stimulated it. Paul deliberately repeated the action, and Sheila reacted shamelessly, almost begging for more. Paul responded by continuously brushing her clit, resulting in Sheila having a massive orgasm. Paul said, 'You really are a little minx, aren't you?' Sheila just nodded.

It was almost time for Sheila's first job. There were five girls all dressed as clowns and five grope boxes. The grope box was shaped like an old telephone box with clear windows. There were apertures and covers on all four sides that could be released by inserting a pound coin. Once the clown was in the box, a punter could pay a pound to release the cover and grope the girl for one minute. The clown could avoid the grope, but not if there were multiple gropers. Apparently, this was a real money maker for the circus.

It was 18.00, and the circus doors opened to the public. The effectively naked female clowns were in their boxes awaiting the punters. One of the clowns was telling Sheila that she had to watch out for fingernails, as the men often scratched. Sheila was not looking forward to this. An avalanche of dirty men, both young and old, suddenly appeared. Coins were deposited, and hands were grabbing at every part of the clowns' bodies.

Sheila had all four corners of the box occupied, as did most of the girls. She tried to fight the hands-off, but they were too strong for her. Her nipples were being tweaked, and fingers were in and out of her fanny. One finger was actually up her bum. As the money ran out, more hands appeared. It was relentless and not the sort of thing a lady did.

As soon as the circus started, she was released. She was supposed to parade around the inside of the big top, but she decided to do a runner. She couldn't find her clothes but decided to leave anyway. She managed to flag down a passing driver who agreed to give her a lift to the station, providing he could take some photos. She also convinced the station master to loan her some money, for a small consideration. She decided that she wasn't a tart, but it was OK to use her body to achieve certain ends.

She couldn't get that song out of her head, 'Send in the Clowns.'

The Human Farm: Part 1

Sheila's daughter-in-law was vegan. In the family, there had often been discussions about the morality of eating meat. Sheila had always enjoyed a good burger and some up-market sausages. She understood both the ethical argument against eating an animal that had a nervous system and the associated environmental issues. She felt that most of these animals would not exist if they had not been bred for food. Anyway, she and her daughter-in-law agreed to disagree. They had a great relationship and were, in many ways, good friends.

Almost as a joke, her daughter-in-law bought Sheila two tickets to experience the Human Farm. This was an organisation set up by vegans to show the general public what it was like to be a farm animal. The difference here was that the attendees became the farm animals. They experienced the farm as an animal. Sheila wasn't that keen on the idea, but the ticket was costly and Sheila felt obligated to attend. What was worse was that a large deposit had to be handed over as well.

In the brochure, it said that the participants must act like animals. If they did not, they would lose their deposit. The brochure made it clear that the organisation would be more than happy to take the deposit for their funds if the animal did not participate properly. It also made it clear that the experience was not designed to be a happy one. The participants would genuinely be treated like animals. It emphasised that there could be physical and sexual abuse, but that this was what animals experienced on farms.

Sheila didn't like the whole idea of getting dirty or spending time in a field, but as so often in life, you are pushed down routes that you don't want to go. Sheila would rather go to the theatre or see an opera dressed in all her finery. She loved having the chance to show off her shapely legs and a great figure. She was a very pretty girl with an enticing smile, a bubbly personality and a great sense of fun. This didn't sound like fun.

Anyway, she turned up on the allotted day. She was met by a farmer who took her to the conference room for women where there were thirty other animals waiting. The speaker explained that this was a genuine working farm, and for the day, they would be treated like animals. If they pulled out now, they would lose their deposits, but they were all free to go.

The speaker displayed the rules on the screen:

No clothes or footwear.
No phones, watches or jewellery.
Participants will pick a card to determine the type of animal they will be.
They will not stand.
They will eat animal feed.
They will be treated exactly like an animal.
Their sexual organs might be touched for breeding purposes.

Three of the women immediately left, and Sheila was tempted to go too, but she was worried about losing the deposit.

They were taken next door to the changing rooms, or

rather where their possessions were deposited. It was a communal area. Each "animal" was given a box to store their clothes. It was amazing how many women were reluctant to let go of their phone. They were then told that when they walked through that door, they would be treated as animals until 17.00. They were then asked to sign a document saying that they accepted this. Sheila noticed that they were effectively handing their bodies over for eight hours. Sheila selected a card to find that she was a cow. 'Hardly romantic,' she thought.

Looking around the room at the naked assembly, she was amazed at the variety of shapes and sizes. Probably most of the participants were middle-aged and overweight. There were two or three pretty ones, but they were the exception. After the forms were signed, the ladies were lined up by the door.

The door was opened, and out they went into a wet, muddy paddock. It was a bit chilly, and Sheila's nipples stiffened. Three men were waiting for them. 'On your knees!' they shouted, and everyone obeyed. One of the farmers explained that they had cattle prods to enforce obedience. The women didn't like their hands and knees getting all muddy, but now they had little choice.

The same man said, 'Cattle to the right, sheep to the left and pigs straight ahead.'

Sheila thought, 'Well, that's hardly realistic—not many animals can follow verbal instructions,' but she did what she was told. They were forced down one of the alleyways with fences on each side. One of the naked women tried to stand up, and she was cattle-prodded. When she offered some verbal abuse, she was cattle-prodded again. It certainly set the scene.

The alley reached a cattle dip which they had to crawl

through. It was full of a cold, detergent-type liquid used to disinfect the heifers. Sheila found it a truly horrible experience, especially as they were in a queue as the first cows were being inspected. She was desperate to get out; her entire body was feeling the cold.

The path started climbing upwards towards the inspection area. Four male farmers were carrying out a thorough inspection. Her turn came. Sheila was effectively on a concrete slab, stark naked, on her hands and knees with a farmer eyeing her up. One of the younger assistants came over with a clipboard and said to the farmer, Roger, 'Looks like we have a pretty heifer here.' Roger had to agree as he admired her dangling breasts and the cut of her arse.

John said, 'She looks like a good breeder to me.'

John opened Sheila's mouth and checked her teeth. He shouted out something, and Roger recorded it on the chart. 'Eyes and ears look fine,' John said.

Roger said, 'What about the tits?'

John grabbed Sheila's left breast and held it in his hand. He rubbed her nipple with his fingers. He said, 'It seems fine to me; quite weighty with a responsive nipple.' Roger said that he would check the other one, which he did. Sheila felt that the responsiveness check on the right nipple was a bit over the top. John ticked the box to state that both breasts were acceptable. Sheila felt quite relieved, although she was pleased that they both had warm hands.

The legs, arms, hands and feet were checked and deemed satisfactory. John said to Roger, 'Who is going to check the vagina?'

Roger said, 'I think that it's your turn.'

John said, 'I did the last two.' Roger agreed to do it. Sheila thought it couldn't be that bad a job. Both men stood behind Sheila, admiring her arse. Roger pulled Sheila's labia apart and pushed his finger into her fanny, which made her jump slightly. John said, 'I thought you were supposed to use gloves.'

Roger said, 'I don't always.'

John said, 'I noticed that you don't bother wearing gloves with the pretty ones.'

Roger said that her fanny was a bit too tight and some lubrication was needed. John took a lump of jelly from a dirty old box and rubbed it over the whole area. Then he efficiently managed to get two fingers into Sheila's cute little pussy. John said that it still felt a bit tight and he wasn't sure if the bull would be able to get in there. Roger said, 'We'd better check. Go and get the bull sizer.' John came back with what looked like a very large dildo.

John rubbed some jelly on the end of the bull sizer and slowly inserted it into Sheila's vagina. He was surprised at how much went in. Sheila wondered if this was standard procedure, but it did make her realise how vulnerable farm animals were. She once knew a man who got arrested for sheep shagging not once but three times. John said, 'I think we can tick the vagina off as satisfactory.' He patted Sheila's bum and pushed her down the corridor.

Sheila couldn't believe what she had just been through. She assumed that it would be easier from there. But she was wrong—very wrong. At the next station, she was going to be tattooed and measured for a suction cup. The two male tattooists were very impressed with the heifer in front of them. One said, 'What a fabulous pair of tits; best we have seen all year.'

The other one said, 'The arse isn't bad either.' They couldn't decide whether to put the tattoo on the breasts or the bottom. They decided to throw a coin: heads for a tattoo on the tits, and tails for a tattoo on the arse. Tails won.

Sheila was manoeuvred into a restraining frame as cows can deliver a very nasty kick. Frank, one of the tattooists, took his job very seriously. He preferred more artistic work but wasn't complaining as he looked directly at Sheila's rear. There were some obvious compensations. He decided to put the tattoo as near to the fanny as he could. One hand was on the fanny holding it in place while the tattooing gun printed six temporary numbers close to it. He accidentally managed to get one of his fingers into her fanny. Strangely, that had happened a few times before with the pretty heifers. Tom, the other tattooist, gently rubbed some lotion over the new tattoo. He also managed to accidentally touch her fanny.

Now it was time for the suction cup. Tom asked Frank what size suction cup he thought she would need for milking. Tom said, 'Hard to tell as they are big tits.' Both Frank and Tom decided to carry out an inspection. They grabbed a tit each and played with them. Sheila had experienced a fair amount of breast massage in her time, but this was ridiculous. Two young men were treating them as stress balls. They were being manipulated every which way: up, down, weighed in their hands, etc. A supervisor came over and said that they were taking too long; a queue was building up. They explained that they weren't sure what size cup was needed. The supervisor bent down, grabbed Sheila's left tit and said a type D would do the job. Sheila winced as his hands were really cold.

Sheila was herded onto the next station, which was the last

one. A man in a lab coat said to a nearby nurse, 'Has she been inseminated?' The nurse replied that she hadn't been. The doctor asked her to schedule it for this afternoon. Sheila was then released into the field.

There were six other 'cows' in the field. Two of them were lying down, which was permitted. They compared their experiences. Most of them had been touched up and most had received various levels of breast manipulation. Two of the cows said that they felt sexually stimulated. They put it down to a loss of control. Young men could do whatever they liked to them. However, none of them wanted to go through it again, but all agreed that it had been a very interesting learning experience.

They debated about what was going to happen next. Apparently, there was going to be some food, and then they were going to be milked. Some of them would also be artificially inseminated. Sheila already knew that she had been nominated for that. In the meantime, they could lounge around the field. Luckily, it was a hot summer's day.

The food arrived—well, a trough of raw vegetables arrived. They had to eat it on their hands and knees. Sheila was surprised at how quickly the women had got used to nudity. There were plenty of men walking by. The women now did not attempt to cover themselves up with their hands. Everything was on display.

A man with a stick rounded them up for milking. It, fortunately, wasn't a long crawl and they were soon put in cages. They were strapped in to avoid posing a danger to themselves and the milkmaids. However, they soon discovered that they were milkmen. The cups that they were measured for were fictitious as this was going to be a hand-milking exercise.

A young lad of nineteen was going to be Sheila's milker. He had never done it before and had an instructor with him.

To be honest, the young lad was much more interested in Sheila's rear. He had never seen a vagina in real life before. The instructor said that since it was his first day, he could feel free to have a good look. He stared at Sheila's private parts in awe. The instructor saw that he was dumbstruck and thought that he would make his day. He walked over to Sheila's fanny and pulled her labia apart so that the young lad could see everything. He gestured to the young lad to touch it. In no time at all, Sheila was being fingered by a virgin. Sheila's cunt couldn't help responding physically. She started to get quite damp.

The supervisor told the lad to get on with the milking as they had a schedule to keep to. It was evident that the lad had little or no experience with breasts. The older man pushed him out of the way and started 'milking' Sheila as if she were a cow. She had never experienced that type of massaging before. It wasn't all bad; it certainly stiffened her nipples. The young lad learnt quickly and did a much better job on the other tit.

The 'cows' were separated into two groups. The older ones went put out to pasture, and the younger ones were sent to the insemination centre. Sheila was quite knackered by the time she crawled there. She was led into a cowshed, which was hardly romantic, she thought.

There was a man there in a white coat, who was probably a vet, and he gave Sheila a quick look-over. He clearly liked what he saw as Sheila spotted an erection forming in his trousers. He said, 'I see that she has passed the bull sizer test.'

A uniformed nurse nodded and said, 'It would probably be worth doing again, as you know what those young lads are like.' The vet agreed, and a bull sizer was called for. This time, it was sprayed with an antiseptic substance.

The vet rubbed some lubrication over Sheila's genitals and gently eased her labia apart. They didn't need much easing as they had been touched up all day. He placed the bull sizer at the entrance of her fanny and gently eased it in. You could tell that he was a professional, especially when he started massaging her clit. All this playing was pushing Sheila towards an orgasm. The nurse came over and said, 'I will play with that bit while you manoeuvre the bull sizer.' The two of them deliberately gave Sheila a fabulous orgasm. They always enjoyed doing that.

The vet asked the nurse if she had the insemination kit ready. Sheila didn't like the looks of it. It looked like one of those tubes you use to put putty around a window frame. Sheila thought, 'I bet cows don't like that up them.' It looked very cold.

The nurse said, 'This cow looks very fit; we could consider a natural insemination?'

The vet said, 'Has she signed the form?'

The nurse checked and said, 'Yes, she signed up for the full experience.'

The vet said, 'In that case, check to see if we have a bullock available.'

Sheila was put into a breeding frame and strapped in to protect all concerned. Cows can get very fruity during the breeding process. Sheila's back legs had been spread apart on the framework to make the job easy for the bull. The vet would have volunteered to be the bull himself, but his wife, the nurse, wouldn't let him. Sheila was a very tasty-looking morsel, standing there naked with all her bits on show. She had quite a few admirers in the room.

A young man with an impressive erection was led into the room. He was one of the men who had signed up for the full 'Human Farm' experience, but he hadn't expected this. He was gobsmacked when he saw Sheila. He was going to fuck this beautiful woman in front of this crowd. The nurse came over and lubricated his cock, which almost made him come.

He approached the frame and entered Sheila without any difficulty. There was no way he could focus on Sheila's needs as the framework was too constraining. He just decided to go for it. He fucked her hard and quickly, thoroughly enjoying the softness of her fanny. He could feel his balls tightening; it wouldn't be long before he came. The nurse came over and squeezed his testicles, which pushed him over the edge. He filled Sheila up. Sheila could feel the hot liquid hitting her fanny walls.

The bull was led away, and the nurse used some surgical linen to wipe Sheila's fanny down. The vet decided to help finish the cleaning operation, which slightly annoyed his wife, but it would be his last chance to play with this delightful creature.

After a brief period in the paddock, the cows were taken back to the changing rooms to get their clothes.

Sheila wasn't too sure if she'd enjoyed the experience or not, but she did book a day for her daughter-in-law and her sister to attend. She ticked the box for the full experience. She still had a second day to experience the Human Farm; they guaranteed that you would be assigned a different animal on the second day.

On the way home, she stopped for a large steak burger and thoroughly enjoyed it.

Her daughter-in-law asked her how the day went. Sheila said that a day on the farm was fucking hard work, but she quite liked the 'bull in her little shop.'

The Human Farm: Part 2

Sheila wasn't too sure if she wanted to experience the second day at the human farm after all. Being a cow had been degrading but also rather erotic. Sheila found the loss of control rather arousing but also disturbing. Did she want to go through it again? In reality, she had little choice as she would lose the substantial deposit she had left if she didn't participate.

Sheila remembered the rules: participants must act like animals. If they did not, they would lose their deposit. The brochure made it clear that they would be happy to take the deposit for their funds. It also made it clear that the experience was not designed to be a happy one. The participants would genuinely be treated like animals. It emphasised that there could be physical and sexual abuse, but that this was what animals experienced on farms.

Anyway, she turned up on the allotted day. She was met by a farmer who took her to the conference room for women where there were thirty-five other animals waiting. The speaker explained that this was a genuine working farm, and for the day, they would be treated like animals. If they pulled out now, they would lose their deposits, but they were all free to go.

The speaker displayed the rules on the screen:

No clothes or footwear.

No phones, watches or jewellery.

Participants will pick a card to determine the type of animal they will be.

They will not stand.

They will eat animal feed.

They will be treated exactly like an animal.

Their sexual organs might be touched for breeding purposes.

Sheila knew the drill: strip off clothes, remove all personal possessions, allocate animal type, sign the form, queue to enter the farm, face the cattle prod if they misbehaved, etc. Sheila was still surprised how many of the female animals were middle-aged and overweight. She couldn't help thinking that she was one of the pretty ones. Sheila had been designated as a sheep, which she thought was probably better than being a pig.

The farm door was opened, and out they went into a wet, muddy paddock. Sheila was directed to the left-hand alleyway. Once again, they had to crawl on their hands and knees through a dip. This time, it was a sheep dip full of cold, smelly detergent. The liquid was just deep enough to cover Sheila's thighs, although her breasts dangled in the water. It immediately made her nipples stiffen. Then a young lad walked up to Sheila and pushed her entire body into the liquid, including her head.

She managed to lift herself up, but she was still sputtering from the fluid in her mouth. She instinctively stood up to wipe her eyes when she was cattle-prodded on her breast. Someone shouted, 'No standing!' She decided that she didn't want any more prodding as the pain was excruciating, albeit temporary. She managed to continue, but she wasn't enjoying it.

A few minutes later, Sheila was dragged out of the dip by two strong men and positioned between the legs of one of them. Effectively, she was sitting on her bum with the young man holding her arms in a stretched position. Apparently, if sheep were put on their back with their front legs being held, they became very docile. Sheila wasn't feeling docile, but she didn't want another prodding.

James came over with a clipboard and spoke to Callum, her handler. 'This is a nice-looking ewe,' Callum said.

James agreed, 'She certainly has a nice pair of udders, and I wouldn't mind getting my hands on that rump.' Sheila could hear what they were saying, but she didn't feel too glamorous with her wet, straggly hair and her shivering body. James said, 'I guess we'd better start the inspection.'

Callum opened Sheila's mouth and shouted out some numbers, which James recorded. Callum fingered her ears and nose, and James ticked a box on the chart. Her eyes also passed the test. Her arms, hands and fingers were checked. Sheila felt like a helpless animal, but then again, that was the objective. James checked each toe, which Sheila quite enjoyed, and then he worked his way up her legs. James said to Callum, 'The hoofs, posterns, cannons and hocks are all OK. They are a fine pair of legs. I'm just going to check the rear flank and the twist.'

While James was doing that, Callum was checking out her breasts. Sheila thought that he was doing a particularly meticulous job, spending a fair amount of time on each breast and even more time on the nipples. At least it was warming her up. She could feel his full erection against her back. James had reached her thighs and gradually pushed her legs farther apart to expose her fanny. He prodded her labia and clitoris and said,

'We need to get this ewe standing up to check out things properly.' Callum agreed, and Sheila got on her hands and knees.

James said to Callum, 'What is your verdict on the tits?'

Callum said, 'I've only just completed a preliminary investigation, but they appear to be satisfactory.'

James said, 'On my chart, I need to record her weight, size and milking capability.' Callum asked if James had completed the checks on the ewe's vagina. James replied that the checks weren't finished. He still needed to check depth, width, lubrication response and the need for wool removal.

Callum suggested that they take a breast each, which they did. James thought that these were the best udders he had reviewed all year. Firm but soft, well-shaped, very responsive nipples, and very attractive, particularly when dangling. The boys had a breast in each hand. They agreed that they weighed two to three kilos. They couldn't agree on the size but settled on a 36C. James just put a tick in the milking capability box, as he had no idea how to measure it, although he was very tempted to give them a good suck.

James said, 'Now, for the fanny.'

Callum stood behind Sheila's naked rear, pulled her labia apart and said, 'It's a very neat-looking fanny; no floppy bits. I will stick my finger in to check the depth.' In went Callum's index finger. Callum said, 'It took my finger OK, but it is a bit tight.'

James said, 'Shouldn't we use the measuring device? I will go and get one.' James came back, lubricated the device and pressed it into Sheila's fanny. It took the full length very easily. James marked on his chart 'XL,' although her vagina seemed perfectly acceptable to him. Callum asked James how he was going to measure the width. James said, 'I just put two of my fingers into the fanny and see how far I can separate them.' Callum volunteered to it, and soon he had two fingers imbedded in Sheila's cute little cunt.

'Two inches,' he shouted.

James said, 'Are you sure?' and inserted his fingers. 'Yes, 2.5 inches, I would say.' Lubrication appeared to be OK. James said, 'The last item on the list is wool inspection.' Callum asked why they checked the hair on the fanny and not the hair on the head. James explained that in the past, they used to shave the head, but there were too many objections, so now they focus on the pubic hair alone. James said, 'Right, let's check this little filly out.' He had a picture of a fanny to mark up. James said to Callum, 'You check, and I will record.'

James shouted out, 'Pubic mount.'

Callum responded, 'Hair removal required.' James then listed right, left and bottom. Every area required shaving. Callum enjoyed this part of the job and made a mental note to check this ewe out after the shaving had been completed. He always thought that a shaved woman looked innocent, like a little girl, but it was still lovely and smooth. Nothing was hidden.

James said, 'I'm wondering if we should give her a fertility boost.'

Callum asked, 'What does that do?'

James replied, 'It makes the ewes very randy, and it works very quickly.' Sheila doubted that it worked.

Callum said, 'Does it work?'

James said, 'It does; I've tried it on my wife, and my cock is still sore. I will prove it to you. Flick her clit before and after the injection, and you will see the difference.'

Callum bent down, found Sheila's clit and gave it a quick flick, which made Sheila jump. James injected her and counted to ten. James then said, 'Go on, flick her clit again.' Callum did as he was told and was astonished to see the reaction. Sheila's clit was on fire—she wiggled her bum every which way. James said, 'We could both fuck her now, and she would say "thank you".

Sheila thought, 'I would say more than thank you.' She continued to wiggle her bum, almost begging for a fuck. Well, to be honest, it was more than begging; she was gagging for it.

James got his pot of yellow paint. Callum asked what it was for. James said, 'We paint the left tit yellow to warn everyone that she has received a fertility boost. Even painting the breast can be dangerous.' James got his brush and liberally painted the breast bright yellow. James said, 'Now, watch this.' He got the brush handle and rubbed it against Sheila's nipple. It sent her into ecstasy; her whole body started moving around, her legs were kicking, and her arms were trying to grab the boys. It took James and Callum quite a bit of effort to restrain her. Both ended up having throbbing erections. You could smell how excited Sheila was.

Callum said, 'I would really like to fuck her.'

James said, 'I know what you mean, but it's more than our job is worth. We need to send her to the next station before we are accused of preference.'

Callum said, 'But it makes such a nice change to get a pretty one, especially one that wants to be fucked.'

They patted Sheila's bum and pushed her back onto the alley towards the next station. On the way, she was guided by a shepherd and two sheep dogs. Well, they weren't actually dogs—they were human lads who were on the programme experiencing farm life. Sheila noticed that both of the dogs had bright yellow, erect cocks. In her current aroused state, she would be very happy to have both of them. Sheila stopped and wiggled her bum to attract their attention, but it wasn't really necessary as the farmer was already struggling to hold them back.

The shepherd used his crook to gently nudge Sheila along. Sheila found the crawling difficult due to the mud and the coldness. There was much more crawling being a sheep than a cow. The shepherd continued to nudge her along by sliding his crook between her buttocks. The fennel at the end of the crook kept rubbing against Sheila's fanny. Sheila thought to herself, 'What am I doing, crawling naked along a muddy path with a walking stick pressing against my cunt?' It just didn't make sense.

Just then, one of the dogs leapt forward and gently bit her bum. The dogs do this to show their dominance over the sheep. As the shepherd hadn't stopped him, the dog leapt forward again, but this time, his large yellow cock entered Sheila's welcoming vagina. The shepherd shouted at Fido to stop, but Fido ignored him and was giving Sheila some serious thrusts. She was being well and truly fucked. The shepherd was having trouble controlling the other dog, who also wanted some of the action.

To be honest, the shepherd wasn't too surprised, as this was an exceptionally attractive ewe and both the ewe and the dog had been treated with the fertility boost. The dog was really going for it, and the shepherd was worried that the ewe might get hurt. Little did he know that Sheila was made of tough stuff and was giving as good as she got. Her fanny was literally grabbing the dog's cock.

The shepherd used the curved end of the crook to grab the dog's testicles. He gave a quick tug, which resulted in the engorged yellow cock being abruptly removed from Sheila's tight, little cunt. This caused the dog to come, and Sheila's arse was sprayed with hot, steaming spunk. The dog was happy, but Sheila felt cheated; she wanted more. The other dog also wanted some. The shepherd only just stopped him from mounting her.

Sheila was approaching the next station which was shearing. One of the shearers, Bill, said to the other shearer, Joe, 'We might have trouble here. Her left tit has been painted yellow.'

Joe said, 'I will get the restraining frame as the yellow-titted ones can be a bit of a handful.'

Bill said, 'It looks like we have got a bit more than a handful—look at those beauties.'

Joe said, 'And I like the look of that arse. What is she down for?'

Bill said, 'Standard wool trim.'

Joe said, 'That sounds good; full removal of the pubic hair, and she has signed the form for the full experience.'

Joe manoeuvred Sheila into the restraining frame. It was designed so that the legs could be spread apart to give full access to the sexual organs. Bill decided that this was a particularly pretty sight. The ewe looked exhausted, but she had a fine pair of dangling tits, and her arse was fully exposed. They could both see an open fanny. They sprayed her rear with disinfectant, as they had no idea where she might have been.

They then sprayed her genitals with shaving cream. They agreed that Bill would shave the right-hand side and Joe would do the rest. Bill switched on the electric shaver and started the trimming process. Sheila had never felt so exposed and vulnerable. Bill's fingers were everywhere, fingering her labia, clit and fanny. He was meticulous in removing her hair. Joe just watched a master at work. Bill handed the shaver over to Joe and said that as he was less experienced, he would recommend putting two fingers into the fanny to steady his hand and then work around the edge before slowly moving inwards. He said to try to avoid giving her an orgasm because he could end up nicking her by mistake.

In fact, Sheila wasn't far off having an orgasm. Bill's excellent manipulation of her vagina had almost pushed her over the edge. Now Joe's two fingers were just too much. Sheila was doing everything she could to stop it. She could tell that Joe was less experienced, as he was quite a bit rougher. Whilst this was going on, Bill was stroking her breast, which didn't help her control her orgasm. Joe said that he was finished, and Bill inspected his work.

Bill pulled the labia farther apart and played with the hood of her clit. He pointed out to Joe where some additional shaving was needed. The job was done, and Sheila was once again nude in the fullest sense of the word. Bill then said, 'Watch this.' He knew that Sheila had been fighting an orgasm. He grabbed a handful of aftershave lotion and dropped it onto Sheila's back. He then rubbed it down each buttock and fingered it into Sheila's love hole. It stung like hell, which pushed Sheila towards a massive orgasm. Bill kept two fingers in her fanny while her whole body just exploded. She bucked and kicked and twisted in ecstasy.

Bill enjoyed having his fingers in that place while this was going on. His fingers enjoyed the feeling of a woman abandoning herself to pure sex. When she finished, Bill started tickling the inner walls of her fanny. Sheila had no objections, as she was still under the control of the drug, and then without warning, Sheila had her second orgasm. Bill quickly removed his fingers as he felt them being crushed by an overactive fanny.

Joe patted Bill on the back and said, 'I've never seen anything like it before.'

Bill said, 'It worked because we have a particularly fruity minx on our hands here. It's a shame to let her go.'

Then Callum turned up. He said, 'I thought I would inspect your work.'

Joe said, 'You just missed Bill giving her two huge orgasms.'

Callum said, 'Did you fuck her?'

Bill said, 'No, I just used my fingers.'

Callum said, 'Could you show me?'

Sheila thought, 'What a cheek; I'm not here for your sexual gratification.' She decided that she was going to complain until she felt the aftershave being poured on her back for a second time. She then decided that she would resist an orgasm, just to show them who was in charge.

All three men stood there and admired Sheila's naked beauty. Every part of her genitalia was on full show. Bill explained that he was going to rub the lotion over each buttock first. He would then rub it down the side of each labia and then the hood of the clit. He would then give the clit a good rubbing, and then he would quickly push two fingers into the fanny. He thought to himself that he might even try three fingers, as she was fairly accommodating at the moment. He then told the boys that she would have a massive orgasm. Sheila knew that this wasn't going to happen.

Sheila enjoyed him massaging her buttocks, and he took a lot more time than before. Her body ached for him to finger her fanny, but she was determined not to come. Bill slowly approached her labia and gently rubbed both sides of them. He very gently rubbed her clit in every direction. Sheila was now fighting the orgasm, but she knew that she would not surrender to it.

She was surprised when he used his tongue on her clit. She was even more surprised when he started chewing it. The chewing and licking grew in its intensity, which made Sheila sweat. She was resisting as hard as she could. Bill knew how a woman's body worked. He stopped chewing and gently poked her fanny with one finger. Sheila started to squirm, and Bill entered a second finger. Sheila squirmed even more. Bill then decided the finish the job off. He gently bit the clit and pushed a third finger into the fanny.

Sheila exploded for the third time. This was the most intense orgasm of her entire life. If she hadn't been in the frame, she would have collapsed. Sheila was dribbling from almost every orifice. It was as if she had lost control of her body. The boys saw Bill as a love god. Bill just basked in their adoration. He said, 'It was a good performance, but then again, I am working with a lovely ewe.'

Callum said, 'It's a real pity that we can't fuck her.'

Bill said, 'It's time to move her on.'

Joe released Sheila from the frame, and she collapsed onto the floor. Joe asked if she was OK. Bill said, 'Just give her a bit of time to recover.' They manhandled her back into the alley. Callum managed to play with her tits and arse in the process.

'Dirty boy,' she thought. She saw the shepherd and his two

dogs approaching and decided to get a move on.

Sheila approached what turned out to be the final station, which was managed by Greg and Tim. Greg said that the ewe looked shagged. Tim said, 'It's unlikely at this stage, but it will definitely be the case in the paddock unless a dog has already got to her.' This was the painting station. Each sheep was coloured to show ownership. Greg used to tell his daughter that the colour on the sheep was the colour of the jumper that would be made from the wool.

Sheila crawled into yet another restraining frame and wondered what humiliation she was going to suffer there. She wasn't sure if she could cope with any more orgasms. Greg said to Tim, 'She may look exhausted, but she has a fine body on her. Look at those boobs, and what a pretty-looking arse. She has gone straight into my top ten for the year.'

Tim said, 'Probably a top five. If her hair were brushed, she might even be "The One".

Greg said, 'Where are we going to paint the bulls-eye?' This was the symbol used by the farm.

Greg said, 'Let me guess—you are going to paint the bulls-eye on her arse.'

Tim said, 'What makes you say that?'

Greg replied, 'That is what you do with all the pretty ones.'

Tim said, 'As a matter of fact, I was thinking of painting it there. Let's get her prepared.' Sheila was manipulated in the frame so that her arse was sticking out. Tim painted the outer circle blue. Greg painted the next circle yellow. Tim then had the job of painting the more intimate bits red, which he always enjoyed.

Before Tim continued, Greg asked him if he was allowed

to fondle the tits. Tim said, 'Please, go ahead, but be gentle as she has been drugged.' Tim started the onerous job of painting the fanny red. He was having some problems getting the paint to adhere as the whole area was somewhat damp. He asked Greg if he could wipe her down. Greg was a bit annoyed as he was enjoying squeezing the breasts together.

Greg found a dirty cloth and started rubbing the fanny to get it dry. The harder he rubbed, the wetter it got. Tim said, 'Give her a blast of the air gun.' This was used to dry the paint. Greg started blasting away. Sheila found it a very unusual experience to have a jet of warm air blasting away at her most private parts. Tim moved the labia to one side to aid the drying process. It seemed to do the trick, and Tim carried on painting. It didn't take long for Sheila to have a bright red fanny.

Sheila was now ready to enter the paddock. She was put back in the alley. The shepherd let the two dogs loose to speed her up. Sheila got to the paddock just in time, before she was mounted again. She wasn't sure why she hurried, as she still fancied a bit more. Another shepherd let her into the paddock, pushing one of the dogs off her.

One of the shepherds said to his colleague, 'This is going to be very interesting; there are five randy rams and one ewe. I must say it is a lovely ewe. I do enjoy watching the ewes get fucked.' Sheila looked up to see five naked rams with yellow erections. She then realised that she was the only ewe in the paddock. In the next paddock, there were twenty ewes and one very exhausted-looking ram. That didn't seem fair.

The five randy rams circled Sheila. They looked at her, and then they looked at each other. Each ram wondered who was going to make the first move. Sheila couldn't monitor them all at once, and with little warning, she soon had a cock in her fanny. He acted just like a ram and ignored her needs.

He just rammed away. The other rams soon joined in. Her breasts were being played with, and she ended up with a cock in her mouth.

The cock in her fanny was soon replaced with another one, and then a third. Breasts were chewed and bitten. Her mouth ended up with a second cock in it, and yet another cock was trying to fight its way into her arse. One shepherd said to the other, 'I think she has been fucked eleven times.'

The other shepherd said, 'But there are only five rams. Perhaps the drug was too potent? We'd better send in the dogs to rescue her.'

Three dogs were sent in—two of them chased the rams away, and one entered Sheila. One shepherd said to the other, 'Not sure if you can call that a rescue.' The dog continued to hump Sheila until he came. Finally, the two shepherds rushed in and intervened.

Sheila managed to get back to the changing room and get dressed. She wasn't sure if she could sit down, and she wasn't sure how many times she had been fucked or how many orgasms she'd had. A lady in a long white gown asked if she had enjoyed the experience. Sheila told her to 'Fuck off.' But it was a good question—had she enjoyed it? She decided that she wouldn't do it again, but she had had the best orgasm of her life.

In the car park, she saw one of the dogs who had taken advantage of her. She kicked him in the balls, thinking to herself, 'That is just another farmyard experience.'

Her husband asked her how the day went. Sheila said that in many ways, it was a dog's life, but you can't have five wolves and one sheep voting on what to have for dinner.

Sheila wondered why a single sheep was called a sheep, and several sheep were called sheep.

Paying the Rent

Sheila had always had a somewhat complicated relationship with her best friend's son, Charles. He was a good-looking, intelligent guy who always searched for ways of avoiding hard work. It wasn't that he was lazy; it was more about him only doing things that he wanted to do. In reality, it was about him. He wasn't interested in anything that didn't benefit him directly. He wanted to be the focus of attention. He also had a growing problem with substance abuse. This was a reflection of twenty-first-century society.

Sheila had always looked out for him, as her best friend wasn't particularly family-orientated. The reverse was not the case, as this tale will tell. One day, Sheila got a phone call from a foreign-sounding gentleman demanding money. He kept saying that she was the guarantor and he wanted his money or there would be consequences. She ignored it as just another junk call, but he was soon back on the phone. She asked him to post the relevant documentation to her.

What arrived in the post the next day, was a copy of Charles's rental agreement. She had signed it nearly a year ago as the guarantor. If Charles didn't pay, then she would have to. To be honest, she had signed it without reading the conditions. Anyway, the document didn't look entirely above-board. She decided to read the clauses carefully. It was clear that if Charles didn't pay, then she would have to. What she didn't like was clause 3.6, which she thought must be illegal.

It said that in the event of the rent being in arrears, the guarantor would be responsible for paying the debt. Until the debt was paid, the guarantor would agree to have sex with the proprietors or their agents. This would continue daily until the debt was paid in full. Sheila couldn't believe what she was reading. She phoned Mr Shah and asked him to confirm that this clause was never actually enforced.

Mr Shah answered the phone and listened to Sheila ranting on about the conditions of the agreement. Sheila made it clear that she thought it was just disgusting, and she asked how he could do business like that. Mr Shah replied that he was the victim here. He had rented a room to Charles in good faith and had not received any payment. What was worse was that the deposit cheque had bounced. Charles had not made any attempt to pay him, and he had just disappeared in the night.

Mr Shah said that all of the conditions were perfectly legal and told her that she could check with her solicitor if she wanted. Sheila said, 'What about the clause relating to sex?' Mr Shah said that it was legal, and he reminded her that she had signed it voluntarily. Sheila said that she hadn't read it. Mr Shah said that Charles had read it carefully and had agreed to every single clause. Sheila found Mr Shah to be quite reasonable, so she asked him why that clause was in there, to begin with.

Mr Shah responded that if he just added additional costs or interest, then they were generally ignored. If a man turned up expecting to have sex, then a solution was usually reached pretty quickly. Sheila could see the logic of it. Mr Shah then said, 'A young man will be knocking on your door at 19.00

tomorrow. Please give him the money or you-know-what. It's up to you.'

Sheila immediately phoned Charles, who answered in a very nonchalant way, 'Hello, Aunty Sheila. I guess that you are phoning about the rent not being paid.'

'That's right,' she said. 'Are you going to pay it today?' Charles said that he wasn't planning to as he'd never liked Mr Shah. He said that he didn't treat his tenants right. Sheila said, 'You haven't paid any of the rent, and the deposit cheque bounced.' Charles said that he knew that, but he still had no intention of paying it. Sheila said, 'You have got to pay; otherwise, I will have to.' Charles said that he knew that.

Sheila was getting very frustrated with Charles. Sheila said, 'Do you have the money to pay?'

Charles said, 'Yes, money is not the problem; it's a matter of principle. I refuse to pay money to a rental shark.'

Sheila said, 'I need to be blunt with you. If you don't pay, then a man will come around tomorrow night to fuck me. That's all because of you.'

Charles said, 'I had thought that was a strange clause, but I don't believe that they will do that.' Sheila wasn't so sure. Charles said that he had to go, as his dinner was getting cold.

Sheila wondered how she got herself into these situations. There was no way that she could pay £12,000. Wormy was still out of work, and her pantomime career had been cut short. Anyway, she tended to agree with Charles in that it was very unlikely that there would be a knock on the door expecting sex, but she would find out tomorrow.

The next day, there was a knock on the door. It was exactly 19.00. Sheila opened the front door to find a tall black guy with only one eye standing on the doorstep. He asked if she had the money. She told him that she didn't have it, and he immediately started taking his trousers off. She asked him what he was doing. He had been told that if she didn't have the money, then he was to have sex with her. Apparently, it had all been arranged. She explained that it wasn't the case. He took his pants off to display a seriously impressive erection.

Sheila dragged him into the house as she didn't want the neighbours to see. Wormy was in the lounge; she didn't want him to know about the guarantee. She was, as they say, in the right tiswas. There was only one thing she could do. She pulled her knickers down, lifted her short skirt and bent over the sofa arm. Sheila said, 'You will need to be quick as my husband is in the lounge. There is some moisturiser on the table. You might find it useful as a lubricant.

And the one-eyed man was quick. He wasted no time lubricating his long, hard cock and gently easing it into Sheila's somewhat tight fanny. He then moved it up a gear and started giving Sheila a real banging. Wormy shouted out, asking if she was OK. Sheila said, 'I'm fine, I'm helping a local lad with some Bible teachings. We are doing Adam and Eve at the moment.'

Wormy said, 'I didn't think you were religious.' Sheila said that she wasn't, but even atheists needed to understand their country's religious heritage.

Sheila asked the young man how he was doing. He said, 'I'm just about to take a bite of the apple.' The bite hit him hard, and Sheila had to put her hand over his mouth to keep him quiet. He said, 'Thank you very much; you are the first white woman I have ever fucked.'

Sheila said, 'Did you enjoy it?'

He said, 'Very much; I'd like to do it again.' Sheila

quickly ushered him out of the door.

Sheila was furious with Charles and got him on the phone. 'Charles,' she said, 'I've just been fucked because of you. Are you going to pay the debt?'

Charles asked, 'Was it a big black guy?'

Sheila said, 'Yes, how did you know that?' Charles explained that he had heard rumours. Sheila again said, 'Are you going to pay it?' Charles said he wasn't going to pay on principle and put the phone down.

Sheila said, 'Bastard, fucking bastard!' But what could she do? She decided to phone Mr Shah. She asked if he could offer extended payment terms. He said that he could, but regardless, Ahmed would be around tomorrow night at 19.00. All the next day, she was nervous. She tried to get Wormy to go to the pub, but he was too lazy even for that. All she could think of was repeating the same exercise, but how long could it go on for? She decided to chat up some old friends to see if they could lend her some money.

Again, there was a knock on the door at precisely 19.00. This time, it was a short Asian man with an extremely large nose, and he was already taking his trousers off. Sheila dragged him in and explained that her husband was in the lounge. She wasn't wearing any knickers in a bid to speed up the process. Once again, she was over the sofa arm.

The Asian lad, or "Nosey", as she nicknamed him, gratefully accepted the lubricant and rubbed it all over Sheila's fanny, making sure that fingers entered places that they shouldn't. He was soon exercising his penis. Sheila was quite enjoying it. He was gentle but firm at the same time. She was starting to respond when Wormy called out, 'Are you all right?'

Sheila replied, 'I'm helping a young man complete a survey. He wants to know if you are happy with your sex life.' Wormy replied that he couldn't be bothered with all that mucky stuff.

Sheila asked Nosey if he liked that sort of mucky stuff. He said that he did and that it wouldn't be much longer before it got even muckier. He had achieved a steady rhythm; Sheila was assisting the best she could as she needed to get him out of the door. Suddenly, the rhythm stopped, and the questionnaire was completed. He said, 'Thank you very much. You are the first white woman I have ever fucked.'

Sheila said, 'Did you enjoy it?'

He said, 'Very much; I'd like to do it again.' Sheila quickly ushered him out of the door.

Sheila had quite enjoyed the experience, but she was still furious with Charles. She got him on the phone again. She said, 'Charles, I've just been fucked for a second time, all because of you.'

Charles said, 'Was it an Asian lad with a large nose?'

Sheila said, 'It was, but how did you know?'

Charles said, 'Mr Shah is following his normal process.'

Sheila said, 'What are you going to do about it?'

Charles said, 'What do you want me to do about it?'

Sheila said, 'I want you to pay that fucking bill. I want you to do it now.' Charles said that he would talk to Mr Shah. Sheila was surprised that he had finally agreed to talk to him.

Charles phoned back later with good news. He was in negotiations with Mr Shah and said that they should reach some sort of compromise in the next few days. In the meantime, Chan would be around tomorrow night at 19.00. Sheila said, 'Why can't he cancel it?' Charles said that Mr

Shah didn't trust him and that it was the best he could do.

Sheila spent another day worrying about the evening spectacle. Wormy could walk in any moment, but she couldn't think of another venue. At precisely 19.00, there was a knock on the door. In walked a very fat Chinese lad.

Sheila was ready for the sofa experience, but there was going to be a problem. It took him a very long time to get his trousers and pants off. When the pants were off, she couldn't see his todger. She thought it would be too rude to lift his enormous stomach. She wondered why life kept throwing these problems at her.

Sheila decided to lie on the floor. Mr Blobby was soon on top of her. She felt something pushing against her gusset; she had forgotten to take her knickers off. At the time, she was much more interested in breathing. It wouldn't be long before she would need oxygen. Wormy shouted out, 'Are you OK? What was all the noise about?'

Sheila shouted back, 'The nice Chinese lad from up the road is showing me a few self-defence moves.'

Sheila asked him how his moves were going when she felt the lad ejaculating onto her knickers. He said, 'Thank you very much. You are the first white woman I have ever fucked; in fact, you are the first woman I've ever touched down there.'

Sheila said, 'Did you enjoy it?'

He said, 'Very much. I'd like to do it again, but maybe I'd prefer it more with the knickers off.' Sheila quickly ushered him out of the door.

Sheila felt that this was getting ridiculous. She was back on the phone to Charles. Sheila shouted into the phone, 'I've just been fucked for the third time; it's got to stop.'

Charles calmly said, 'Was it a very fat Chinese lad?'

Sheila said, 'It was—is this still Mr Shah's normal process?

Charles said, 'Yes, but it doesn't matter as I've paid the bill. It's all sorted.'

Sheila said, 'Why couldn't you have done it earlier?' Charles apologised. There was lots of laughter in the background. She even thought she could hear Mr Shah's voice. Charles said, 'Good night, Aunty Sheila.'

Charles turned to his mates and said, 'Hand over the money, now.' They hadn't believed him when he'd said that he could get his mother's best friend, who was a real looker, to fuck a one-eyed black man, a large-nosed Asian and a very fat Chinese man over three consecutive nights.

Sheila decided that she was never going to help Charles again. Wormy asked why there had been so many knocks on the door recently. Sheila said, 'I'm not really sure, but I had sex with each of them.'

Wormy said, 'Why would you want someone else when you have got me?'

The Postman, the Gardener and the Window Cleaner

Sheila had always enjoyed sex. She enjoyed looking pretty and buying sexy clothes. She enjoyed the warm embrace and gentle cuddling that sexual copulation provided. She enjoyed a man caressing her breasts. She enjoyed a man wanting her. She enjoyed teasing a man. She enjoyed her climaxes. She enjoyed being alive.

One day, Sheila woke up with an urge. Every now and then, she just wanted—no, needed—a hard cock in her fanny. It was just one of those things. It was a strong biological urge that had to be satisfied. She thought that it wasn't her fault that she had these needs. But she was slightly worried that she couldn't trust herself when she was on the hunt for cock.

Later that day, there was a knock on the door from the postman. He was a good-looking young man in shorts with firm, tanned legs. 'Mrs Allen,' he said, 'I have a parcel for you that has been damaged in the post. I need to check with you that the contents are OK. If not, I can organise its return. I couldn't help noticing that it appears to be a negligee.'

He passed the damaged parcel to Sheila. It was indeed a black, semi-transparent nightie that left very little to the imagination. He asked if it was damaged. Sheila said that it was hard to tell. In a very cheeky voice, he said, 'Why don't you try it on?'

Sheila looked him in the eyes and said 'OK.'

She removed her top and let her skirt fall to the floor. She stood there in a very sexy bra and knicker set. She could feel her nipples getting erect. She continued looking at his eyes when she unclipped her bra. Both her boobs bounced free. She was proud of them; they were large, firm and beautifully proportioned. He just stared in disbelief. She continued staring at his eyes while pulling her knickers down.

She saw him looking at her pubes. He was simply staring at her little black triangle. His tongue was almost hanging out in total shock. Sheila loved it. She was in control. She picked up the nightie, making sure that he had a good look at her arse and the crack in between, which was starting to feel moist. She pulled the nightie over her head, making sure that her boobs were pushed out in the process.

She could see the effect she was having on him. She knew how to excite a man. Her legs alone were simply stunning. She could see his erection through his shorts. The nightie covered her boobs but not her fanny, but since the fabric was semi-transparent, the coverage made little difference. She asked him what he thought. He stuttered that the nightie didn't appear to be damaged.

Sheila pushed the young man onto the sofa and pulled his todger out of his shorts. 'Not bad,' she thought. It was fully erect and ready to burst. She could see the veins pulsating. It was just what she wanted to satisfy the needs of her fanny. She grabbed his cock and licked the top of it. This immediately made him twitch. She continued licking and increasing the pressure on his glans, which caused him to twist and turn. As soon as she started sucking, he came—big time. Sheila's face was covered in warm, sticky cum.

He apologised profusely, pulled his shorts up and ran out of the door. What a blow. Sheila felt deflated. Her fanny ached even more as she had been mentally preparing herself for a good todgering.

It was a beautiful summer's day, so she decided to put her washing on the line. There was no point in getting dressed as the garden was secluded. She hadn't realised that her part-time gardener was there, as he turned up whenever it suited him. He was working his way through the flowerbeds when he spotted Sheila. He had always fancied her and often took to spying on her to get a glimpse of her legs. On one occasion, he had seen her sunbathing topless, which kept him going for months.

He couldn't believe his luck. Here she was in a tiny transparent nightie. Everything was on show—her tight and cute little bum, her fanny and her impressive boobs. He kept behind a large bush, staring at Sheila's well-trimmed bush, thinking that watching her beat gardening any day. Sheila was putting the washing on the line when she spotted the gardener's shoes under the bushes. She knew that he fancied her and had caught him spying on her before.

The gardener was just getting more and more excited. He pulled his todger out and started moving the foreskin up and down. He wasn't far away from an orgasm.

Most women would get angry, but Sheila thought that it was rather sweet. She changed her position so that he could get a better view. She turned her back to him and bent over, pretending to pick some pegs up. He stared at her fully exposed fanny. No imagination was needed; he could see her moist vagina in all its glory. He thought about how much he would like to fuck her. Little did he know that the opportunity was right there. Sheila was begging for it.

Sheila wiggled her bum and turned to put her finger into the entrance of her fanny. She wondered what else she would have to do to get the message across. A real man would have already thrown her on the grass and taken her. This was too much for the gardener, who shouted out and came, with semen spraying all over his shorts. Sheila walked around the bush to confront a bald man trying to put his todger back into his trousers. She couldn't help noticing the stains.

'Hello, Sheila,' he said. 'I'm off home now to get my lunch.' She had never seen him move so fast. Sheila had also never felt so randy. She started to consider the use of mechanical stimulation, but for her, a vibrator was no substitute for a nice, hard cock.

Sometimes it is strange how fate plays little tricks on you. While the gardener was running out of the house, the window cleaner turned up. Sheila continued putting the washing on the line and then returned indoors. As she entered the lounge, she came face to face with the window cleaner through a pane of glass. He just stared at her in amazement. Here was a beautiful woman, more or less naked, staring at him.

The window cleaner lost his footing and fell off the ladder, with the ladder and bucket of water landing on top of him. Sheila rushed outside to help. He looked to be in bad shape, as he was rubbing his back. He was soaked. Sheila helped him remove his soaking wet shirt and trousers. He could hardly believe it—a naked woman was undressing him. He couldn't help noticing a beautiful pair of tits and an exposed fanny. His erection was pushing against the fabric of his pants.

Sheila noticed it too and quickly removed his underwear. The window cleaner was still lying on his back with an excellent erection pointing upwards. Sheila wasted no time and crouched over him so that his cock was rubbing against her clit. After minimal rubbing, she had her first orgasm. Sometimes you can't beat a slow, gentle fuck. In this case, Sheila wanted it hard and fast. She pushed her cunt against his throbbing cock, totally enveloping it. She just did the equivalent of jumping up and down in a crouching position. She was violent and aggressive. It looked like he was in pain, but she just carried on. Her orgasm was almost there—one last push should do the job. When it came, it was a monster: a magical once-in-a-lifetime-type orgasm.

Sheila stood up, said 'Thank you very much,' and walked off. It tickled her to think that he was probably desperate to come. Serves him right, she thought.

The Worm Turns

Sheila and Wormy had been married for umpteen years. Sheila knew exactly how many, and Wormy had no idea, but he knew it was a lot. Sheila knew that their marriage was a pathetic, unfulfilling sham. Wormy just drifted along from one day to another, and then from one year to another. He knew that their marriage was reasonably sound, but some of the magic had gone out of it. Sheila could send out extensive search parties, and the last thing they would find would be magic.

Wormy started to think about what he wanted from life. It was probably a mid-life crisis arriving a bit on the late side, but then again, Wormy was always late. In fact, he had made lateness a lifestyle. There was one memorable occasion when he was nearly early, but that was because he'd got the date wrong in his diary. Sheila was always nagging him about his time-keeping, or lack thereof. Sheila spent her life nagging him, but he didn't disagree that he usually deserved it.

After giving it a fair amount of thought, the problem was evident to him. The problem was Sheila. She may have been a gorgeous woman, but she was not attractive. She didn't have that X-factor; she didn't know what a man wanted or needed. She certainly didn't understand Wormy's needs. None of his friends fancied her, so it couldn't just be him. But then he wondered what friends he was referring to. He tried to remember when they'd last made love, but his memory wasn't that good anymore.

It was now apparent to him that he needed a bit on the side. It wasn't fair to Sheila as she had been faithful to him for all those years. As far as he could see, Sheila had never looked at another man. Thinking about it, why would she? However, what he needed was someone exotic. He needed a real woman who could get a man's juices bubbling. He mentally worked his way through a list of Sheila's friends and chose the obvious one: Ida, a black lady from Jamaica.

Wormy hatched his plan. He put a note through Ida's door, offering her free-of-charge house maintenance and gardening work. It worked, as Ida was soon on the phone. Sheila took the call and was a bit surprised to find that she wanted to talk to Wormy. All Sheila could hear was Wormy saying, 'Yes, no problem, I will be around first thing tomorrow. It won't be a problem; I can get the materials free of charge.' Sheila asked Wormy what was going on. Wormy just said, 'I'm not having an affair.'

Sheila immediately wondered if he was having an affair, but then it was just too ridiculous to contemplate. Nonetheless, she made a mental note to keep an eye on it. It was one thing for her to fuck other women's men, but no woman was having hers. But then she reconsidered and decided that anyone could have him, with her approval. But why, Ida?

Ida was a large Jamaican woman. For reasons only known to her, she had grown a huge bum. It was one of those bums that you could use as a mantlepiece. You could place several candelabra on it. The size of her tits nicely counterbalanced the size of her bum. They were large, pendulous love bags that she could sling over her shoulders. The nipples could be used for knitting a jumper.

274

Sheila suspected that she was a bit of a love god as she had already killed off two husbands. On the positive side, she had a generous personality, a huge, happy smile and a genuine willingness to help the underprivileged.

Wormy turned up at Ida's house early in the morning. Ida was still in her nightwear. Wormy had made efforts to present himself in the best possible light. He shaved, plastered himself with Brut and even brushed his hair—well, what was left of it. He tried manipulating his hair to cover up the large bald patch, but it was beyond him. His shoes were clean, and he was wearing a fresh pair of pants. He had his fingers crossed.

Ida let him in. Wormy couldn't help noticing the cut of her jib. It was undoubtedly a large jib. Wormy admired the way her buttocks squeezed together and then parted. He was mesmerized by the swinging motion of her fabulous breasts. He almost thought he saw a large red nipple. It was all too much for him. He was starting to feel faint with desire. His two-inch penis was fully erect. He was still having problems with the foreskin being too tight, but he was sure that he could cope with it.

Ida had not had a man in five years. Her loins were aching for a stiff one. She wasn't too sure if this was the one, but she could see the little bald man admiring her assets. The essence of Brut was getting to her, dulling her resistance. If he acted quickly, he could take her. She thought, 'Be quick, but be gentle.' Wormy looked into her eyes. His tiny erection was pushing against his underwear, his mouth had gone dry with anticipation, and he said, 'Let's have a cup of tea.'

Ida put the kettle on, but she did not attempt to cover herself up. Wormy loved her hefty black legs supporting an arse and a half. Well, nearer three arses, but she knew how to move. Her eleven bellies cascaded down from her chin, enticing poor, helpless Wormy. What could he do, when presented with such feminine loveliness? Wormy said to Ida, 'I've always wanted you, prepare to be fucked.' Wormy stood up and tried to push Ida onto the kitchen table. It wasn't easy; she was two or three times his size. In the end, he managed to lift one leg.

Ida was not having any of it. She picked Wormy up, threw him over her shoulder and took him upstairs. She literally ripped his clothes off. She spent some time looking for his cock. She'd never had that problem with Jamaican men. Eventually, she spotted it hiding behind one of Wormy's testicles. It appeared to be erect and sensitive, but just so very small. What was she going to do? Her fanny was demanding action. She just grabbed Wormy's head and crushed it against her clit, which was larger than Wormy's cock.

Wormy could hardly breathe, but he started sucking. He just sucked and sucked. He struggled to hold on, as Ida was very physical. She tossed and turned, throwing poor Wormy all over the place. He was getting severely bruised in the process. At one stage, he was using her nipples as handles to hold onto. She was seriously fruity and almost violent. Wormy had never experienced anything like it. Sheila hardly moved, and she certainly didn't throw him around—but then again, the whole process only took two minutes usually. Here, it seemed to be going on for hours.

Wormy wasn't sure if Ida had climaxed or not, as he had never experienced a female orgasm before. She was certainly making a lot of noise, swearing and cursing and shouting at him to chew her nipples. He attempted to move upwards, but it was a tough climb. He got there eventually, but it had made him sweat. Then her nipple was in his mouth, and he started sucking.

Ida was a woman in heat. Every part of her body was scorching hot. Her fanny was like an oven; her breath was on fire. Her whole body just rippled with lust. She was insatiable. It was very likely that Wormy's cock had entered her fanny, but neither one of them was too sure that it had. Certainly, Wormy had come, and Ida had experienced a series of multiple orgasms.

Ida finally realised why Sheila was such a happy soul. With a man like that, any woman would be satisfied. 'Well,' she thought. 'This is my man now.' She instinctively knew that she'd have to tell Wormy what to do. She told him to go and make a pot of tea and bring her breakfast in bed. He obeyed, saying, 'Yes, Mistress.' Ida was onto a winner here.

She then told him to go home and get his clothes and come straight back. He did as he was told. At Sheila's house, he started packing. Sheila asked what he was up to, and he said, 'I'm moving in with the woman I love.'

Sheila said, 'And who is that?'

He said, 'Glennis Brown.'

Sheila never saw Wormy or Glennis again. Ida was devastated.

Anyway, Sheila thought a Wormy in the hand was worth two in the bush.

The Removal Men

After the divorce, Sheila decided that she needed a change in her life. It was time for a new house, a new job, a new car and possibly a new man. Firstly, she brought a brand new, cream Mini Cooper with all the trimmings. She loved it; it suited her personality perfectly. She then found a lovely flat in London, put her house up for sale, got a buyer and was ready to move. Everything was going swimmingly well.

Moving day arrived, and the removal van turned up on time. The removers were keen to get on the road as it was a relatively long journey. It was a warm, spring day, and Sheila was in a short, denim skirt that showed her very shapely legs off to perfection. She had meant to go back indoors and put a bra on, but with all the hustle and bustle, she'd never got around to it, but her cotton top protected her modesty.

She couldn't believe how much stuff she had, but it wasn't long before everything was loaded and they were ready to go. She took one final look at her old home and rushed by the lorry to take a photo. In doing so, she managed to rip off her skirt on the tailgate. The three removers just stared at her standing there in a semi-transparent pair of knickers. Bill, the older man, and his two sons, Jake and Fred, admired her legs. Bill asked if she had another skirt, she could put on. Sheila said, 'Not really, they are all packed.'

Bill said it wouldn't be a problem since she'd be sitting in the front of the van with them. She would be quite safe. Sheila had heard that before, but there was no alternative. They got on their way. Sheila was very conscious about sitting there in her tiny panties, especially as the two burly sons kept taking a sneaky peek. She thought she had nothing to be ashamed of, anyway.

After two hours, they decided to stop for a coffee and a toilet break. The three men seemed to forget that Sheila was not fully dressed, but she needed to go to the loo. She got lots of wolf whistles from the drivers in Chieveley Services as she walked by in her underwear. She didn't mind, as she had three strong men to protect her. While they were drinking their coffee, the heavens opened up. It just poured down. Bill said, 'That's global warming for you.' They waited for half an hour, and then Bill said, 'We can't wait any longer, or we will run out of time.'

All four of them ran for it, trying to avoid the huge puddles that had appeared. The rain was just torrential, and Sheila was drenched. It wasn't so bad for the men, as they had sturdy industrial clothes on. At the van, Bill said to Sheila, 'You need to get out of those soaking wet clothes, or they will be the death of you.' Jake grabbed Sheila's top and pulled it off, releasing two fabulous tits. Fred whipped her knickers down and pushed her into the van.

Sheila couldn't believe what had just happened. She was sitting naked in the front seat of a removal van with three husky men. They all had grins on their faces as they took in the view: great tits, great arse and a black bush fully on show. They put the heater on high and attempted to wipe Sheila down with an old, dirty cloth. Fred was making considerable efforts to get her breasts dry, which made her nipples erect. They got on their way. The poor road surface, with all its potholes, made the van jump around, causing Sheila's boobs to bounce all over the place. Jake and Fred found it difficult to take their eyes off them.

The vibration of the vehicle and the fact that the heaters were on full made Sheila drowsy. This was quite normal for Sheila, as she found dozing in a car one of life's great pleasures. She did, however, have the ability to sleep and listen to conversations at the same time. As Sheila dozed, Jake and Fred tried to make things more comfortable for her, and she ended up lying across their laps. The boys had the challenge of stopping Sheila from falling off, which is the same problem one encounters with a sleeping cat.

Fred held Sheila just under the boobs. Actually, he had her boobs resting on his arms, which he thoroughly enjoyed. Jake was holding her tightly by the hips, and his arm was resting on her fanny. As Bill turned to his left to survey the situation, he could see a beautiful, naked woman lying across the laps of his two sons. Both her boobs and fanny were being well protected. He laughed at the antics of his boys, but then he was sitting there driving a Luton with a huge erection.

They all assumed that Sheila was fast off. Fred asked his dad if they were going to fuck her. Bill said, 'I've told you before that we don't fuck customers.'

Fred said, 'What about Mrs Wilson?'

Bill blushed and said, 'She was an exception.' Fred asked if this could be an exception too, as Sheila had fantastic boobs. He took the opportunity to gently stroke them. Sheila kept quiet, keen to see how the conversation would develop— although she was a bit concerned. She didn't want to be the target of a gang-bang.

Jake said, 'We are not going to get that many opportunities to fuck such a beautiful woman.' Bill agreed that she was exceptionally pretty, as he took another glance at her pussy. Jake said, 'She is fast off, we could do whatever we like,' and he rubbed her bush to emphasise the point. Jake said, 'I could be in and out of her pussy before she knew.' He managed to find her clit and started caressing it.

Bill said in a stern voice, 'I will not have this sort of behaviour in my van. It's unacceptable.' But he realised that his boys were young, and it wasn't every day that they had such a gorgeous, naked girl in their laps. In his day, she would have been having his babies by now. Jake was still playing with Sheila's clit, which was getting Sheila hot. She could feel her fanny moistening. It didn't help that Fred was giving her nipples a good work out as well.

Jake said to his dad, 'I don't think she is objecting, as her fanny is getting very juicy.' Bill leaned over and put his finger in Sheila's vagina.

Bill said, 'I think you are right, but this has got to stop now.' Sheila didn't want it to stop.

Sheila groaned and moaned as the two boys continued to play with her very willing body. Jake had a finger gently caressing the inside walls of Sheila's vagina. He had got a steady rhythm going that sent waves of pleasure down her spine. Her fanny was getting steadily wetter and wetter, and it had reached the point that Jake needed to dab it down with his hanky. There was an overpowering smell of musk in the cab. In fact, the windows in the cab were getting quite fogged up.

Fred wanted a share of the delights hidden in Sheila's cute little cunt, and he inserted his finger. Bill wondered if she could take three, as she certainly looked moist enough, and he joined the two boys in her fanny. It certainly made driving a little bit tricky.

Sheila wondered how she had got herself into this situation, driving along the M25, stark naked, lying across the laps of two young men with three fingers belonging to three different men in her fanny. No one would believe it in a film or book. The sheer naughtiness of the situation, the rhythmic movement of the truck and the traffic in her fanny was getting too much for her. Sometimes her climaxes were like the tingle you get from touching an electric fence; other times, they felt like a bomb exploding in her mind, and she'd lose all control. This was a bomb—she lost all control. Her legs went rigid. She nearly broke the boys' fingers.

Jake said to his father, 'What happened?'

Bill said, 'Looks like an orgasm to me. Very tricky things are women. I remember my ex-wife having an orgasm once. I was downstairs watching the TV when it happened. I ran upstairs to find her incapacitated with a cucumber in a very private place. It put me off salads for years.' Jake said that they looked quite dangerous.

Fred was wiping blood off his nose. Bill asked, 'What happened?' Fred said that the orgasm had caused him physical harm. Apparently, while he was caressing one of Sheila's nipples, her leg shot out and smashed against his nose. Bill and Jake laughed, but Fred found it quite painful. Sheila, still lying down, couldn't help laughing. She did feel sorry for Fred, but Bill had warned him.

They were approaching Sheila's new downstairs flat. Sheila sat up, covering her breasts with her arms. She noticed that her nipples were still very erect, but they were also a bit sore. She wondered how she was going to get into the house in her current state of undress. Bill said, 'Don't worry, we will sort it.' Bill took the key to unlock the front door, and Sheila edged her way out of the cab. The boys picked her up and rushed her into the flat.

Joyce, Sheila's new next-door neighbour, said to Norman, her husband, 'You won't believe this, but three burly men have just rushed a naked girl into the vacant flat next door.' Norman rushed over, annoyed that he had missed all the action.

Norman asked, 'What did she look like?'

Joyce said, 'Well, it was all quite quick, but I could see that she had dark hair, a slim figure and big breasts.'

Norm asked, 'How big?'

Joyce said, 'Big enough. Perhaps she has been kidnapped.' Joyce and Norman were not the sort to interfere, but they kept a strict watch on the neighbourhood.

Sheila welcomed the chance to stand up after all that lying down. She had enjoyed her orgasm, but she never felt satisfied until she had been properly fucked. Sheila bent over, leaning on a small coffee table that the previous owners had left behind. 'Who's first? I need to christen the flat,' Sheila said. The three men looked at each other, and without any discussion, Fred dropped his trousers.

Fred positioned himself behind Sheila's welcoming fanny. He couldn't let the others know that he was still a virgin, and hopefully, he wouldn't be for much longer. Like a virgin, he plunged right in. There was no finesse, just inexperienced humping. Sheila was well and truly humped. The humping soon ended when gallons of spunk erupted from his immature cock. He was so excited. He gave Sheila a passionate but amateurish kiss on the lips. Sheila thought, 'How sweet.'

Jake looked at his dad, who nodded his approval. Jake's

erect cock was in Sheila's fanny in no time at all. He didn't think he would last very long because he had been so very aroused on the journey. He was right, and Sheila received her second deposit that day.

Bill looked at his sons and thought, 'Amateurs.' Bill took off his trousers and carefully folded them up. He did the same with his pants. His sons were impressed with the length and girth of their father's cock. It was a monster—a real king of cocks. Jake wondered if Sheila's fanny could cope with it, but then he remembered that she could cope with three fingers at once. Bill walked towards Sheila with the look of a matador. He would show the lads how it was done.

He grabbed the sides of Sheila's buttocks, and with no help from his hands, he entered Sheila's vagina. It was a forceful, but delicate, entry from a man who knew what he was doing. His penis fucked her head on; he switched the direction to the inside right of the fanny, then the inside left. Then up, then down—his penis was hunting for the 'G' spot. He put it on automatic so that it repeated the cycle again and again: straight ahead, left, right, up and down. Sheila's head was swimming. She had never been fucked by a food mixer before. Her fanny would have turned it off given a chance, but the mixer just speeded up. She had never seen, or felt, anything like it.

The boys were entranced. The sight of Sheila's sweet little pussy being fucked relentlessly was almost too much to bear. Jake was at the point of telling his dad to stop when there were two mighty screams. Both had come simultaneously. Bill pulled out to send a torrent of spunk flying through the air towards the window, where they saw the faces of two elderly people appear and then quickly duck.

Sheila was exhausted. Fred had lost his virginity. Jake was just so impressed with his dad. 'What a man,' he thought. Bill thought that it was the first time that the three of them had mixed their semen in one woman. Norman hadn't known that he could still get an erection. Joyce had discovered that he could, shouting, 'Harder, Norm, harder!'

Sheila never received a bill from Bill, but she did get a Christmas card in the post.

One Last Time

Sheila had been divorced from Wormy for about three years. It had been an amicable divorce, with both parties in full agreement. There had been no furious arguments or anger. The marriage had never really worked; Sheila was treated more like an unpaid care worker looking after her husband and three children than a wife. Wormy had been in a mental hospital a few times. He had suffered from depression most of his life, especially when one of the children had been born, which was a time when help from her husband was most needed. He had been more of a burden than a help to Sheila, especially as he had lost one poorly paid job after another.

And to cap it all off, he was a disaster in bed. He was never that interested in sex. He had no idea how to meet the needs of a woman. In Wormy's world, the important person was Wormy. Sheila remembered that he used to kiss her breasts as if they were a plastic toy. She couldn't stand the strange kissing noises he used to make. He had no idea where her fanny was, and she always had to help him enter her. Sheila often wondered how she'd managed to have three fine, strapping boys with that man.

In the end, they'd drifted apart, ending up in separate bedrooms with totally independent lives. Sheila initiated the divorce, but it was something that Wormy had wanted for some time, hadn't it been?

Sheila had been thinking about Wormy as he was coming around at 12.00 for a chat. He wouldn't say on the phone what it was about. She decided that she would have a bath at 11.00 and be ready to meet him at noon. 'Probably a waste of a day,' she thought.

Wormy rang the doorbell at 11.00 when Sheila was getting in the bath. 'That's typical of Wormy,' she thought. Sheila quickly wrapped a towel around herself and let him in. 'You are early,' she said.

Wormy said, 'Well, you always accused me of being late, so I thought I would make an effort.' Sheila organised some coffee, and they sat around the dining room table.

Wormy said, 'It's really good to see you; you know that in my own way, I have always loved you.'

Sheila said, 'You rarely showed it.'

Wormy said, 'That's not true, what about all the holidays we went on?'

Sheila said, 'Come on, I booked the holidays, I did the packing, I organised the food and the cooking, and I paid for it. What did you do?'

Wormy said that he did some of the driving. Sheila laughed and pointed out that he was generally too tired to do much of it. He used to stop on the hard shoulder of the motorway and refuse to go any further. It didn't matter how tired she was. Sheila said, 'What about that time when you were driving back from Colette's wedding? It was minus nineteen, the coldest day of the year. You got lost on the M4 and ended up in South Wales. We lived in Brighton.' Wormy agreed that neither his navigation nor his driving skills were the best.

Wormy said, 'I always bought presents for you at

Christmas and on your birthday.' Sheila couldn't believe that he raised that point.

'Wormy,' she said in a very aggressive voice, 'your presents were the worst ever. One year, you bought me bin liners, salt, washing up liquid and pencils. I was so angry with you. I didn't want expensive presents. I just wanted something romantic, or even girlie.'

Wormy said, 'I bought you socks one year.'

Sheila responded, 'Wormy, you bought me socks eight years in a row. You even moaned when you didn't get enough presents for yourself.'

Wormy said that he did the cooking sometimes. Again, Sheila laughed and said, 'Wormy, you only did the cooking when it suited you. Then you would just cook something you wanted and ignored me. I did the cooking almost every day of our marriage. You never helped with the shopping. You never put it away. You never helped when guests came around. You never did any housework.'

Wormy said, 'I used to cut the lawn.' She replied, 'Only after I asked you over and over again. And to make it worse, your pruning was a bit like deforestation.' Wormy agreed that his gardening skills were somewhat limited.

'Anyway,' Wormy said, 'I had my art to consider.' Sheila agreed that some of his paintings were quite good, but most of his other creations were a disaster. Sheila pointed out that after he left, she had to hire two skips to take his rubbish away. It had taken months to sort the house out.

Sheila didn't want it to become an argument. Time had passed, she had moved on, and she was more than happy without him. She asked Wormy what he wanted.

'Well,' he said, 'I thought I would update you on my

position. I'm still suffering from depression, and I have some very black days. I hate my little flat; there is not enough room to do my art. The flat needs a good clean, and I can't stand doing the washing or ironing. I'm not eating properly. I can go days without talking to anyone. I've no one to spend Christmas with. And to cap it all, I've not had sex for more than three years.'

Sheila said, 'I'm sorry to hear all that. That would certainly get me down. Who did you have sex with?' Wormy asked what she meant. Sheila said, 'You mentioned that you had not had sex for three years. The last time you had sex with me was about six years ago.'

Wormy said, 'In that case, I've not had sex for six years.'

Sheila then asked, 'What has any of that got to do with me?'

Wormy said, 'As you don't seem to have a man, I thought it would make sense for me to move in with you. We don't have to get married, but we could have sex if you wanted to.'

Sheila was somewhat shocked and said, 'You want to move in here?' Wormy said, 'I thought you would agree. I've got some of my stuff in the car. You can help me get the rest later.'

Sheila almost shouted as she said, 'No. You are not moving in. What would be in it for me?'

Wormy said, 'Companionship, more money, safety, a loving relationship and the kids would like it.'

Sheila said, 'The answer is no. I'm really enjoying myself. I don't need you back in my life.' Wormy's face dropped. He thought that Sheila would go for it. Sheila could see that he was distraught.

Sheila said, 'Wormy, I'm sorry if this has upset you, but

it's for the best.' He said that it was not the best for him. He was looking forward to a loving relationship. He was looking forward to having sex again. She asked if he had considered using the services of a prostitute. He said that he had, but they cost £100 a time. He was willing to pay it, but he was just too shy. Anyway, she was the only person that he had ever had sex with. With a grin, he said that he would be willing to pay her £100 for sex.

Sheila thought that for all these years, he had got it for free, and now he was willing to pay for it. 'Wormy,' she said, 'I'm not a prostitute.'

'I know,' he said, 'but I'm really desperate. If I don't have a woman soon, I will commit suicide.' While he was chatting, he couldn't help noticing the curve of her breasts as the towel had slipped. She had always been a beautiful woman. Although he was never sex-mad, he had always enjoyed her perfectly proportioned breasts and her exquisite pair of legs.

Sheila saw him looking at her breasts, and she allowed the towel to slip a bit further so that her nipples were exposed. She wasn't sure why she did that, but she was enjoying teasing him. Wormy stared. Sheila said, 'So you are offering me £100 for a shag?'

Wormy said, 'I could offer more than that.'

Sheila said, 'Go on.'

'£200,' he said.

She carried on looking at him, and he increased it to £500. Sheila said, 'So you are offering me £500 for full sexual intercourse.'

'Yes,' he replied.

Sheila realised that she was negotiating over the price, but in her mind, she was not sure if she wanted to go ahead or not.

She then asked what she would have to do. He said, 'Just lie on the bed with your hands holding your legs apart. I will fuck you and then give you £500.' Sheila said that she wanted the money upfront, knowing that he wouldn't have it. He called her bluff and then counted and handed over £500 in cash.

She felt that she now had no choice, and they both walked upstairs to the master bedroom. Sheila took her towel off and laid it on the bed in case he was messy. It was slightly strange, but she felt a bit shy being naked in front of a man who had fucked her many times. She got in position with her hands holding her legs apart. Wormy quickly undressed.

Sheila looked at what was in front of her: a weak, pathetic little man with a very skinny two-inch cock. Usually, she couldn't feel anything. Wormy said that he had never seen her fanny before. Sheila thought about it and agreed that that was probably true. Hard to believe that a married man had never seen his wife's fanny, but then she had rarely seen his cock. It was clear that he wasn't sure what to do. 'Come here,' she said, and she quickly put his penis into her vagina.

Wormy grunted, and the job was done. Sheila had felt nothing. There was no sign of any semen, but she assumed that he had come. Wormy kissed her on the cheek. He asked if he could see her next month. Sheila said, 'No.' On the way out, Sheila said, 'Don't expect a Christmas present.' She felt guilty about the whole thing for a few minutes, but then she thought, 'It's my body, I can do anything I like with it.'

But she'd decided that he wasn't going to worm his way back into her life.

Best Friends: Part 1

Sheila was having a nice cup of coffee at The Ritz and waiting for her two best friends to turn up. Sheila always liked coffee in a bone china cup. 'That's how it should be done,' she thought to herself.

She was a little nervous, as she wasn't sure how her two best friends were going to react to her latest scheme—writing a soft-porn book for women. She knew that it had been done before, but her angle was to make outlandish situations seem possible. Just thinking about the stories made her a bit frisky, but then she felt that her libido was a bit stronger than most women's.

Carol and Margot turned up as planned, and Sheila organised two teas for them. The girls chatted about their family and holidays and all the local gossip. There was much laughter and joviality. These were three friends who knew each other well and enjoyed each other's company. Sometimes the laughter got a bit raucous, and the other customers nearby gave them a stern look.

Carol used to be a bit of a head-turner in her day, with her slim figure, blonde hair and cheeky smile, but the years had taken their toll. Margot, who was Cypriot, had also seen better days, as she had developed a Mediterranean bottom that was a few sizes too large. They were both a bit jealous of Sheila, as time had treated her so well. To put it simply, Sheila was still gorgeous with her very shapely legs, well-proportioned bosom, great figure and one of the most infectious smiles you could ever ask for.

They were still chatting away when Sheila announced that she intended to write a soft-porn book. Both Carol and Margot stopped in their tracks and said, 'What? Are you serious?' Sheila nodded.

Margot asked, 'Is it going to be like 50 Shades of Grey?'

Sheila said, 'Not really. It's going to be a series of sexy stories. Typically, a young, attractive woman, who might be called Sheila, is put into awkward positions where she has to strip or have sex.

Carol said, 'What sorts of positions are you thinking of?'

Margot blurted out, 'The doggy position,' and they all laughed.

Sheila said, 'I'm not talking about sex positions, but more situations—like having to strip for a charity calendar.' Her friends thought that this was typical of Sheila, but they knew that when she had an idea, she usually followed through with it. Writing a naughty book certainly would suit her bubbly personality. She would love all the attention she got if the book were published.

Sheila told them that she had written quite a few stories already, but she was now looking for new ideas and needed some fresh inspiration. Neither Carol nor Margot was particularly creative. Sheila was pretty sure that neither woman was having sex with her husband or had the energy for an affair. Sheila couldn't imagine a world without the occasional 'bonk.'

Sheila said to her friends, 'You must have at least one story that I could use.'

There was lots of hesitation, and then Carol eventually said, 'I do have one story, but you must swear that it will remain a secret.' Sheila said that keeping it secret would be a bit tricky considering she planned to put it in a book. Carol said, 'I know that. You would need to change the name and never tell anyone that the inspiration for it was me.' Both Sheila and Margot were suddenly very intrigued, and both swore to keep the secret. Sheila was wondering who she could tell.

Carol said, 'This has always been a secret, but it would do me good to tell it. David must never know about it.

'When I was nineteen, I fell madly in love with a biker. You know what it is like when you are that age—love is absolutely everything. Anyway, Nigel was fabulous; I would do anything for him. I also loved his Harley. You probably don't know that I've always been keen on bikes.

'Anyway, he was part of a gang, and to be his girlfriend I had to be initiated into the chapter. I had my suspicions as to what it meant, but I was keen that Nigel should give me a really good seeing to. I was desperate to lose my virginity. I had also heard stories that I might be gang-banged as part of the ceremony, but if Nigel didn't mind, then neither did I.

'I sat on the back of his massive bike. I could feel the rumble through my short skirt and flimsy knickers. My arms hugged Nigel's leathers. The smell of oil and leather and the constant rumbling and tumbling of the bike was getting to me. My fanny was more than damp.

'We arrived at a clearing where about six other bikers were waiting. It was a warm, moonlit evening with a slight breeze. The chapter leader said, "So, this is your intended girlfriend?" And Nigel introduced me to all the chapter members who were slowly disrobing. Getting the leathers off is always a bit time-consuming.

'The chapter leader said to Nigel, "I take it that you and Carol know the rules and that you are happy to go ahead?"

'Nigel said, "Yes", and I nodded.

'The leader looked at me and said, "Can you confirm that you are happy to go ahead?"

'I said, "Yes", very enthusiastically.' He then told Nigel to get me ready.

'Nigel walked me over to his bike. He made sure that the stand was firmly in place. He then laid me face-down on the bike with my legs stretched to each side. My bottom was sticking over the end of the seat, and my head was resting on the fuel tank. He then used leather straps firmly to attach me to the bike. I could hardly move a muscle or even see what was going on.

'It looked like the ceremony was going to start. My short skirt was undone and removed. I heard Nigel say, "I willingly give this cunt to the Chapter".

'I thought, "How rude". Then I felt my knickers being cut off with a knife. My cunt, as they put it, was now fully exposed to the gang. I couldn't imagine what it looked like, but it couldn't have left anything to the imagination. It was looking like I was going to lose my virginity to Nigel very soon.

'I could feel the cool breeze against my fanny. I was then surprised that a thick, cold liquid was splashed against my private parts and rubbed in. I had never felt a man's hand rubbing my pussy before. It was a strange sensation—the cold breeze, the oily liquid substance, the warm hand and the humiliation of the situation. I later learnt that it was used engine oil that had been used to lubricate me.

'Before I could give any more thought to the situation, a large penis had taken my virginity. After a merciless pounding, there was a large grunt. I assumed that Nigel must have come, but with all the fluid sloshing around, it was hard to tell. I was so disappointed—no flashing lights, no sensuous buzz and no feeling of euphoria. It was all such an anti-climax.

'I was expecting to be cut free when a second penis entered my vagina. This penis was a bit more thoughtful; a bit gentler. I started to get some delightful tingling sensations. I was just beginning to enjoy it when there was another grunt, and my pussy was empty again.

'But not for long. A very large penis started to enjoy the inside of my fanny. It seemed to be very experienced, as it gradually increased its rhythm. It was almost musical. My body responded to the music. It was contracting and convulsing to the rhythm, or the rhythm of life, as I called it. It entered me and withdrew, entered and withdrawn, faster and faster. I could feel my body perched on the edge of something, and then he grunted, and my pussy was empty once again.

'"Well", I thought, "most girls don't have three cocks up them on the day they lose their virginity". Then a correction was needed—it was four cocks, as another one entered. Compared to the others, it was small and pathetic. It was soon out. I nearly shouted out, "Call that a fuck?" but then again, I was hardly experienced myself. Then I worked out that including Nigel, there were seven men present.

'Number five arrived and did a pretty good job. I could feel his cock rubbing enthusiastically against the side of my vagina. I started to respond to his gentle pounding. He steadily got more intense and pushed harder and harder. I heard someone say, "Steady, John, it's an expensive bike". But there wasn't any concern for my fanny. John wasn't too concerned either, and he came with a powerful thrust. This time, I thought I felt semen spraying my intimate parts.

'The sixth fuck was just excellent. He was a big man. He struggled to get his penis into my almost virgin hole. Someone asked him if he needed any more lubrication. He said, "No, this chick just needs to get used to a big one". In no time at all, I got used to him. I never realised that my cunt could handle such a monster. He pumped and pounded, and pushed, and heaved his member into me. I was more than willing to take it. I was a rag doll; I was his. I was never too sure if he came, but I certainly did. This time, it was flashing lights—it was a huge, sensuous buzz and totally euphoric. I lost myself in the splendour of the moment. "What a pussy", I thought. I was now a woman.

'I thought it was strange that the last one was the best when another cock entered me. I had had enough by then. Had more bikers turned up? The young lad soon finished. I was now able to judge a man's age by his performance. The next one was even younger. While he was pumping away, I heard the chapter leader say that I was now fully initiated. The straps were being cut away while the lad's penis was still inside me. I felt it slip out when I stood up.

'Nigel gave me an odd look. I got on his bike knickerless with a mixture of spunk and oil running down the side of the engine cover. When I got home, Nigel held my hand quite lovingly and said, "I don't want to see you again, you whore". He got on his bike and left.

'I was devastated; I had given my virginity away and been fucked by a whole biker gang.

'I later learnt that there had been six bikers present, and

two of them had fucked me twice. Nigel hadn't fucked me after all. It appeared that he never fucked any of the girls he brought to the chapter meetings. He was the best "girl finder" they had.'

At the end of the story, both Sheila and Margot held Carol's hands, as she had a tear in her eye. Margot said that she would tell her story next time.

Best Friends: Part 2

Sheila, Carol and Margot were back at The Ritz for their monthly get-together. They had been in the V&A Museum all morning and were now having a well-deserved drinks break. After hearing Carol's story the last time, Sheila was eager to get details on Margot's sexual adventures. It was still hard to believe that Carol was tied to a motorcycle and gang-banged. Although she wanted to keep it quiet, she seemed secretly proud of her encounter.

They had their refreshments and Sheila moved the conversation onto her new book. Carol once again emphasised how important it was to keep her story anonymous. Margot said, 'I suppose you want my story now, on how I lost my virginity? Although looking back, the whole episode was rather shameful.' Sheila said that she had her notepad ready and asked her to proceed.

Margot started, 'As you know, I was born in Nicosia in Cyprus. The years after the Second World War were very tough. The British Government had no money, Cyprus had no money, and my family had no money. As a country, we wanted independence from the UK, which meant that British aid was somewhat limited.

'It's hard to believe, but a good wage at the time was £2–3 per week. A pound was a serious amount of money. I was the youngest of six, but we were all expected to contribute to the family's finances. My eldest sister was a real beauty; she had at one time been the Cypriot National Beauty Queen. Anyway, unbeknownst to my parents, she was charging men to view her body. She was charging the equivalent of 50p to see her boobs or fanny and £1 to see her naked.

'She was raking the money in. She was earning more money than my father, who was a fisherman. Eventually, she had enough money to put down a deposit on a house. I'm not sure how she got away with it. I'm not even sure how she marketed her services. As far as I know, things never went any further than a peep show. Things were a lot more innocent in those days. There was no whiff of a scandal. I've never even mentioned it to her in the last twenty-odd years.

'I spotted this dress in the local shop, and I was determined to have it. To be honest, I was fixated on it. It became the sole objective of my life. There was no way my parents could afford it, and I certainly didn't have the money. I approached my "rich" sister, and she said, "There is no way I'm buying that dress for you. You have got a nice pair of boobs and a fanny; you can earn it the hard way".

'I wiped the tears away, but I never truly forgave my sister. I thought, "She's right; let's put my assets on show". I started locally. One of my male friends was always asking to see my boobs, as young men do, so I said that it would cost him 25p. The next day, he came back with the money, and I lifted my top. In those days, I never wore a bra as they were too expensive. Anyway, my boobs were firm, and they didn't need much support. He started fondling them. I wasn't sure if it was allowed or not, but I enjoyed it.

'He tried to move his hand downstairs. I stopped him and said that if he wanted to see my fanny, it would be another 25p.

300

The next day, he turned up with two of his mates. I took 25p off each of them. I then pulled my knickers down and lifted my skirt. The look of awe on their faces was amazing. I suddenly realised how powerful a fanny was. They asked if they could touch it, and I nodded. Three young lads were touching my fanny—there was no penetration, but I still enjoyed it.

'I rushed to the shop to buy the dress of my dreams. But now I wanted a bra and a nice pair of shoes, too. I figured that it shouldn't take too long to earn enough for that, and it didn't. My top was up, my knickers were down, and the money came pouring in. Despite all of this, I knew practically nothing about sex. I had never seen a todger, but I knew that I got hot thinking about it.

'Then, one fateful day, Danny turned up. He was older than my usual clients—more sophisticated and worldly. He had a cheeky look about him. It was love at first sight. He asked how much he could get for a fiver. He was brandishing a crisp note in his hands. I had never seen a five-pound note before. I'm not even sure that my parents had.

'I didn't know what to say when he said, "Do you go all the way? I innocently nodded. He grabbed my hand and rushed me down to the beach. In Cyprus, you are never far from the beach. He laid his jacket on the sand, more or less pushed me onto my back and quickly whipped my knickers off. Before you could say, "Have you considered safe sex?" his prick was in my fanny. Before you could say, "Have a nice day", the job was done, and he gave me a fiver. I just wondered what all the fuss was about. I cleaned up my private parts with a hanky and pulled my knickers up. That's when I saw my father fishing on the beach.

'The following week, I was back on the beach with another fiver in my hands. I purchased all the clothes I needed. Danny even commented on the nicer knickers I was now wearing—not that he spent much time looking at them, as they were soon off as we got down to business.

'The weeks went on, and I was building up a very nice kitty. Danny never changed the routine. It was always hello, jacket on the beach, knickers off, cock in the fanny, a quick spurt, £5 in my hand and he was off. He never even helped me put my knickers back on.

'Then, the inevitable happened. I started to put on weight and felt slightly sick in the mornings. My eldest sister noticed it first. She gave me the name of a lady in St Pauls who could cure my problem. Perhaps she hadn't been the pure little angel she pretended to be after all. I mentioned it to Danny, and he immediately proposed marriage. He was an honourable man, after all.

'As you know, we have now been married for twenty-five years. The strange thing is that our three children were all conceived on Brighton Beach. It's the only way he can get his rocks off.'

The three girls all laughed, finished their drinks and left. On the way back home, Margot said to Carol, 'The annoying thing is that I paid the deposit on our house in Cyprus from the money Danny gave me. He effectively got half his money back.'

Best Friends: Part 3

Sheila, Carol and Margot were back at The Ritz for their monthly get-together. This time, they were joined by Monica, an attractive and exuberant Caribbean lady. They had just visited Buckingham Palace, and as a treat, Sheila offered to buy them a cream tea.

Sheila explained to Margot that she was writing a series of erotic stories that she hoped to get published. She was looking to her for a sexual adventure that she could put in the book. She stated that it went without saying that all names would be changed to protect both the guilty and the innocent.

Monica decided to tell her story. Her daughter Linda and Linda's husband were having financial problems, as John was between jobs. She sold her little flat to help them catch up on their mortgage arrears in exchange for moving in with them. She wasn't sure if she was doing the right thing for them or herself.

Monica had been divorced for over twenty years, but she still had several gentleman callers. This was not surprising as she was an attractive woman who looked at least twenty years younger than she was. She had put a little bit of weight on, but it only seemed to accentuate the curves of her breasts and arse. She was definitely a head-turner, especially with her fabulous, shapely legs and her long, black hair.

It also helped that she wore colourful trendy clothes that

made her happy. Monica always saw the bright side of life. Her bubbly, infectious attitude put a smile on everyone's face. It always put a smile on John's face. He had always secretly admired her—well, sometimes not that secretly.

Linda, on the other hand, was a studious and serious woman who liked to button-up her dowdy blouse. John had never really seen her naked. He wasn't too sure if he wanted to. Ten years of marriage had dulled his ardour to the point where he had considered divorce.

Monica was concerned about moving in, as she had always been an independent woman. She was also concerned about having both mother and daughter in the same house; everyone said that it never worked out. Who was going to be the boss? But she had always enjoyed John's company. He was good fun—a manly sort of man who still played rugby at a reasonable level.

The day had come for her to move in. It was a hot August day, the kind of day when everything and everyone was sticky. The removal guys had finished their work, and she was desperate to wash. As no one else was in the house, she quickly stripped down to her knickers and bent over the bath to wash her hair.

She heard the front door go and shouted to let the person know that she was upstairs. John opened the bathroom door and just stared. Here was his mother-in-law bending over the bath in a tiny pair of knickers. Her gorgeous breasts were fully exposed and dangling over the edge of the tub.

Monica could see John looking at her through the mirror tiles. She was soaking wet as the water poured over her head. She thought about grabbing a towel, but instead, she just wiggled her bum. John grabbed her and took his cock out of his trousers.

He pulled her knickers to one side and simply entered her. There was no discussion and no agreement. He just entered her and pumped and pumped until he came with an enormous roar. She had no chance of coming as the whole thing was so quick—she was just a fuck-toy.

He said sorry, zipped up and walked off. He was apprehensive about what would happen next. Effectively, he had just raped his mother-in-law, but then she had wiggled her bum. Would she tell Linda? He never thought that he was the sort of man who could do that, but there was just so much pent-up frustration.

The next day at breakfast, Monica passed John a note without Linda seeing it. It just said, "Never again". He felt both relief and guilt. He decided that it would never happen again, but Monica secretly wanted more. She liked a man who took what he wanted. She would not initiate anything, but she might just tease him.

Monica made sure that occasionally too much leg was on show, or perhaps her breasts were not covered as much as they should be. On one occasion, they were watching TV when John couldn't help noticing Monica's little black triangle as her skirt rose. Her nightie, late at night, was often too skimpy and too transparent. John was having far too many hard-ons.

Monica and John were actually making love without touching each other. John knew what Monica was doing, but he kept his hands to himself. Linda could not even sense the tension in the house. John desperately wanted to fuck Monica again, but what could he do?

Then life solved the problem. Monica was in the garden in a tiny pair of shorts and a skimpy top with no bra. John had been secretly watching her from the window and occasionally catching a glimpse of her boobs. He often did this when Linda was away.

Monica was stung on the bottom by a bee. She ran inside screaming. John rushed to her assistance and quickly removed her shorts to expose her naked body. He rubbed cream on the sting, and then he proceeded to rub her fanny. Monica offered no resistance whatsoever.

He almost brought her to a climax with his hand, but he stopped to remove his trousers to expose the largest, hardest cock she had ever seen. As she stroked it, it got even harder. She positioned herself so that he could easily enter her.

She could tell that he was desperate, but he was still gentle. He slowly entered and withdrew, entered and withdrew. She could feel an orgasm building in her. He could sense it also. He continued his gentle but steady pressure on her fanny, and every now and then, he would fondle her clit. The pressure continued to build until Monica just screamed in ecstasy. It was the best fuck of her life. She didn't know what to say.

But before she could rest, he started again. He entered her slowly and then withdrew. He gradually increased the speed and pressure, making her orgasm again and again. Then he upped the game and increased both the rate and pressure until they both exploded in an orgy of sensuality. Monica had never experienced anything like it, and she mopped up a torrent of spunk that was running down her leg.

They spent the rest of the day cuddling, kissing and exploring each other's body. The next day over breakfast, Monica handed John a note which said, 'Never again?' They both knew that it would happen over and over again.

Life continued, and John and Monica made love regularly.

Linda was often away with her work, which helped a lot. Neither of them knew if Linda realised what was going on. One day, Linda announced that she wanted a baby, which annoyed Monica as it meant that she would be using John's body for her own needs. But life goes on.

Monica explained that she had another story for Sheila's collection. It related to her first husband, Bob.

Best Friends: Part 4—The Biology Lesson

Sheila had asked Monica to provide a sexy story for her new soft porn book, and here it is:

Monica had been a member of the Parent-Teacher Association for many years, as she had always been very involved in her children's education. By contrast, her husband, Bob, had shown little interest. This had been the cause of many arguments over the years.

Bob had often promised to help, but there had been no action on his part thus far. There had been little action in other aspects of their life together as well. She was trying to remember when they had last made love. But her life was hectic, what with being a taxi service for the children as she escorted them to their various activities.

At the last Parent-Teacher meeting, she vaguely agreed to assist with finding a volunteer to help with the biology class. They needed a man, which was going to be a bit daunting, as Clifford High was a very strict all-girls Catholic school for students up to the age of eighteen.

It was the best school in the area, and it had taken a lot of work for her to get her ten-year-old daughter in. She'd forgotten about her assignment until the previous meeting's minutes came in the post. Then she panicked because they needed the man for the next night.

When Bob returned from work, she showed him the minutes and said that this was his chance to finally do his bit. He immediately protested, but Monica put her foot down, and he reluctantly agreed. He asked what he had to do, but Monica had no idea. She said to take the minutes, go to the Biology Department and ask for Miss Dunn.

The next day, Bob put his best suit on, brushed his hair and arrived at the school at the designated time. He asked for Miss Dunn and was directed to the Biology Department. He rather nervously knocked on the door, as he could hear lots of giggly voices on the other side.

A very attractive brunette opened the door and said, 'You must be the model?' He nodded, not understanding what she meant. He introduced himself as Bob. He was surprised at how young and vivacious she was; he thought teachers were supposed to be rather dull and boring.

The room went quiet as he walked in. It was full of girls in their final year. They looked quite innocent in their school uniforms. However, he couldn't help noticing their short skirts and that there were several panties on show as they were sitting on the laboratory benches.

Miss Dunn said that the girls were quite excited because they had not had many practical sessions in their biology class. She asked him to remove his trousers and pants and stand on the stool. 'Pardon me?' he said. She asked him again to remove everything below the waist and stand on the stool. This time, she used a much more authoritative voice.

He was not sure what Monica had agreed to, so he started taking his trousers down. The girls giggled. He then took his pants down, exposing his genitals. The girls giggled some more and chatted loudly amongst themselves. Miss Dunn told them to be quiet.

'Now girls,' she said, 'some of you have seen your brothers naked, but this is a full-grown man. I'm going to take you through the male anatomy. You will get a chance to touch it later.' Miss Dunn walked over and lifted Bob's penis to expose his testicles. She caressed them to show the girls. Fortunately, her hands were quite warm.

'These are testicles, often known as "balls". There are two of them. They are contained in a sack called a scrotum. This is where the sperm are produced. The testicles are kept outside of the body to aid sperm development. They don't like it too hot.

'Most men like to have their testicles played with. Are you married?' she asked, looking into Bob's eyes. He nodded. 'Well, Bob, do you like your testicles being played with?' He nodded, and the girls laughed.

'OK girls, I would like you to line up in a row so that you can all get a chance to fondle the testicles. Please be rather gentle as they can be quite sensitive. You don't have to do it; this is voluntary,' One by one, each girl fondled Bob's balls. One was a bit rough, which made him jerk. While this was going on, Miss Dunn was holding up his cock so that the girls could get easy access to his balls. She must have felt it harden.

'Now, please sit down,' she said to the girls. 'Let's now look at the penis. It's an extendable shaft that is used to penetrate the female's genital opening. When excited, it grows in length and width. You probably noticed that Bob's is already larger than it was when he first came in.

'The penis, which is known by lots of rude names, such as cock, todger, etc., transfers the sperm from the testicles into the female's vagina.'

One of the girls put her hand up, 'Yes, Sally?' Miss Dunn said.

'What makes the sperm transfer?'

Miss Dunn, said, 'Well, Sally, the penis has to be excited. As it gets steadily more excited, it eventually orgasms. This is where the sperm shoots out of an opening at the end of the penis. Men find this very pleasurable.' Miss Dunn looked Bob in the eye again and asked if he found it very pleasurable. He nodded vigorously. The girls laughed out loud.

Sally couldn't keep quiet and raised her hand again. 'Yes, Sally?' said Miss Dunn.

'How does the penis get excited?'

'Sometimes, just the sight of a naked woman is enough to get the man excited, but normally, the penis has to be continuously stroked. Just like this.' She took Bob's penis and moved the foreskin back and forth. 'By the way, girls the skin that moves is called a foreskin.'

Looking at the girls, she said, 'There is no definite way of getting the man excited; every couple learn their own techniques, but I find that constant rubbing back and forth seems to work best before it is placed in the vagina.' Looking at Bob again, she asked if he agreed. He nodded once again.

While this was going on, Miss Dunn was constantly rubbing Bob's cock. She whispered, 'Don't you dare come, yet.' He wondered what that meant.

'Now, girls. It's time for you to have a turn handling the penis,' she said. 'Once again, it's totally voluntary.' The girls lined up to have a play. It was amazing to see how different their handling was. Some gingerly touched it and ran off. Others gave it a good old tug. Bob was finding it hard to control himself. After all, how many men get their todger played with by a dozen teenaged girls?

Bob thought, 'It looks like Monica is going to get a good seeing to tonight,' as he prepared to put his clothes back on. But then he noticed Miss Dunn was taking her dress off. Her bra and knickers quickly followed.

She walked over and bent in front of him, leaning on a table. 'Bob, could you place your penis at the entrance to my vagina, please?' she said. Bob felt his penis throb and decided to obey.

'Now, girls. Can you all see?'

'Yes,' they all responded.

Sally said, 'Miss, it looks too big to enter your little hole.'

Miss Dunn said, 'Don't worry, I'm sure that it will be OK.'

Miss Dunn asked Bob to insert his penis fully into her fanny. He obliged. The girls all went quiet. Miss Dunn asked Bob to continue, and he repeatedly plunged into Miss Dunn's tight little pussy. The girls noticed that Miss Dunn was dribbling from her fanny and that her breathing was getting quicker and quicker. Miss Dunn agreed that her pussy was a bit on the small size for his engorged cock.

Miss Dunn could tell that Bob was starting to reach his climax and asked him to pull out before he came. She explained that she wanted the girls to see what happens when a man climaxes. She was a bit annoyed about missing out on her climax, but then she thought that she would be ready for a good todgering from her boyfriend that night.

Bob could tell that he was almost there and pulled out. He orgasmed, and there was a spray of semen all over Miss Dunn's bum. The girls screamed. Bob screamed, and even Miss Dunn screamed as she'd orgasmed after all. Bob was embarrassed by how much spunk there was and how far it shot through the air.

Miss Dunn thanked Bob for a job well done. The girls giggled their approval. Bob dressed and went home.

When Bob got home, Monica asked how it went. He explained that it was tough, gruelling work. She asked if being a man had been necessary for the exercise. He nodded. He said that he had given some thought to her comments regarding helping out more. Reluctantly, he said he had agreed to a further ten sessions at the school.

Monica now knew why she loved him. She asked Bob if he fancied an early night. He said he did, but he had work tomorrow.

The Human Zoo

Sheila had another meeting fixed with Ken, her agent, as he had another opportunity for her. She had always enjoyed her encounters with Ken, but now there was the added complication of his very jealous wife. Usually, she would be looking forward to a quick but erotic fuck, but after the other evening, her fanny needed a rest.

'Morning Ken', Sheila beamed, 'How are you today.'

Ken said, 'You seem to be even more full of the joys of Spring than usual.' Ken had always enjoyed his meetings with this beautiful woman. Her smiling face made him feel years younger. She was one of those glorious women who enjoyed her body, and indeed, enjoyed a good fuck, how he missed the joys of her fanny. He wondered how he could engineer a clandestine meeting, but his wife kept him on a very short chain.

Ken said, 'I hear that you were not too keen on the last job.'

Sheila said, 'It was an experience as I was fucked eighteen times in eight hours. I think it was an all-time record for me, not one that I want to repeat.' I assume that your new opportunity requires nudity and some fucking.

Ken said, 'It does. It's the Human Zoo.'

Sheila said, 'Do you mean that commune that lives as animals in a biosphere?'

Ken said, 'Yes, it's a bit like the Eden Project, but instead of plants they have naked human beings.'

Ken said. 'They are looking for a pretty girl for two weeks. They need to jazz everything up a bit. The General Public can see what is going on 24 hours a day, but they a bit bored looking at grumpy middle-aged women getting the occasional leg-over.

Sheila said, 'What about grumpy middle-aged men?' It appears to be mostly men who log onto their site, probably hoping to see a bit of "How's your father". Well, that's just what the owners what to give them.'

Sheila said, 'So what you want me to do, is to go into the biosphere, and fuck everything in sight, and to make it as public as possible.'

Ken said, 'That's my girl.'

Sheila said, 'Ken, I've had enough of being a fuck-toy, there must be something else I could do?'

Ken said, 'I need to be honest, I do have lots of other opportunities, but you either don't have the skills or your CV wouldn't get you in. Entertainment is very competitive nowadays. You have a unique niche. I would advise you to go for it, and you will get £8k for two weeks, providing you fuck five of the ten men.'

Sheila said, 'What if I can't seduce five men?'

Ken said, 'Then you don't get paid.'

Sheila asked, 'What are the other woman going to think?'

Ken said, 'They are probably going to hate you, don't expect any help.' Sheila decided to take the challenge, and Ken gave her a file to read.

The biosphere consisted of ten men and ten women. There were no formal relationships as they were banned, but informal arrangements had been established. There were four single people and eight couples. At least one of the men was gay. It was not going to be as easy as she thought.

Sheila arrived at the Biosphere Visitor Centre at the designated time and was asked to meet the Site Director. He explained the rules to Sheila, emphasising that she would not be let out for two weeks. He also emphasised that both her nudity and any sexual activities, need to be as public as possible. The objective was to increase visitor sales, especially digital ones.

His secretary came in with a box, and he asked Sheila to place her clothes and any personal property in it. Sheila said, 'You want me to strip here?'

The Director said, 'Yes please, there is no point being shy, you are going to be naked for two weeks.' Sheila couldn't help agreeing, and took off her top and skirt. She knew the type of man he was and decided to pander to his tastes. She very slowly removed her bra, letting her ample breasts burst free.

The Director couldn't help admiring them. Perky but voluptuous, well rounded and curvaceous. He desperately wanted to get his hands on them. Sheila very slowly pulled her panties down, firstly exposing her bum, and then slowly putting her vagina on public display. The Director admired her shapely legs, the curve of her arse, the flat stomach and the little black triangle. To put it simply, she was a serious looker. He couldn't stop looking at her fanny. He was now jealous of the inmates, as he saw them. He wanted to take her, there and then.

The Director put his arm around Sheila's waist and said, let me introduce you to the press. He walked Sheila to a large assembly area. In the process, he managed to touch both of

Sheila's breasts and her fanny. He now stood behind her, with his hand on her bum. In front of Sheila was fifty plus press representatives, who were busily taking photos. The Director spun Sheila around so that the press could see every facet of her body. He gently bent her over so that they could get a better view of her fanny. Sheila wondered how many millions of people were going to see a naked picture of her.

The Director then walked Sheila over to the biosphere entrance, unlocked the door and gently pushed her in. Then that was that she was alone. She had no idea where to go, no idea where the humans lived, no idea what to do next. It wasn't cold, and she wasn't hungry, but she needed a plan. Anyway, she thought to herself the Biosphere is only about 30 acres in size, that is no distance at all.

As she was thinking, she heard a man's voice shouting, 'Who is there?'

Sheila shouted back, 'It's me, Sheila.'

He shouted back, 'Who is Sheila?'

Sheila shouted back, 'I'm the latest recruit for the experiment.' Then she saw him, a tall thin naked man with grey hair, and a long thin penis.

He stopped and stared at Sheila, and said, 'You are a sight for sore eyes, and as he looked, his penis rose in admiration or was it anticipation.

Sheila thought, 'It's not quite as thin as I first thought.'

Sheila wondered what type of interaction was expected, but she soon found that it was the same old thing. He quickly grabbed Sheila, bent her over, and entered her vagina from behind. She thought that there would at least be some pleasantries first, but no, just a regular humping. He huffed and puffed, and then came with a series of chunky spurts. He withdrew his penis and patted Sheila on her back, and said, 'Well done, that was just what was required, a man has needs you know.'

Sheila thought, 'Four to go.'

Sheila asked what his name was.

'Donald,' he said, 'You can call me Don.' Sheila asked him where the others were.

Don said, 'Most of them live in a series of huts in the centre, but you don't want to go there.'

'Why not?' she asked.

Don said, 'They are very set in their ways; they treat women as slaves.' Sheila had no idea what he was talking about.

The Director asked his secretary for the latest figures. She said that Sheila had made an immediate impact. In the first hour, she had been fucked by Don, which led to the viewing figures increasing by 15%. Just shows you what a beautiful, naked woman can do. We need more, and we need Sheila to continue her journey. Fortunately, Sheila had just that objective in mind.

Sheila continued her travels with Don following behind. He was mostly following so he could continue to admire her nudity. He simply enjoyed the way her arse swung backwards and forwards. He decided that he was going to have her again, in the very near future.

It didn't take long before Sheila encountered the huts; in reality, it's a very small biosphere. There were at least five ramshackle huts. They weren't huts, more like shacks with no roofs. Inside there were several women tied up to posts. The women immediately started shouting at Sheila to release them. It would appear that the men were using them to satisfy their sexual needs.

Sheila was trying to remove the women's bonds when four of the men turned up. They liked the look of the new meat that had arrived. Sheila could tell, as they showed their excitement in a, particularly masculine way. As two of the men held her, a third man entered her. Sheila wasn't sure if this was rape or not, as she was there with the express objective of getting them to fuck her. It didn't take him long to unload his seed.

He was soon replaced by a larger man with a long grey beard. Sheila expected him to take his time, but she was wrong. He came in record time. Sheila was actually a bit disappointed.

Sheila was dragged outside and bent over a rock. While this was going on, the Secretary called for the Director. She said, 'Sheila has been raped by two of the men in one of the huts. Jeremy has now bent her over one of the rocks.' The Director was studying the video images very carefully. He was looking forward to seeing another cock enter Sheila's sweet little cunt. He didn't have to wait long. Jeremy held Sheila's arms behind her back and forced his way into her fanny. Sheila thought to herself, 'Force wasn't needed, I want them to take me.'

The Director felt his own cock harden. He wanted to be Jeremy. He wanted to feel the sensation of entering Sheila's cunt. His secretary was also feeling randy. She was fingering her fanny. The Director told Miriam, his secretary, to prepare to be fucked. Miriam pulled her knickers down, lifted her dress, and bent over so that the Director could enter her from behind, and watch the video at the same time.

The Director entered his engorged cock into Miriam's

juicy fanny. Miriam was grateful that she had the foresight to lubricate herself before she entered the room. She knew what the Director was like; he just fucked and fucked without any consideration for the woman. She knew that he was metaphorically fucking Sheila.

Where in reality, it was Jeremy who was fucking Sheila. He was doing quite a good job. He was fucking her from every direction, using a mixture of long and short strokes, and varying the speed. The Director was emulating his technique with Miriam. Both Sheila and Miriam were enjoying themselves. Miriam wasn't so keen when the Director shouted at Jeremy to fuck her harder. Somehow Jeremy took it on-board and started fucking Sheila hard, which made her come two or three times.

The Director followed suit and started fucking Miriam harder and harder. Miriam came like she had never come before. This didn't stop the Director. He just kept pumping away until he released his load. He then wiped his cock on her knickers and pushed her out of the way. Miriam loved this man. He took what he wanted. She thought, 'What more could a woman want.'

In Sheila's case, the next man, Bob simply pushed Jeremy out of the way. Bob had decided that it was his turn. Sheila felt Jeremy's cock exit her vagina. As far as she was concerned, it had been a good cock, and she was sorry to see it go. Bob, however, was also doing a good job, but you could tell that he was over-eager. Sheila could easily tell when a cock was ready, and she tensed her vaginal muscles to push him over the edge. Within seconds she could feel his ejaculation.

The Director asked how the figures were going. Miriam said that the number of viewers had increased by 50%, and were still increasing. The Director said that they were going to make a fortune out of selling the repeats.

Sheila stood up to find a torrent of spunk running down her leg. She tried to find a cloth, but Bob pointed towards a leaf. Sheila thought to herself, 'What am I doing wiping my fanny down with a dock leaf. I want to get back to civilisation.' Sheila decided to make a run for it. And run for it she did.

Three of the men were running after her, but she easily outpaced them. Later she learnt that they were under-nourished, and consequently, they lacked stamina. She thought that was a bit strange, as they certainly had enough strength to fuck her. She reached the edge of the dome when she was grabbed from behind by Don. He pushed her against the glass wall so that her entire body was spread-eagled. Her boobs were pushed flat like large pancakes, with a cherry in the middle.

She knew that Don had his needs, and he was soon satisfying them. Sheila, as everyone knew, enjoyed a good fuck, but this was pretty uncomfortable. She would have felt even more uncomfortable if she had known that there was a large party of press photographers on the other side of the glass wall. She couldn't see them, but they could definitely see her. They could see Don's large cock enter her pretty little cunt. They could see Don fondling her clit. They could see her voluptuous boobs pressing against the glass wall. They could see her hips gyrate in response to Don's thrusts. They could see Sheila's heavy breathing as she prepared herself for another climax. They could see Don's spunk running down her leg. They saw everything. The Director also saw everything.

Don withdrew and kissed Sheila on the cheek. Thank you he said with his eyes. Don showed her the exit door. The Director didn't want to let her out, but it was too good a press opportunity. The glass door opened and Sheila stepped back into the sunlight and the artificial light of what seemed to be thousands of cameras.

The Director pushed Sheila towards his offices, through a huddle of photographers, most of which took the opportunity to pat Sheila's bum. In the office, Sheila explained what was going on in the dome, but it was evident that the Director wasn't interested. Miriam brought Sheila's box of clothes in. The Director said that you could have the box back if you do one last job.

The Director pulled his erect cock out of his trousers. Miriam thought, 'What a man.'

Sheila bent down, took his cock and put it in her mouth, and then bit it hard. Very hard. The Director screamed, and Sheila ran for the door. Once again, she was sitting naked in a taxi on her way home. She didn't think she bit him hard enough to bleed, but it must have hurt. Anyway, she decided that the bastard deserved it.

Miriam rubbed the Director's cock with an ice pack. Sheila's agent managed to get the full fee from the customer, even though she only spent a day there. They got every penny back in countless replays. The women in the village were eventually freed except for the ones who liked being tied up.

The moral of the story is, 'If you go into the lion's den, expect to be fucked.'